MW00906407

M I N D   W A L K E R

Shays work
416 - 621 - 4982 numba

chanelle
647-678-9108

Own by:
Evangelie Renov

MIND WALKER

A NOVEL

ROY McCONNELL

iUniverse, Inc.
New York   Bloomington

iUniverse books may be ordered through booksellers or by contacting:

iUniverse
1663 Liberty Drive
Bloomington, IN 47403
www.iuniverse.com
1-800-Authors (1-800-288-4677)

Because of the dynamic nature of the Internet, any Web addresses or links contained in this book may have changed since publication and may no longer be valid. The views expressed in this work are solely those of the author and do not necessarily reflect the views of the publisher, and the publisher hereby disclaims any responsibility for them.

ISBN: 978-1-4401-6866-6 (sc)
ISBN: 978-1-4401-6864-2 (dj)
ISBN: 978-1-4401-6865-9 (ebook)

Printed in the United States of America

iUniverse rev. date: 09/14/09

Acknowledgments

A very special thanks goes to my wife, Rosemary, who put up with all of my thinking out loud, and provided tireless editing services. I am grateful to Vali, my writing mentor throughout a major portion of this book. Thanks to my writing friends and first readers. They gave me plenty of feedback, especially Ellen MK, whose yellow-sticky edition of one of my first drafts still adorns my office.

Most of all, thanks to my mom who gifted me with perseverance and a passion for living.

CHAPTER ONE

WOLF'S FIERCE WORDS RESOUNDED off the concrete walls of the small room. Tara watched, frozen in place, as her father's face tightened with anger and his deep brown eyes boiled dark. Perspiration soaked the edges of his short, black hair. His tall, ominous form loomed even larger as he raised his long arms and shook them in frustration. His thick fingers looked long and powerful enough to easily snap her neck.

Tara grasped the tight red curls of her short hair, as if protecting herself from his onslaught. She had never seen her father so angry and was terrified of what he might do to her. But—damn it—she had to stand her ground, no matter how much he yelled.

When he lunged at her, she jerked her head back, but she didn't try to dodge to the side or step back. She could feel his hot breath on her face as he continued to yell. Tara refused to cry, even though tears welled up in her eyes.

"Since you were fourteen," Wolf said, "I've tried to teach you about the family business, but you've screwed up everything I've ever asked you to do. Your problem is that you are weak. You care too much about people."

Overcoming her fear, Tara glared fiercely into Wolf's nearly black eyes.

"All you do is pile up a fortune on the back of other people's troubles. What you call weakness, I call compassion."

"As far as I'm concerned, compassion and weakness are both the same, and neither will get you far in business or life," Wolf shouted, waving his hand dismissively. "You'll be twenty-one in two weeks, and it's time you demonstrated some family loyalty. This is your last chance to prove to me that you're capable of taking my place someday. You need to toughen up and become an Ostermann I can respect." Pointing toward the centre of the room, Wolf continued. "I caught this bastard, one of my own guards, planting a bug in my office phone. I want you to help me question him to find out who the hell he's working for and what they're after."

Tara looked around the room, which she had never seen until tonight. Her father had led her into it through a sliding door in the back of his office closet. The small, concrete room was empty except for a chair in the centre where a bound man was seated. He looked to be middle-aged with dark brown hair and soft features. A high-wattage lamp stood in front of him, pointing directly at his face. The blazing bulb was so bright that Tara was sure it would blind the man. She winced at the sight of ropes twisted around his wrists, turning his hands grey-white. Sweat poured down his face, merging with blood trickling from the corner of his mouth, sending a gory, red stream along the side of his neck and into the collar of his sweat-soaked shirt. A rope tightly strung around his forehead and tied to the back of the chair pulled his head back, denying reprieve from the lamp's glaring light.

This was the shocking sight that had sparked the argument with her father, an argument she was determined to win. Born of German and Irish ancestry, Tara had inherited a double dose of stubbornness, which her mother often said came directly from her father's side of the family.

Tara closed her eyes in an attempt to block out the horrific scene. Her body trembled, and her hands were cold and clammy. She choked back the acid-laced bile that surged into her throat and held her body very still. After her lurching stomach began to calm, she turned to face her father.

"You should untie this man and report him to the police. If he was really doing what you said, he'll be dealt with."

"Dear ..."

"Don't call me 'dear,' you cruel son of a bitch. I will never contribute to this ... horror. As far as I'm concerned, you're no longer my father."

"Do you mean that?"

"Damn right I do."

Wolf's dark eyes narrowed; his fingers clenched; his body went rigid. As his anger filled the room, Tara's fear rose. If she stayed any longer, he might strangle her or worse. Without saying another word, she fled. Her vision impaired by hatred and rage, she raced into the garden.

Though it was a warm, British Columbia summer day and circular plots of brightly coloured roses, dahlias, lilies, and well-manicured lawns surrounded her, she paid no attention. She focused entirely on dispelling the rancid smell of blood and sweat that lingered in her nose and on shattering the image of the man's bloody face.

After a few minutes Tara slowed down, exhausted more by her intense emotional state than by physical exertion. She turned to the garden, seeing the exquisite flowers that reminded her of her father's dichotomy.

How can he grow such lovely flowers and, at the same time, be so cold? What is wrong with him?

Tara made her way to a stone bench at the end of the path and slumped down. She stared straight ahead, wondering what to do.

"Tara."

She turned at the sound of her name and saw Chris Landry approaching. Chris was her bodyguard whenever she left the estate as well as her father's handpicked security guru. She'd been attracted to Chris from the first day she had met him. She'd been instantly drawn in by his kind smile, confident attitude, and of course, his toned physique and those light blue eyes. He was a man who could obviously deal with anything that came his way. Her recent fantasies involved her and Chris curled up naked together, her fingers sifting through his blond, wavy hair. Maybe he could help her? Could she trust him? No, it was best not to tell him anything. Chris worked for her father.

"Tara."

"Hey, Chris."

"Are you okay?"

"Yes, just thinking. Why don't you sit down?" she offered through a forced smile.

She could see that he hesitated, and she knew why. If any male employee came within five feet of her, her father would fire him. But after what she'd seen this morning, she knew the punishment might even be worse.

Chris sat down at the end of the bench, maintaining a respectful distance between them.

"Dad and I had a major argument this morning. I told him that as far as I'm concerned, he's no longer my father."

"What happened? He seems to love you very much."

"He doesn't love me. He loves what he wants from me and that's to continue his legacy. He wants a clone, not a daughter with a mind of her own. I don't want any part of his greedy empire. I've made a decision."

"What's that?"

"I'm leaving here tomorrow morning, and I'm never coming back."

"Are you sure you want to do that? The world's not as great a place as you may think."

"It's not safe here either. Promise me you won't tell Mom or George Ferguson, the chauffeur. If they find out, they'll try to keep me here. I'll send them a letter to let them know where I am once I've settled somewhere."

"Don't be too disappointed if it's not everything you expect."

"Believe me, Chris, I can't be any more disappointed than I am right now."

"I hope not," he said, standing up and putting his hand on her shoulder. "Best of luck, Tara."

So much for not telling him anything, she thought, as she watched him walk away.

CHAPTER TWO

SLEEP ELUDED CHRIS AS he worried about Tara. He knew that security was too tight for her to get off the estate, but he worried about the treatment she was receiving from her father. Wolf was going to destroy her if something wasn't done about it. Chris thought that maybe he should take her away himself—someplace where her father couldn't find her. He had become very fond of Tara. He would hate to see any harm come to her, knowing that he could have prevented it. Losing his job wasn't a concern; he'd saved enough money to support him and Tara for several years.

Chris drifted off to sleep.

In his world of dreams, he sensed the delicate pleasure of a soft hand drawing up and down the full length of his rigid shaft. He saw Tara brush back his blond hair and smile knowingly while her smooth, narrow fingers brought him intense pleasure. Her delicate scent drew him dangerously close to eruption as he kissed her full moist lips, their tongues thirstily probing each other's mouths. Tara's firm breasts heaved as Chris hurriedly unbuttoned her blouse, pulling it down over her shoulders, revealing her innocence. Lightly kissing her tender, smooth neck and her chest, his tongue lingered on the swell of her breast, tracing increasingly smaller circles around the nipple. She trembled as he sucked and teased her nipple with the tip of his tongue. The moist entrance of her vagina gave way to his fingers—sliding in and out, taunting her clitoris, driving her to dizzying passion, her thighs clenching in a shuddering orgasm.

Breathlessly, Tara looked at Chris and whispered, "It's your turn, now."

Chris closed his eyes in anticipation as Tara lowered her face toward his hardened cock and said, "Chris, I love you so much."

Chris smiled. Those were the most wonderful words he'd ever heard.

Gently, ever so gently, she licked the tip of his cock, grasping at the base and taking it deep into her mouth. At the brink, she took her lips away and momentarily left him throbbing in the cool air. Leaning over, she folded her perfect, soft, creamy breasts around him letting his cock slide easily between her fleshy mounds. He came, semen spilling out in pulsing waves, splashing into a pool of white on her chest.

In the midst of his dream, Chris did not hear the barely audible sound of a snapping lid or of his bedroom door closing as he settled into an even deeper, dream-filled sleep.

CHAPTER THREE

A SPEAR SLAMMED INTO the tree beside Tara, just missing her, but she kept running after the soldier. The biting frost stung her lips and nose, and her heavy breathing created a constant mist in front of her. The soldier's head was topped with a metal helmet. Chain mail draped from the back of his head to the base of his neck, and metal plating covered his chest and parts of his legs. Blood dripped from his right calf, where an arrow had grazed him, leaving a spotted trail of red in the snow.

Tara could hear the thundering hooves of horses pursuing them. Her hands were freezing; her wool overcoat and pants were soaked; and her undergarments clung to her sweaty skin. As always, a strange female voice told her to keep going, to not stop. The voice had a thick accent—German, she thought. She couldn't explain why, but it sounded ancient. Possibly, she'd heard it before.

The soldier, even at a distance, appeared extremely tall and muscular, almost giant-like. His pace slowed slightly, but he continued running, body leaning forward, arms rapidly gouging the air, and legs visibly straining to propel him onward. His form reminded Tara of the racing thoroughbreds that her parents had taken her to see on her sixteenth birthday. Their muscular thighs had rippled with every thrust as their hooves had exploded against the dirt track.

The soldier stopped just as the searing pain in her lungs threatened meltdown. Like a marionette with its strings cut, she slumped sideways to the ground, leaning against a large oak tree, positioning herself to keep an eye on the soldier. Tara lay panting like a spent hound, breathing so loudly that she was terrified he could hear her.

She saw the soldier lean forward, hands on his knees, mouth wide open, greedily gulping every breath, and eyes darting, anxiously surveying his surroundings. He did not seem as strong and fearless as Tara had first thought.

Turning to the left, the soldier stared at something and then spun around in a fluid motion. It was obviously something significant. Tara shifted to get a better view of what he was looking at. It looked like an opening below a stone cliff, possibly a cave. The soldier rose to full stature and was about to move when a spear grazed his side below the chest plate, ripping away flesh and piercing the ground behind him. He staggered backward. Holding his side to slow the bleeding, he hobbled toward the cave. An arrow pierced the air where his head had been.

Pushing herself up, Tara grabbed a low-hanging branch of a nearby oak tree to steady her fatigued body. She was barely on her feet when a troop of soldiers raced by, almost knocking her down. She was surprised they hadn't seen the soldier's blood trail leading to the cave. Dragging her tired, unwilling body along and using the trees for cover, Tara crept closer to the cave. As she approached, she saw that the mouth of the cave was twice the height of an average man. An imposing hornbeam tree cast its shadow over the entrance, blocking sunlight from the threshold and making it appear impenetrable.

The sight of the cave flooded her mind with images of men and women from different time periods. She recognized some of the faces as her ancestors. Seeing her own image caused a surge of energy to course through her with such intensity that she clutched the trunk of tree to keep from falling.

She twisted around to see the cave. The soldier was crouched just inside the entrance, holding his side, his hand covered with blood. Tara watched with heightened anticipation as he slowly stood and vanished into the abyss.

With her last bit of strength, she screamed, "Don't go in there."

There was no response. He was gone.

A suffocating fear overtook her as she let out another scream, forcing her from a deep sleep.

Now AWAKE, EYES WIDE and riveted to the ceiling, her body drenched with perspiration and hands numb from gripping the bedsheets that replaced the weathered bark of the tree, Tara was unable to think clearly.

"Tara, breathe," she said.

At first, her breathing came in jagged bursts, but it smoothed as she concentrated on calming herself. With less apprehension, she recalled the scenes of her nightmare, playing them over and over again. Like a horror movie, after watching it a few times, it gradually lost hold. Collecting her thoughts, she realized that the dream was the same one she'd had many times before. So why was she terrified? It wasn't the voice, though the first time she'd heard the voice, it had frightened her, making her think that someone was directing her dream. However, she was used to it now, and Tara knew her fear was caused by something else.

Recalling the images that flashed through her mind at the sight of the cave created a feeling of dread. She couldn't envision any of the faces now, but she knew she had recognized most of them. Many of the figures had been dressed in clothing from different time periods. Why did those images, or even the thought of them, scare her so much? She couldn't explain it, but thinking of them made her tense, especially when she recalled seeing herself in the succession of faces.

The ember glow of the numbers on her clock radio showed three o'clock. Tara couldn't believe it. It seemed as if she'd been asleep much longer. She turned on the bedside lamp to orient herself and began to think about her plans to leave the estate. She'd leave late in the morning, and never return. Would she be able to survive in the world alone? What would she do? Where would she go? She had to make it on her own and prove herself capable. She hated the thought of never seeing her mother again.

Tara switched off the bedside lamp and watched the night sky through her large bedroom window, hoping it would calm her. She needed to relax. The full moon's glow and the abundance of brilliant stars displaced the galaxy's darkness. At first, the stars seemed random, as if a giant had dropped a huge crystal vase on a black onyx floor, dispersing crystalline fragments across its vastness. But Tara knew they weren't randomly placed. She could make out the large and small dippers, along with constellations. If the stars were not randomly arranged, then how had they been formed and placed?

She knew that everything from the smallest insect to the largest mammal had a purpose, so this orderly display must be the work of something more—a superior being that she couldn't comprehend. The thought of something larger than herself, something with a greater, more profound purpose, always helped her put things in perspective.

After all, it was just a bad dream, she mused.

Tara thought of her privileged life as she settled back under the covers. Her days were filled with learning and recreation. Her university tutor came in the morning, her harp instructor came after lunch, and the rest of the day was spent reading, swimming, playing tennis, horseback riding, or going shopping—it was the only life she knew. She wondered how she would cope with life outside the estate.

She heard a scuffing noise. Her body tensed. She propped herself up on her elbows and peered into the darkness, straining to hear more. When she reached to turn on the bedside lamp, she spotted a shadow moving quickly toward her. A large hand slammed into her chest, pushing her down and knocking the wind out of her. Another hand covered her face. She could smell something sweet. She tried to scream for help. But no sound came out—only choked gasps.

Tara's left arm instinctively swung toward her attacker, but she missed, slamming her hand into the bedside lamp and shattering the glass shade. She felt something run down her arm and assumed it was blood. Ignoring it, she continued to swing at her attacker, missing each time.

An oddly pleasant-smelling cloth descended over her face as the attacker's firm grip pushed her head deep into the pillow. The smell overcame her, ending her last attempts to fight back.

CHAPTER FOUR

"TARA, ARE YOU IN there?"

This was the third time Una Ostermann had knocked on her daughter's bedroom door without a response. She was concerned because no sound came from the bedroom, not even of the drum of the shower or the buzz of a hair dryer. Tara had to be in there.

Call it a mother's instinct, but Una knew something was wrong. Tara was a creature of habit. It wasn't like her daughter to be up and out before eight o'clock on a weekday. They always ate breakfast together before Tara's tutor arrived. Una's stomach twisted in knots as her hand slipped over the doorknob and she pushed the door open.

"Tara, are you in there? Tara, answer ... " Una's body froze, her throat constricted. The bedding was sprayed with blood; there was blood on the nightstand—blood everywhere. The Tiffany bedside lamp was smashed, and pieces of it were strewn across the floor. Her knees weakened. She rubbed her arms. She felt cold, a clammy cold. When Una noticed that the window was open, a primal scream erupted and her mind reeled with images of her precious only child being taken from her room.

Despite her shaky legs, Una's instincts took over. She ran down the hallway, descended the stairs two at a time, and collapsed onto the marble floor at the bottom. Ignoring the searing pain in her shoulder, she leapt to her feet, flew across the foyer, and burst into Wolf's private reading room.

"Wolf, Tara's gone," she yelled. "There's blood all over her bedroom."

Wolf's head snapped away from the book he was reading. His wife stood before him in a half-open robe. Her usually flushed face was grey with anguish; her dainty hands were clenched into tight balls at the ends of her pale, thin arms. He stood and went to her, putting his arm around her.

"Una, what happened? What did you see?"

"Our daughter's been kidnapped," she stammered.

"Tell me exactly what you saw," he said, holding her firmly.

"I told you. Blood everywhere. Don't just stand there. What the hell's wrong with you? Go and see for yourself!"

"I will, but first, I must know what you saw."

"I was getting Tara up to have breakfast with me. I knocked on her bedroom door a few times. When she didn't answer, I went in, and there was blood everywhere. Tara's been kidnapped," she said. "There's so much blood. Wolf, what if she's dead?"

"I'm sure she's not dead."

"How can you be sure?"

"Kidnappers abduct people for money. Until they collect on their ransom demand, Tara will be safe."

"I hope you're right."

"I know I am. Let me help you over to the couch," he said, taking her by the arm. Una collapsed onto the couch. Tears filled her eyes. "Don't cry, Una. We'll get her back."

"Don't you want to see the room?" Una anxiously pressed.

"Not yet. I believe what you've told me. We need to keep calm and start searching immediately."

"Are you calling the police?"

"No."

"Why not? Shouldn't we call the police? What if we waste too much time and she is killed? Isn't that how it always happens?" Una said, her voice growing louder.

"You've watched too many crime shows. As I've already told you, the abductors won't kill her until they get their money. I have a man on my staff who's more than capable of handling this situation—certainly better than the police."

"I don't believe one man can do more than a whole police force," she said, picking up the phone. "I don't care what you say, I'm calling the police."

Wolf yanked the phone from Una's hand and slammed it into its cradle.

"Una, I know you're distraught but you must give me a chance to do what I know is best. The police will waste too much time with formalities. My man will get right to work. I'm only thinking of Tara. I want her found as quickly as possible, just as you do."

Pulling her body straight up and hardening her emotions, Una glared at her husband. "Who is he? I want to meet this man and decide for myself if I can trust him to bring our daughter home."

"I'm calling right now," Wolf said as he quickly punched in Chris's cell phone number. "Chris, it's Wolf. Something's happened. Come to my private reading room immediately."

"Is he coming?" Una asked.

"Yes."

Chris had awakened before Wolf had phoned. He didn't feel very rested, which was odd, because he'd slept quite well in the last couple of months. His nightmares had mostly subsided. Faces of people he'd assassinated in the name of national security had invaded his sleep less frequently, but that night he had felt strangely uneasy and confused.

A gnawing feeling told him something was terribly wrong.

Hearing a knock at the door, Wolf called for Chris to come in.

Una immediately recognized Chris as the guard who watched over Tara when she was off the estate.

"Wolf, tell me that you're not trusting our daughter's life to this one young man? He can't possibly be experienced enough to handle such a detailed investigation. He doesn't look much older than Tara."

"You must believe me, Una. This man has more experience than any of my senior guards. This type of assignment is exactly what he's trained for. I'm not trusting our daughter's safety to anyone else."

"Remember, Wolf, she's my daughter too. I'm part of this decision."

Una stood and strutted over to Chris, looked him straight in the eye, and asked, "How old are you?"

"Twenty-six."

"Twenty-six!" A look of dismay crossed Una's face, but then she quickly composed herself. "Please don't take this the wrong way. My daughter's disappeared, and I'd be happier if the man charged with finding her had more experience."

"What's happened to Tara?" Chris asked.

"Tara's gone missing," Una blurted out before Wolf could speak.

"When?"

"Sometime during the night," Una said, beginning to warm to this young man. His concern seemed genuine enough. Could he get her daughter back? "I only need you to answer one question for me. Can you bring my daughter safely home to me?"

"Mrs. Ostermann, I made a promise to protect Tara no matter what happened, and I plan to do just that. I was trained by the FBI," Chris lied, not wanting to divulge that he was actually CIA, "and before I was hired by Mr. Ostermann, I put a number of kidnappers behind bars."

Una looked closely at Chris. His square jaw and tight skin made his face look strong; his light blue eyes levelled on her with intensity, waiting for her evaluation. Chris suddenly seemed older than his twenty-six years. She sensed that he was prepared to do whatever it took to find Tara. She just hoped that it was enough.

"Una, are you satisfied?" Wolf said.

"I'm not finished yet. Chris, I suppose you'll want to see her bedroom."

"Yes, of course."

"What are we waiting for?" Una asked.

"While you're inspecting the room," Wolf said, "I'll check with my chief guard to see if any incidents were reported last night. Chris, after you've finished, meet me in my office."

Una and Chris walked to Tara's bedroom in silence, both deep in thought. Chris paused at the doorway to view the scene. He swallowed hard, struggling to maintain his professionalism. As he walked toward the blood-sprayed bed, scenes of how the horrific event might have unfolded played in his mind.

"Do you think she's dead?" Una asked.

Turning toward her and making eye contact, Chris answered, "No. The whole purpose behind kidnapping someone is to get—"

"Money."

"Yes."

"That's what Wolf said, too."

"He's right."

Chris walked toward the large walk-in closet in the north wall of the bedroom.

"Why are you looking in there? The crime scene is the bed."

"Mrs. Ostermann, the crime scene is this whole bedroom. I suspect the culprit was hiding in here waiting for Tara to fall asleep. The evidence by the bed indicates a struggle, which means he miscalculated. As he approached the bed, he probably noticed that she wasn't fully asleep, causing him to use extra force to prevent her from screaming and alerting you or the guards, while he tried, at the same time, to cover her face with, I suspect, a chloroform-soaked cloth. He would've probably used chloroform simply because it's the quickest and easiest way to render a person unconscious. In her last few seconds, she must have been wildly swinging her arms to fend him off. Her hand could have crashed into the lamp, cutting her. The spray of blood indicates that she continued flailing until she was out."

"Sorry I interrupted you," she said, "I just feel so helpless."

"Right now, the best thing you can do is let me finish investigating. Then we'll talk."

"Okay." Una said, turning toward the south wall to divert her eyes from the gruesome scene.

Chris could hear the tone of resignation in her voice and knew he had gained some measure of her confidence.

Upon exiting the closet, Chris got down on his knees, and moving slowly, he closely examined the floor between the closet and the bed, looking for further evidence.

"Mrs. Ostermann."

When she didn't answer, Chris looked up to see that Tara's mother's gaze was fixed on a collection of stuffed animals that were neatly compartmentalized on half of some shelves covering the south wall. The other half of the shelves was filled with jade, crystal, and porcelain collectibles from around the world.

Chris walked over and tapped her on the shoulder.

"Mrs. Ostermann."

"Sorry," she said, "I was just remembering when Tara got each of those stuffed animals and how much she loved them at the time," she paused. "Did you find anything, Chris?"

"My initial check of the room hasn't uncovered any sign of anyone other than Tara having been in this room."

"That can't be. Someone stole my daughter."

"I know, and I'm going to get him." He paused. "Mrs. Ostermann, there's one more thing."

"What's that?"

"Well," he started hesitantly, "I can't see how a kidnapper could've gotten onto this estate without inside help."

CHAPTER FIVE

ONCE MORE, TARA DREAMED about the soldier. Again she was struck with horror, as he was about to go into the cave. Images flooded her mind as before—photographs from the past.

"Everything will be okay. Don't worry," said the familiar Germanic voice.

With a reassuring tone, the voice encouraged Tara to enter the cave and follow the soldier. As if releasing a lifeline, she gradually let go of the tree and took her first step toward the entrance. She'd only walked a short distance when one of her feet snagged on a twig, sending her facedown into the snow. The cold, white crystals bit at her face as she lay on the snow-encrusted ground, praying the nightmare would end.

"Get up, Tara, get up. You must keep going."

"Why?" She was desperate to know.

"It's your destiny."

"What destiny?"

"You have to see for yourself."

Not understanding but wanting it all to end, she struggled to her feet and continued. As she got closer, the cave's gaping cavity loomed larger than she had first thought. Thick layers of rock created an uneven ceiling that framed the entrance. The bright, morning sun illuminating the threshold was gradually replaced by the deep blackness of the inner chamber as Tara stepped forward and peered into the void. Her body shook more from fear than the cold. In the silence she could hear her rapidly thumping heart pounding in her chest.

"Tara, be calm. This is your legacy," the voice urged.

What legacy? She wondered how this gut-wrenching terror could be a legacy. She inched deeper into the cave but stopped just beyond the entrance, eyeing the passage with trepidation. Using her outstretched hands as antennae, she proceeded as the outside light gradually disappeared, leaving her encased in dank blackness.

Tara's imagination conjured up all sorts of possible terrors: spiderwebs blocking her path, bat wings flapping overhead, and small animals scurrying around her feet. Suddenly, her foot landed on something long and round. *A snake*, she thought in panic, breaking into a run, fleeing as though her most frightening childhood monster was chasing her. She nearly ran into a large boulder that was silhouetted by a distant glow.

The faint light illuminated the cave enough for her to make out what was in front of her. As Tara got closer, she saw two figures standing in the middle of an open area with the light between them. One of them, she was certain, was the soldier. He nodded his head as if responding to someone, but she didn't recognize the other person, who appeared to be about ten feet tall. His head was bald, and his neck looked like a sloping mountain falling toward cliff-like shoulders. His stout, unyielding arms were folded in front of him like seasoned tree branches.

The gentle, even-toned voice spoke to her again, "Everything isn't always as it appears. Go closer."

Tara eased onto her hands and knees, crawling carefully so as not to startle the two figures in the distance. At least one of them was male, she knew, but the tall one? She wasn't quite sure of it yet and didn't even know if it was human. Getting as close as she could, she watched from behind a large rock.

The light glowed very brightly, allowing her to see the strange figure clearly. Staring at the massive shape, she remained uncertain of its origin, but its large protruding eyes looked like great gemstones without visible pupils. The soldier nodded his head again as if agreeing with something the hulking giant had said.

The voice spoke to Tara again. "Your time is near, Tara. Wake up."

Tara struggled to open her eyes, wondering what the voice had meant when it had said that her time was near.

Awake, she felt dizzy, and her head thumped with pain. Her thoughts were murky, as if she were looking through a steamy window on a cold, winter day. What had happened? Where was she?

Her arms and legs were frozen in place. The surface beneath her felt hard, and she could hear her own muddled thoughts through her still foggy brain. Was she asleep or awake? Was the strange, giant creature an alien? Had it captured her and taken her to its spacecraft? Her eyes were open, but she was unable to see. Had he blinded her? Was he going to subject her to some painful experiments and then toss her back to earth like useless waste?

"What the hell's going on?" she screamed. However, her words never left her mouth because her lips had been sealed shut, her mouth bound so tightly she couldn't make a sound. Tara desperately tried to free herself as tears streamed from her eyes. Questions stormed her mind. Why would anyone do this to her? Was she being held for ransom? Had she been raped? Just the possibility of having been raped made her feel dirty and worthless. She could only hope that this was a sick joke or a nightmare that would soon end.

The air reeked with a sterile odour, reminding her of the time when she and her mother had visited Aunt Josephine in the hospital. Suddenly, Tara recalled smelling a sweet chemical odour just before she had blacked out. Her light-headedness was slowly lifting.

She heard a loud male voice. "Hey, the spoiled little rich girl is waking up."

"Shut up, you," a sharp, female voice rebuked.

These were not alien voices, Tara decided. These were human. Even though she couldn't see, Tara sensed that her legs were stretched open and she had been hoisted into a raised position. Cruel bindings held her ankles and wrists in place.

"What the hell are you doing to me?" she demanded, making short, inarticulate, guttural sounds, her mind filled with venomous words.

"It's okay, sweetie," a voice answered. "Don't mind that jerk. This will all be over before you know it. You won't feel a thing, which is really unfortunate, because it feels so much better when done the natural way."

Tara's mind swirled, she barely heard the woman speak. Her stomach churned and she swallowed hard to keep from vomiting, forcing back the rising bile in her throat. She tried breathing deeply to calm herself. She shuddered as cool air ran along her thighs, between her legs, and across her belly, increasing her awareness that she was fully exposed to whoever was in the room. Once more, she exploded with fearsome anger. Tara rocked violently back and forth, yanking at the restraints, desperately trying to free herself. Then, just as whatever she was lying on started to tilt to one side, a large pair of rough hands hammered her shoulders into the hard metal surface, sending a sharp piercing pain through her head as it slammed down.

"Easy, you dumb fuck, you're going to injure the poor girl, and you know what he'll do to you if anything happens to her before the baby is born."

Had she heard that right? Tara froze. She wasn't having a baby. She'd never even been with a man. But maybe they had raped her—the bastards! She struggled to free herself once more, but the man's determined grip held her still.

"Hand me the syringe," the woman ordered.

At her command, the man lifted one hand from Tara's shoulders and pressed the other one into her chest, nearly taking her breath away, making sure she would not be able move as he handed over the liquid-filled tube.

CHAPTER SIX

Wolf Ostermann relaxed in his high-back, leather chair, satisfied with himself. He thought of the men before him who had contributed to the massive fortune he enjoyed. His eyes embraced the rich, Victorian office furnishings that his grandfather and father had acquired over the years. Childhood memories surfaced, and he recalled himself sitting at the rolltop desk in the corner of the office as a young boy, doing his studies under his father's stern tutelage. As a child, Wolf had taken his carefree life for granted, but it had all changed on his twenty-first birthday. That was when he had found out the secret to his family's wealth—a secret he had hoped to share with Tara. His anger frothed, as he thought of her stubborn refusal to carry on the family legacy.

"What the hell," Wolf shouted, startled by the blaring, high-pitched sound of the motion detector surrounding his office. He quickly flicked the switch on the console under his desk as he watched Chris's approach on the monitor. He then turned toward the immense picture window in the north wall; it delivered a magnificent view of the Douglas fir trees along the fifty-foot ridge where Ostermann Falls descended. Prior to building the tall, stone wall around the property, he had been able to watch the falls meld with the stream below, raising a steady mist that sparkled in the afternoon sun. Now he could only see it through a remote camera that he had had installed—the price of his paranoia. With power beyond any man's imagination, he still had no control over Mother Nature, and he knew he must respect her if he wanted to continue enjoying her great beauty.

Wolf considered himself very fortunate that his grandfather had purchased and maintained this magnificent parcel of paradise in British Columbia's Fraser Valley. Communities to the north—Promontory, Ryder Lake, and Sardis—were growing rapidly, but due to his grandfather's foresight, the Ostermann family would never have to worry about being surrounded by development.

Christopher Landry was quickly approaching Wolf's office door. Chris had received a second PhD from the Massachusetts Institute of Technology at age twenty, by the next year he had completed his training for the CIA, and within another year, he had become a top operative. Last April, Wolf had offered Chris three times his CIA salary to come to work for him. Wolf recalled Chris's response when he had asked him why someone of his intelligence had become a sniper. He had said it was better than the alternative.

"And what was that?" Wolf had asked.

"Conforming to my parents wishes."

Chris was about to knock on the office door when Wolf pressed the intercom button and told him to come in. Unflinching, he turned the brass knob on the solid, oak door and strode into the office, exuding the confidence and strength of someone twice his age and experience. Wolf motioned for Chris to sit down.

Chris sat down as Wolf hurried to cover a document on his desk with one of his gardening magazines but not before Chris had read the title: "NSTC—Nano Security Technology Corp: A Prospectus."

Wolf stared at Chris for a few seconds, sizing him up.

"Well, what have you found out about my daughter's disappearance?"

"Sir ..."

"Call me Wolf."

"Other than the fact that it's obvious that she's been kidnapped, it also appears the perpetrator had help from someone on your staff."

"Why do you believe a staff member was involved?"

"Based on my experience and given the number of guards, alarms, and video monitors you have in place, it would be next to impossible for someone to get onto this estate, let alone leave carrying a body, without being seen. Also, the northwest floodlight passes by Tara's bedroom window every twenty seconds. He had to have at least one accomplice, maybe more."

"What's your plan, Chris?"

"First, I'm going to recruit some outside help."

"No."

"What do you mean, 'no'?"

"I don't want anyone except you involved in this investigation. I don't want the rest of the world knowing about this. Not even my other guards."

"Your daughter is missing, and you're worried about publicity?"

"You have to understand, Chris. If I'm seen as vulnerable, my family will be in further danger. I have a lot of confidence in you. I'm sure you can get my daughter back before anyone else finds out she's missing. By the way, we still haven't received any ransom demand. How soon do you think that will happen?"

"Usually within twenty-four to forty-eight hours. Since I'm doing this alone, I'd better get to work. I need you to order all staff members to remain on the estate for the next seventy-two hours, and anyone who is currently off the estate must return. I'm going to interview each of them. If anyone raises my suspicions, I'll do a deep background check on him. I won't rest until I find Tara."

"Thanks, Chris. What reason should I give my staff for detaining them for so long?"

"Tell them someone has stolen a rare and valuable painting from your personal art collection. The accomplice in Tara's kidnapping will know it's a ruse, but that doesn't matter. His or her guilt will be revealed when I'm done," he answered, standing to leave. "However, I have another question," Chris said.

"Yes."

"You seem very concerned about Tara now, but yesterday she told me you had disowned her and told her she'd have to leave. Is that true?"

"Are you insinuating that I had something to do with my daughter's disappearance?"

"No, but I have to investigate everything that's happened over the last few days. It's possible your argument with Tara triggered her to call someone she thought she could trust ..."

"I understand. It's true that we had a big argument, and I said some things I now regret, but it was she who disowned me. I offered to let her move out for a while to find herself, and, of course, to finance her completely until she could figure out what she wanted to do with her life, but she flatly refused my help."

Chris eyed Wolf suspiciously, wondering how much he could trust him. "I'll find her," he said, as he turned to leave.

After the office door clicked shut, Wolf picked up the office phone, "Did you hear everything?"

"Yes."

"Don't let Chris out of your sight. And do whatever you have to," Wolf ordered.

"Yes, sir."

CHAPTER SEVEN

IT WAS THREE IN the morning. Wolf rotated the combination lock on the wall safe behind his desk, his sharp hearing capturing the clicks of the final tumbler falling into place. He turned the short lever toward the floor and opened the small door. Inside, on the bottom of the four-cubic-inch safe, was a single green button. He pressed it, allowing a section of the wall behind the desk to slide open.

Wolf walked through the opening, and immediately the door closed behind him. He picked up a box of wooden matches from a shallow alcove in the stone wall and lit the end of the long, wooden, tapered torch he'd retrieved from its angled holder on the wall. Instantly, the area was illuminated by a natural fiery glow. He had often considered installing electricity in the secret room, but he liked the torchlight. It was nostalgic and brought back memories of the only two people he had ever loved: his father and his grandfather. Wolf had not known his grandfather very well, as he had been so young when the elderly man had died, but Wolf cherished the many stories his father had told him about the great man. Mostly, he recalled the delicate touch of his grandfather's hand affectionately caressing his head.

Wolf remembered the day his father had told him about the family legacy that had been passed down to each generation for the past five centuries. It was the day of his twenty-first birthday and his father had invited him to join him in his office.

Wolf thought his father must have had a special birthday gift for him—maybe the keys to his very own car—he hoped. His father walked over to the wardrobe on the far right wall as Wolf's stomach tightened with anticipation. His father returned with a chain suspended between his hands. It had a medallion hanging from it. As he got closer, Wolf could see that the necklace was an octagon-shaped, gold pendant with a triangular silver stone embedded in the centre.

"Father, why …?" Wolf stopped himself, knowing that he must have looked quite disappointed with what appeared to be a very minor trinket to mark such a major birthday.

"It was first given to a soldier—a very distant relative of yours," his father had said.

"A soldier?"

"Yes, a member of the legendary Black Army of the Hungarian king named Matthias Corvinus, in the mid-1400s. It was winter, and he was running through the forest away from a battle they were losing against the Bohemians. During his escape, he spotted a cave that looked like a good hiding place."

Wolf couldn't believe what he was hearing. Fear overtook him. He stared in disbelief—he felt sick to his stomach. In his mind, he could clearly see the soldier's face, intense, deep black eyes, his ruddy weathered skin, and frozen moustache. He had dreamt about him running in the forest so many times.

Without thinking, Wolf blurted out the question, "What was the soldier's name?"

Instantly, his body tightened, as if preparing to be slapped for rudely interrupting his father, who remained surprisingly silent while staring at Wolf with arched eyebrows and a sly, paper-thin smile on his lips. His expression said, *I know what you're thinking, son. I've been there myself.*

But his father's answer didn't come immediately. He continued to torture Wolf with a long, unsettling pause until he finally spoke.

"His name was Erich Eberhard. Over the years we've translated Erich's journals, and this is what he wrote about the incident."

Wolf's father lifted a heavy, black, leather-bound book from his desk. Pulling on the red ribbon that protruded from the bottom to open it, he began to read.

> *I was barely in the cave when I saw a light shining*
> *farther down the tunnel. I inched my way along the*
> *wall. Gradually, the light source came into view. It was*
> *a tall, round lamp, emitting light from its dome-shaped*
> *top. Edging my head around the corner, I saw someone*
> *standing in front of it. At first, it looked like a very tall*
> *man. As my eyes adjusted, I could see that he didn't look*
> *human. He stood about eight feet tall and was staring*

straight ahead with wide, silver, octagon-shaped eyes
that rested on either side of his long, hooked, hawk-like
nose. The light glared off the front of his bald head. His
body was wrapped in an unfamiliar tight-fitting, gold-
coloured suit.

Suddenly, I became powerless and no longer felt any
pain. My eyes fixed on the creature. My thoughts were
like stone. I walked to within a couple of feet the lamp,
which was giving off heat as well as light. Its warmth
penetrated my clothing, right down to my grateful,
damp, cold flesh. Because of the creature's solid silver
eyes, I couldn't tell if he was looking at me or if he even
knew I was there. Without warning, his massive legs
flexed and he squatted down, but after a few seconds,
he straightened his back and stretched out his hands,
revealing a chain identical to one that was draped
around his thick muscular neck.

Then, he stood up—straight and steady like a
massive horse. When he reached his full height, he leaned
toward me, hands outstretched, holding the necklace
between them. It was then that I noticed he had only
three fingers on each hand, and the backs of his hands
were covered with bumps that resembled large warts. I
was convinced that he was not of this place—but from
what evil place had he come? I wondered.

Gently, as if sensing my fear, he placed the chain
around my neck, and then placed his hands on each side
of my face. I tried to yank my head free but his strong
grip held me firm. At first I felt comforting warmth
from his hands, but the intensity increased until my
face burned as if lit by a thousand torches. However, as
fast as the temperature rose, it quickly cooled. I touched
my hand to my side. In astonishment, I found that the
wound was no longer there.

Suddenly, there was a voice in my head telling me
about an accident, about crashing into planet X15. I
figured the voice could only be coming from the monster

before me. No, he wasn't a monster. With his powerful strength, he could have crushed me at any time but instead he shared his warmth, healed my wounds, and treated me with kindness. Somehow, I could hear him in my head. He must have realized my confusion, because he went on to explain that X15 was his people's name for this world. He told me that his own people would soon come to rescue him. He asked if I would stay with him for a while, because he had been alone for a long time. I wondered if he could also hear me, so I thought the words, "Sure, I'll stay with you," and nodded my head.

We mentally engaged each other, exchanging thoughts about our worlds. Mostly, I listened in awe as he described his home planet and his journey to our planet—how he had traveled millions of our years in twenty of his own. He talked of folding space to make time go faster. This traveler from a distant star told me fantastic things about my world: that it was round and mostly covered with water and had many separate masses of land. Everything he told me was extraordinary and unbelievable, but yet there he stood—evidence that what he was saying was possibly true. I wasn't sure how much time had passed when he told me I could leave because his people would soon arrive. I asked him how we had been able to talk to each other without speaking. He said that he had given me the ability when he had held my face in his hands, and the necklace allowed us to understand each other's language. I asked him if I could keep the necklace as a token of our meeting. He nodded 'yes,' mimicking my earlier gesture.

Without warning, a shaft of light consumed him. When it faded, he was gone, and so was the lamp, along with all evidence that he had ever existed, except the necklace.

Wolf stepped toward the stairwell and descended into the cavern below the house. Over the years, the steps had been worn smooth by numerous footfalls. His feet landed with determination on each of the twenty stairs.

Tonight was special. He would activate an important step in his plan, which, when complete, would allow the legacy started by his great ancestor, Erich Eberhard, to continue.

Now, Wolf surveyed the cavern as if it was his twenty-first birthday all over again and he was seeing it for the first time. He marvelled at the intricate white-painted stone floor with its small ruts and irregular surface that made it resemble the terrain of the snow-laden forest that Erich had trod through and on which Wolf had fallen many times in his youthful dreams. There were also the artfully constructed bushes at the cave's mouth. But best of all was the hand-carved, craggy old hornbeam tree. It was a shame Grandfather hadn't lived long enough to see the tree's completion. Beyond the hornbeam was the cave entrance, complete with the layered stone ceiling. It was as dark as the threshold that Erich must have first crossed in the fifteenth century.

After generations of searching, no one had ever found the original Bohemian cave. They only knew the description of it from their dreams and from the chronicles that Erich had left behind.

Wolf stepped into the blackness. Inside the inner chamber, which had been designed to resemble the location where Erich had first met the alien, he placed the torch in the middle of a low stone monument that protruded from the floor. His father had told him that it represented the warm light device that had stood between Erich and the alien.

Wolf knelt down, planting his knees on the fibre mat in front of him, his legs jutting out behind him and his back as straight as an iron gate. He bent forward, reaching toward the monument, and then inserted his right hand into a slight recess at its base. He lifted out the necklace that his father had given him, held it high and thought about his plan to enter the minds of Chris and Una to make them forget what they knew and make them believe that Tara had runaway.

"This one's for you, father," he said, before going into his trance.

CHAPTER EIGHT

CHRIS SHOOK WILLIAM'S HAND and asked him to take a seat in the chair on the other side of the table, and then flipped through the man's information sheet. One of Chris's many CIA contacts who owed him a favour had provided him with a profile on each of the Ostermann staff members—no questions asked. This provided a baseline of personal information not usually found on a resume or job application, allowing Chris to ask questions to establish each staff member's level of honesty.

"Do you know why you're here, William?" Chris asked.

"I heard somebody stole one of the boss' paintings. I hope you catch the son of a bitch."

"So do I. How long have you worked for Mr. Ostermann?"

"Three years."

"Are you happy working here?"

"It's number one."

"Why do you like it here so much?" Chris asked.

"The money, mostly."

"Directness, I like that."

Chris had gotten used to the direct, snappy answers from the other guards. He knew they resented him. He was the newest guard, and he was interviewing them as if they were all criminals.

"I like to be direct, and you're going to get more of it," William said.

"Where did you work before you came here?"

"I drove for an armoured car company."

"How long did you work for them?"

"Twenty years."

"Why did you quit after such a long time? You must've been close to retirement?"

"I could've retired in ten years but Ostermann offered me twice the salary. Couldn't turn that down. Anyways, I can't afford to retire."

"Why?" Chris asked.

"Wife and kids."

"How many children?"

"Three girls and a boy."

"That's a big family. Must cost a lot to keep them fed and clothed."

"Damn right," William said. "Especially my two older girls. It seems they need a new pair of shoes every couple of weeks. And clothes ... they're always buying the latest fashion. Gonna spend me into poverty, they are. And my son eats like I own a grocery store."

"I guess it would be tempting to make a few extra dollars if the opportunity presented itself."

"It would but not at the risk of losing this job. Ostermann has treated me very well, and I wouldn't do anything to betray him, if that's what you're implying."

"Don't you have another major expense?" Chris asked.

"What are you suggesting?"

"You have difficulty staying away from the horse track. Isn't that right?"

"Whoever told you that is full of it."

"Who said anyone told me?"

"You bastard. You've been following me?"

"No, I just happened to see you there one night, and you certainly didn't have the relaxed demeanour of someone who only goes to the track a few times a year. And believe me, I know the difference between a hardened gambler and someone who plays the horses periodically."

"So what if I gamble a little more than I should?" William snapped. "What makes you such an expert?"

"It's a long story. And, anyway, I'm the one asking the questions. This schedule indicates you were working Wednesday night when the painting went missing. Do you remember seeing anything suspicious?"

"No, not really," William answered, his face turning red, clearly infuriated by Chris's style of questioning.

"What do you mean, not really?"

"Well, the lights were on in Ostermann's office between four and five AM He's often there late at night but not that late."

"Did you check it out?"

"I thought about it, but no," William said.

"Why not?"

"We're not to go near the big guy's office. It's a rule."

"Who was on shift with you that night?"

"Gordo."

"Do you mean Gordon Macklin?"

"Yes."

"Did either of you leave your post for any reason?"

"I left for a two-minute pee break. That's all," William admitted.

"So, you're saying Gordon was alone for two minutes. And, in fact, so were you."

"Yes, but—"

"Thanks, William. You can go, but I remind you not to leave the estate in case I have more questions."

"Yeah, yeah, seventy-two hours …"

Chris stood abruptly and walked away, pretending not to listen to anything further. He'd done something similar with each of the guards, instilling doubt and uncertainty in their minds. He hoped one of them would panic and make a mistake. However, like most of the staff, William was fairly average. Sure, he had a gambling problem but what man didn't have at least one vice? And when pushed, he'd admitted it.

Chris had interviewed all of Wolf's fifty-three staff members, and only a couple of them had raised an inkling of suspicion. He would do a further background search on them, but Chris was certain he'd find nothing substantial. It was frustrating to be no further ahead than he was. Wolf's staff was either very loyal or very smart.

Chris had slept very little during the past twenty-four hours. He'd been having strange dreams in which he'd heard a voice that sounded like Wolf's. Even though he tried hard, he couldn't remember what the voice had said to him. The only thing he could remember was hearing Tara's name. Chris had also begun to doubt his original premise that Tara had been kidnapped. He was starting to think that she had simply run away. It was a gut feeling, and through experience, he had learned not to ignore his gut. Yes, her bed had been a bit dishevelled and her window had been left open, but none of that proved she'd been kidnapped. Besides, Wolf still had not received a ransom note.

Chris returned to Tara's bedroom and got down on his hands and knees to comb the carpet one last time, desperate for clues, any clues. Having decided to proceed on the theory that she may have left the estate of her own accord, he hoped to find something he might have missed that would support his theory.

Chris stood, turned toward the bedroom wall, and noticed that the bottom drawer of the dresser was slightly open. When he opened the drawer fully, he was astonished by what he saw. Tara's clothes were organized in matched sets of shirts with pants and blouses with skirts. He thought this was highly unusual for a young woman, but Tara was no ordinary young woman. There were four empty spaces. He wondered why he hadn't checked this before. It wasn't like him to miss something so obvious. He knew her clothes were laundered every day, so if any pieces of clothing were missing, it was because she was either wearing them or had taken them with her. *She must have changed into a set of fresh clothes.* This was an indication that she had run away, confirming his most recent theory.

A sudden noise interrupted his thoughts. He spun around to find Una standing by the bedroom door.

"How long have you been there?" Chris asked.

"About thirty seconds. Have you found any new leads?"

"It's possible. But before you say anything I must tell you something else."

"What?" Una asked.

"Well, I'm beginning to think that Tara actually ran away and was not kidnapped."

"Yesterday you were so convinced that she'd been kidnapped. Why do you now think she's run away?"

"It's a …" he hesitated to mention gut feelings, especially to Tara's mother who deserved better, " … based on my interviews with the estate's staff. None of them seemed like they would betray your family. If that's true, I can't ignore the idea that she could've run away. There's also this," he said, motioning toward the dresser.

"What?"

"Missing clothes."

She walked over and looked into the open drawer. "It does look like she left on her own, but what about the broken lamp? Doesn't that mean she struggled with someone?"

"Maybe she was in such a rush to leave, and with the light off, she miscalculated where the nightstand was and knocked the lamp over."

"How would she have gotten off the estate without help? You said that would be nearly impossible."

"I still believe someone helped her, and I'll find out who it was."

"How could she hate us so much to leave this way?"

"I don't know. None of this makes any sense."

Frustrated, Chris stared at the dresser as if hoping a major clue would present itself like a gift. Nothing came. He considered his conversation with Tara two days before in the garden, but he couldn't recall anything of importance. They'd just chatted about the nice weather and beautiful gardens. He wished he'd engaged her further and asked more probing questions. Maybe she would have imparted something that could help him now.

He was about to leave when he saw two evenly spaced indentations in the carpet.

"What are those from?" He asked.

"What?" Una asked, squinting to see.

"Those two indentations in the carpet, near the wall between the end of the dresser and the closet door."

"They look like they're from Tara's backpack. She must have run away."

The two of them silently looked at each other. Chris clasped her hands. Their eyes met briefly. In that instant, he knew they had a common connection—their shared fondness for Tara.

"Chris, when you find Tara, tell her she doesn't have to return to us. As much as I'd like her to, I just want to know she's safe and well."

"Me, too," he said.

Una walked away, leaving Chris deep in thought. Even if Tara did run away, she must have had help. Who could it have been? Chris suddenly remembered there was one other man, in addition to Wolf, the chief guard, and himself, who had level-four security—George Ferguson, the chauffeur. George could exit the main gate without reporting to the guards. Chris hadn't interviewed him because George's name had not been on the list that Wolf had provided.

I guess Wolf trusts him so implicitly that he doesn't even consider him a suspect, Chris thought. But it was hard to believe that Wolf Ostermann trusted anyone that much.

George Ferguson's short, black hair was beginning to turn grey along the edges. His face barely gave away his sixty-plus years. The only signs of his age were a couple of shallow lines on his forehead and hardly noticeable crow's feet trailing out from the corners of his eyes. The rest of his face was resolute and finished off by a strong, square jaw. He was about six and a half feet tall with a fit, medium build.

Chris knew that George respected him, because the chauffeur had once told Chris that he wasn't like the other guards and that there was something more professional about him. Chris had simply told George that he was very astute. What else could he say? His previous employer, the CIA, had sworn Chris to secrecy. Fortunately, George had responded with a knowing nod, and hadn't pressed Chris for more information.

George usually smiled and waved at Chris when their paths crossed on the estate, but that day, George had an uninviting expression on his face.

"Hi, George," Chris prompted, waving cheerfully, using his best nonchalant approach.

George focused his eyes, as if seeing Chris for the first time, even though he'd been staring in his direction. Raising his right arm slightly and forcing a smile, he half-heartedly waved back.

"What's the matter, George?"

"Can't fool you, can I, Chris?"

"You should know better than to try."

"Something's wrong, all right," George said in a low voice.

"What?"

"Chris, one of my side jobs here is to keep a cursory eye on young Tara—well, not so young anymore, nearly a woman."

"Really? I thought I was her bodyguard."

"Wolf always has a backup. He never trusts anyone completely. Every morning, I watch Tara and her mother sitting together on the breakfast terrace, just long enough to make sure she's okay. Neither of them was there the last two mornings. I also check on her other times throughout the day, but I haven't been able to find her anywhere. I'd have known if they'd gone on a trip, because, of course, I would've driven them. I'm naturally suspicious when something doesn't match established norms. I've asked Wolf where she is, but he's not telling me anything. Do you know what's going on?"

Chris was a good judge of character, and George seemed genuinely concerned about Tara. But he could also tell by his conversations with George over the last year that he was cloaking his past. He had to be careful of anyone so guarded.

"George, let's take a walk. There are some questions I'd like to ask you."

The two men walked in silence until they reached Ostermann Falls outside the estate walls. The rushing water tumbled over the high cliff, steadily crashing into a man-made wading pool before flowing into the stream below—the lifeblood of Ostermann Valley. The rippling water glinted in the early afternoon's sunlight, reminding Chris of Tara's sparkling green eyes.

"Chris, what's with the paranoia? Why are we standing here close to the falls? So the noise will drown out our voices?"

"Taking no chances. I don't know who I can trust. As you know, one of Wolf's rare paintings was stolen—"

"Don't bullshit me, Chris. I know that's a cover story. I've worked for Ostermann for nearly twenty-three years, and he'd do anything to hide something that might embarrass him in front of his snub-nosed friends. Something's happened to Tara, hasn't it?" George grabbed Chris by the arm, his unyielding grip holding him firmly. "Chris, tell me what's happened."

George's words were direct. Chris knew he would win if he engaged George in hand-to-hand combat, but that wouldn't be necessary. He could trust George, who obviously cared a great deal about Tara and didn't want any harm to come to her.

"Okay, George, you can let go. What I'm about to tell you is only known by Tara's parents and myself."

"I'm listening."

"This will come as a shock, but for the benefit of anyone who's watching, I want you to laugh as if I am telling you a joke."

"I can handle that."

"Good. Here goes. Tara's gone missing."

Anyone watching the two men through very powerful binoculars with detailed attentiveness might have seen the microsecond of pain in George's eyes as he threw back his head in boisterous laughter, slapped his hand on his thigh and proclaimed what a great joke it was.

With a thin smile on his face, he asked, "Missing? What do you mean missing?"

"No one has seen her since she went to bed two nights ago. She wasn't in her room Thursday morning, and there were no conclusive signs of a struggle. It looks like she might have run away."

"Have the police been called?"

"No. Wolf wants to keep this quiet, so he has me looking for her."

"He couldn't have picked a better man. Is there some way I can help?"

"Right now, I just want you to tell me if you've seen anything out of the ordinary going on around here."

"You suspect she had inside help?"

"It's either that or there's a secret tunnel out of here."

"Of course, I'll help you find her. This feels a bit like old times."

"Old times?" Chris mimicked, raising his eyebrows.

"Yes. Since we're being honest with each other, I want to confess—I was with Delta Force. What about you?"

"CIA."

"Chris, I don't know how closely you've watched what goes on around here. Wolf's behaviour is very strange. To start with, it's not natural for a father to be so distant from his daughter, especially one as sweet as Tara."

"I actually thought they were very close."

"Oh sure, he plays the part of the loving father. They spend time together—walking, horseback riding, and eating together as a family—but I've watched as they've grown indifferent toward each other over the last few years as Tara's gotten older. Most people wouldn't notice, but I've worked for this family since before Tara was born. Wolf often works very late at night. One night, I spied on him in his office. I watched him open a panel in the wall behind his desk with a button that's hidden in a small safe behind the painting of his grandfather. He walked through the opening, and the panel closed behind him. I never did find out what was behind that wall. And lately, when travelling in the limousine, I've overheard him in conversations with people whose names I don't recognize."

"What were the conversations about?"

"They were usually very terse and indecipherable, but about a week ago, I overheard an argument between him and some guy named Tim. Wolf argued that, for the amount of money he was paying him, Tim would keep her as long as he wanted him to. At the time, I figured it was some kind of labour dispute at one of his many companies. It sounded like one of his senior executives who didn't care for someone he'd hired and wanted to get rid of her, but Wolf wanted to keep her around."

"Are you insinuating that Wolf might have had something to do with the abduction of his own daughter?" Chris asked.

"It wouldn't be the first time a father wanted to get rid of his child."

"That's true, George. And I know Wolf can be a hard-nosed bastard. What possible reason could he have for wanting to get rid of Tara?"

"I don't know. I just think we need to be open to all possibilities," George said.

"Yes, we have to be open-minded, but I think you're way off on this one. I'm positive she's just run away and we'll find her or she'll come back on her own," Chris said.

"I hope so. Just don't close your eyes when it comes to Wolf."

"I won't," Chris said, before suddenly jerking back.

Chris didn't hear the sound, but he saw the deadly results when blood spurted from George's forehead. With adept swiftness, Chris pulled George to the ground, flattening himself beside him on the opposite side of the stone barrier surrounding the base of the falls—away from the direction of the bullet. He yanked his gun from his shoulder holster, prepared to return fire. He waited for at least five minutes; no more bullets came. All he could hear was crashing water as he held George Ferguson's lifeless body.

CHAPTER NINE

THE BLINDFOLD WAS SO tight it felt as if it might separate the top of Tara's head from the rest of her body. She had been cast into a world where day and night no longer measured time, and each second was a tick of fear and uncertainty. The best she could tell, two people, a man and a woman, held her captive. As yet, she had not heard any other voices.

What did they want with her? Whose semen had they injected her with? Was she being illegally used as a guinea pig for some kind of experimental drug? Was the semen infected with some disease like HIV? Question after question pummelled her mind, trapping her in endless dread.

Tara drifted in and out of short, nightmarish bouts of sleep. She had just awoken from a nightmare in which she'd been screaming into the face of an ugly, scar-faced man claiming to be the father of her unborn child. She'd been thrashing and yelling for him to leave her alone. During the throes of her nightmare, the gown they'd dressed her in had bunched up and tightened uncomfortably around her body. She wished she could use her hands to loosen it. It was just one more irritation to add to her extreme discomfort.

Tara figured at least two days had passed. They had offered to feed her six times—or had it been four? She couldn't remember, because she'd refused all of them, except for the last one. She'd eaten only because somehow, in the melee of madness, she had realized that if she didn't eat something and managed to find an opportunity to escape, she'd be too weak to run. The drum riff in her head had lessened to an irritating throb, offset only by a dull pain in her shoulders from when the asshole had grabbed her with his huge meat clamps and slammed her into the hard surface she had been lying on when they injected her. She wanted to stand up and walk around, if only for a few minutes. She knew that she must have been moved to an actual bed because it was much softer and her upper body was raised at a slight angle. Wrapped handcuffs tethered to the bed restrained her arms and ankles.

With tape no longer wrapped around her mouth, Tara screamed, "You bastards, what the hell do you want with me?"

Tara heard the door latch release and felt a slight shift in the still air as it was exchanged for a waft of cooler air from outside the room.

"It's not what we want. It's what the man who's paying us wants," said the familiar female voice.

"And what the fuck does he want?"

"Silly girl. Your child, of course."

"Why the hell doesn't he just pay some willing woman to have his child for him? What does he need me for? And how the hell do I know I'm even pregnant? For all I know, this is some kind of major con."

"Frankly, I don't care what you think."

The smell of porridge filled Tara's nostrils. It was not just any porridge but porridge with brown sugar. The smell charged her with memories of breakfast with Mom and Dad on wintry Sunday mornings. She had almost forgotten what it was like—those days when they were more like a family and her father would sit her on his knee and tell her stories about the old country. Those were the best times.

She envisioned herself as a young child looking out from her bedroom window across the valley of Douglas fir and hemlock trees surrounding the edges of their estate, thinking that she could command them and the animals living there to do her bidding. Tara used to pretend that the glittering stream running through the valley was her magical pathway. She and her parents had spent many hours riding their horses along the valley trails. She had had her own special pony named Coco, and his coat was a dull reddish-brown colour. They had sauntered leisurely along the seemingly endless trails of Ostermann Valley, which had been named after her great-grandfather. When they weren't riding, they were usually swimming or relaxing around their massive pool, which was divided into a wave area, a stream of rapids, and a deep swimming area.

On most rainy afternoons or winter days, the family spent time in the games room, playing everything from basketball to billiards. In the evenings, the three of them would curl up by the large fieldstone fireplace in the library. Sometimes, her mother and father read her stories of mythology or of damsels in distress and princes who rescued them. Other times, they read stories from the old country—true tales of bravery and strength about men and women who fought to survive and expand their kingdoms. Tara's dad especially liked reading about a certain Hungarian king named Matthias. King Matthias boasted of a very large army called the Black Army. As a young girl, just the name—Black Army— had sounded shadowy and intriguing. She would always ask her dad to read more, because she knew he loved reading about those adventures, and anyway, the longer he read, the later she got to stay up. Sometimes Mom read stories about Ireland during the days before the Great Potato Famine—the disastrous event that had brought her family to Canada.

Tara's childhood was like a fairytale. However, as she got older, she began to get lonely and questioned why she wasn't able to go to school like other children. Why did she always have tutors? Why could she never go outside the walls of the Ostermann Estate? At first, Dad had told her that she was unique, and she couldn't be around other children because she might get hurt. At the time, his explanation seemed reasonable. Tara did feel very special.

"How did you sleep?" said the familiar female voice, intruding on her daydream.

"Like shit."

"Eat some of this, and you'll feel better."

"I tell you I slept like shit, and you think a bit of food is going to change that. How is food going to make me feel better after you've invaded me, injecting me with the semen of who-knows-what kind of despicable human being? He's probably so goddamn ugly it isn't possible for him to get anyone to do this legally. If that isn't bad enough, you continue to degrade me by keeping me blindfolded and tethered to this bed day and night. Even jailed murderers and rapists get to go out in a yard for a short stint each day."

"You'll be glad to hear that, starting tomorrow, you'll be allowed two hours of escorted exercise outside. One hour in the morning, and one hour in the afternoon. We have to keep that valuable body fit for a healthy birth."

"Who's the baby's father?"

"I don't know."

"What do you mean, you don't know? How do I know you didn't inject me with infected semen?"

"Why would we inject you with infected semen?"

"So you can try out some experimental drug."

"It will be a healthy baby. Don't ask me any more questions."

"Why do I need to be strapped to this bed? Why can't I be free to move around? Where the hell would I go other than 'flippyville' in this stifling room? And why do my eyes need to be covered?"

"We have to restrain you to prevent a miscarriage and keep you from hurting yourself. Wouldn't want to mess up now, would we?"

"What kind of monster do you think I am? Just because you sick bastards rammed this thing into me doesn't mean I'm going to harm it or myself. Not that you care much about me. With any luck, I'll have a miscarriage."

"We have to do what we have to do. Now shut up and eat to keep up your strength."

Knowing the woman was right, Tara reluctantly gave in. If she was ever going to escape, she had to maintain her strength.

The wet spoon touched her dry lips. The soft, hot, creamy porridge filled her mouth. Her taste buds acquiesced to the mixture of oatmeal, brown sugar, and milk. The scent of yesterday's memories coursed through her nose. The comfort food was little solace for her misery, but any respite was welcomed.

"Would you like a drink of orange juice?"

"Yes," she answered, gladly accepting the cold, fruity liquid into her mouth, savouring each sip.

When Tara finished eating, the woman said, "If you need anything else, just ring the buzzer, but don't make a nuisance of yourself."

"There is one thing I need before you leave."

"What's that?"

"To go to the washroom," she said, knowing it was the only way she'd have a chance to stretch her legs.

When she first stood up, she felt dizzy and nearly fell down. She grabbed the side of the bed and managed to remain standing. When they got into the washroom, it was the usual degrading routine—the part she hated the most, the reason she put off going as long as possible.

The woman guided her to the toilet, saying, "Do what you came to do," she snapped the command like a leather-clad dominatrix.

Tara lifted her gown and sat on the toilet. The woman watched the whole time, even while Tara sat on the can. Inside, Tara smiled deeply as her evil side kept hoping she would have to shit a lot and stink up the bathroom with such a stench that the woman would have to leave. Nothing seemed bad enough to send that bitch away.

"You've got two minutes left, so you'd better hurry."

Tara took her time. She knew the woman wouldn't harm her, especially, as the woman kept reminding her, she was carrying a baby somebody had gone to a lot of trouble for. She still couldn't believe that anyone would go to such lengths to have a child. She knew there had to be something more to this.

After Tara finished, the woman walked her back to the bed and rebound her hands and feet. Tara ignored the woman and idly drifted back to when she was fourteen, a day when she had argued with her father about a video he had insisted she watch. Ironically, it had been called something like *What to Do if You're Ever Kidnapped*.

"Why do I need to watch that stupid video?" she had yelled at him. "Nobody can get to me behind these huge stone walls laden with prison guards and the multitude of spy cams and the high-tech alarm system on the property."

"Tara, they're not prison guards. They're security guards. Their job is to protect this family and keep our property safe."

"Whenever I hear the words 'protect' and 'safe' in the same sentence, it makes me want to puke." Defiantly, she had opened her mouth and shoved her finger down her throat, pretending to gag herself. "I'm sick of hearing about protection and safety. The only thing I'm protected from is the chance to be a normal teenager," she had screamed at him as she had slammed the door and left the reading room that day.

As much as Tara hated her father, she would even have been glad to see him right then or any other familiar face. She knew her mother would be worried about her. She couldn't remember the last time she'd hugged her or told her that she loved her. Tears filling her eyes, Tara regressed to a childlike state. She longed to be home sleeping in her own comfortable bed—her soft, cozy bed surrounded by her own things. She could see her stuffed animals on the shelves above the dresser and the full bookcase underneath the large window, each of the book titles staring back at her, especially her favourite, *Gone with the Wind*, which was a little more worn than the rest. Tara longed to have breakfast with her mother on the terrace. She would tell her how much she loved her and how much she regretted her behaviour when she had been younger, especially her impatience and sarcasm.

According to the kidnapping video she had watched, Tara was supposed to engage her captives in small talk. So much for that, she thought. Until now, she'd mostly been belligerent and argumentative. She was also supposed to behave and cooperate with them to have a better chance of getting out alive. *Time for a change in attitude,* she promised herself.

CHAPTER TEN

Tara began meditating to get some reprieve from the persistent questions badgering her mind. Repeating her favourite mantra—"Coco"—she began to envision herself riding her childhood pony through the meadows of Ostermann Valley along the winding stream. Her anxiety slowly lifted as her mind transported to that special place of joy where naivety was once a virtue. She felt a wisp of breeze on the hairs of her arms while the heat from the late morning sun filtered through the trees and warmed her face. A smile caressed her.

Then, unexpectedly, the scenery dramatically shifted. The forest greens and sky blues changed to shimmering black and dull shades of grey. Long, feathery, grey shapes floated above—*clouds*, she thought. Coco had vanished, and she was walking on a rippled, granular surface that felt like beach sand underfoot.

Confused and frightened, she wondered what was happening to her. In what seemed like a short time, she had transitioned from emotional horror to a place of beauty to an unsettling, colourless world.

A voice spoke to her, "Tara, I can teach you, but you must relax."

The voice was familiar. Tara thought it sounded like the same German accent she heard in her dream about the soldier.

Astonished, she blurted out, "Who are you? What are you doing here? What is this place? You sound like the voice from my dream."

"I was the first."

Tara only understood the word first.

"What do you mean first? What's your name?"

"My name is Rhea. I was the first female born with the power, and you are the second. There are many things to teach you. To begin with, I was better than the males. When you fully grow into your power, you'll be more powerful than I was."

"Power. What are you talking about? Are you even real?"

"Yes, Tara, I've waited for you for over three hundred years—"

"Three hundred years ... that's not possible."

Tara knew what was happening. She'd fallen asleep. She was dreaming again, but this time it was different. Had she reached a further stage of her recurring nightmare?

"You're not dreaming."

"How did you know my thoughts?"

"I know everything."

"That's not possible. No one knows everything."

"Tara, give me a chance to prove it to you. Still your mind, and feel the energy. Feel it move through you. Imagine yourself lying naked on the soft, silt bed of a shallow stream with your face just below the surface as the water ripples over and around you. It's part of you, and you're part of it. You're fluid. Your body melds with the cool, natural liquid."

"Naked, water, stream," Tara, chanted.

Tara knew that she must have finally passed over the line between sane and insane. But her resistance weakened, as Rhea's repetitive words became her thoughts as well. She could see and feel the cool water swish around her skin, quenching her hungry soul, filling the painful gaps in her life that ached for substance. The ripples gradually increased as the water slowly swirled around her, building into a dizzying force and wrenching her from her solitude. She felt as if she was being sucked into a giant eddy. She tried to resist, her hands helplessly reaching for a lifeline that never appeared.

Rhea continued talking, "You're fluid. The energy isn't controlling you. It is you. You are the energy."

Tara didn't understand and closed her eyes tightly, wishing the torment would end and hoping to wake up. In the darkness, there was no more spinning. A surge of extraordinary power coursed through her body. She immediately felt stronger and much more capable. Fear no longer controlled her; nothing could harm her. She opened her eyes and determined that the swirling funnel of water was actually an encompassing energy that flowed through and around her.

Tara sensed another person's presence, not in the room but standing next to her in that place. It must be Rhea, she thought. Up until now, the voice had only been words in her dream, but now it seemed real and somehow physical, as if it was standing right beside her. Except it wasn't; it kept moving. It was a separate stream of energy that flowed like a tributary into her energy—*a link to the past*, she mused.

"How do you feel, Tara?"

"Like a god."

"By human standards, you are."

"What?"

"I guess maybe a small demonstration is in order. Think about Chris Landry, your bodyguard."

"Why would I want to think about Chris?"

"Because he is being deceived, and only you can open his mind to the truth."

Tara decided to play along, hoping that, if this was real, it might be her means of escape from captivity.

She thought about Chris. She pictured him that last day, sitting on the bench at the entrance to her father's gardens. She could see his calm face and those liquid blue eyes, like tropical coves capturing her every word, absorbing them into his mind.

Another powerful surge of energy cut through her body, threatening to explode through her skull. She was bombarded with emotion—pain, anger, and deceit—none of it hers. Where was it coming from? Suffocating confusion overwhelmed her. But somehow she could still hear Rhea telling her to keep thinking of Chris. With her last morsel of will, she forced herself once more to think of Chris. Tara repeated his name over and over and gradually the cyclone of emotions subsided. She felt peaceful again.

"What was that?"

"It was the collective thoughts of everyone—awake and asleep—in the world."

"Damn. It felt like my brain was being shredded into small pieces by a threshing machine."

"I'm sorry. I'd forgotten how overwhelming it is the first time."

"Overwhelming! That's the understatement of the millennium."

"Tara, continue to think about Chris."

She continued. He was in front of her, lying on the ground by Ostermann Falls. There was somebody beside him, and even though she couldn't see his face because Chris was blocking her view, she could tell by the way he was dressed that it was George, the chauffer. *Why is Chris lying on the ground with George?* she wondered. Then she noticed the gun in Chris's hand. Chris moved, revealing the gruesome bullet wound in George's forehead and blood running down the side of his face, pooling on the ground.

"Chris has shot George! Why would he shoot George?"

"Tara, Chris didn't shoot George. You must listen to his thoughts. Everything isn't as it seems."

She concentrated. A scene of George being shot played in her mind along with other disturbing thoughts.

"You're right, he didn't shoot George. He also thinks that I ran away from home. Why would he think that?"

"Because those thoughts were put into his mind by your father."

"I don't understand why my father would want him to think I ran away. And how could he implant those thoughts? None of this makes sense."

"Your father is the reason you're here, Tara."

"I don't believe you. Why would he do such a thing? I know he doesn't care about me, but I doubt that he hates me this much to put me through such an ordeal."

"He has a five-hundred-year-old reason, dear."

"What is that supposed to mean? Stop speaking in riddles."

"Okay. I'll give you the short version. Otherwise, it'll take too long. Five hundred years ago, an ancestor of yours by the name of Erich Eberhard, the soldier in your dream, found a strange being in a cave while he was trying to escape the advancing Bohemian army. I've since come to realize it was an alien."

"So, this Erich what's-his-name was a coward."

"No. His army was being slaughtered. There was no longer any point in them standing and fighting. Anyway, as I was saying, the alien introduced Erich to a power by placing his hands on the side of his head. I remember his journal describing it as being as hot as a thousand torches. And then the alien gave Erich a chain with a medallion on it that allowed him to hear the alien's thoughts.

"What the alien didn't realize was that by doing this, he had caused a genetic change in Erich. The mutated gene was passed down to future generations. However, no one really understood or figured out the power until I was born. I soon discovered that at any time or any place, I was able to exercise the power of mind walking—as it's come to be known. Whereas the men—as I learned through observing my son—could only go into people's minds when they were asleep. Before I died, I had a vision that the next female mind walker would be born in the third generation of the twentieth century, and that she would be even more powerful than I. I was able to remain in this place until the day of your maturity, hiding secretly in a suspended state from the men who have continually abused the power."

"Why is only one child born in each generation?" Tara asked.

"In the beginning, multiple children were born with the power. Ignorance at the time raised fears that too many births might dilute the power and it would eventually disappear. My great-grandson decided that from his time on, each generation would only have one child, a practice that continues today."

"Assuming I believe you, if you've been here all this time, why haven't you stopped the men from abusing the power?"

"I lost any ability to use the power when I died, but my life force was able to remain. For a while, I thought you might succumb to your father's wishes and continue the legacy of greed and self-interest perpetuated by the men of this family. You can't imagine my joy when you denounced your father. I know that sounds terrible, but you'll soon understand why it was necessary. I only have so long in this place to teach you. We must continue because my strength is fading. Go back into Chris's mind."

"I'm there," Tara shouted.

"Good. Visualize his thought pattern of you running away and trace it back."

"I see it."

"What do you see?"

"It looks like the filament from a light bulb, only longer and pulsing with electrical charges. I can also hear the stream of thought about my running away."

"Follow it backward, Tara"

"How?"

"Listen to the words as they emit from the energy but start from the last word and listen to them in reverse until you get to the beginning."

Tara tried and failed the first four times. Her natural instinct was to listen forward. She was about to give up when finally it began to make sense. She realized that it wasn't enough to listen to the words in reverse but if she could visualize each word it was easier to backtrack through Chris's thoughts. With every word it got easier. She reached the end of the filament—or was it the beginning? She wasn't sure. Something was blocking her from going any further. Tara could see a knot of energy—a place where the filament had been entwined into a ball, with sparks propelling from its surface, making a sound like radio static.

"Rhea, there's a sparking energy ball."

"I know. You have to destroy it."

"How?"

"It can only be destroyed by tracing it through. Continue to follow the energy stream through the knot. When you get to the centre, you might get a bit disoriented because the lines will start to cross over each other, but you must keep going until you get past the knot. That is the only way to destroy it. It requires a lot of discipline and concentration to stay focused and not go the wrong way while tracing through a memory block. I know you can do it."

Without hesitation, Tara continued to follow the string of energy as it twisted and turned. She could feel her focus shifting as she concentrated on the path ahead. Alternate courses appeared in front of her. She got confused, wondering if she was on the right trail. She closed her eyes for a second to reorient herself; that only made things worse. Her head was spinning, and she lost her balance.

Tara abruptly opened her eyes, and the path became clearer; she hoped it was the right one. She continued. She soon rounded another curve. She could see a straight line before her—no more multiple lines, just one—and it was straight ahead. She heard an explosion and when she looked back the knot was gone.

Tara listened once more to Chris's thoughts, and he now remembered seeing the blood-covered bed, the evidence of a struggle the night Tara had disappeared. She could sense his bewilderment as he wondered why George had been shot and why he had thought she had run away when she'd obviously been kidnapped. He should have known better. What the fuck was wrong with him? He didn't make stupid mistakes like that.

Tara hated to hear him rebuke himself.

"I did it, Rhea!"

"That's wonderful. Now there's one more thing I have to show you before my time here is finished. You need to permanently block your father from entering Chris's mind."

"That's great, but how?"

"We create something that I call an empty mind. You flood a stream of nonsensical words and phrases to surround Chris's mind. Once you've done that, when your father searches for Chris, he will hit the wall of random thoughts and won't be able to locate him. From Wolf's viewpoint, Chris will appear to be dead. You will create a nothing kind of mind, a barrier around his real mind that doesn't project his name or real thoughts, thereby protecting him from access."

"How long does this barrier stay in place?"

"Stay in place?"

"How long does it last?"

"Only you have the power to remove it. At some point, believing that the person is dead, Wolf will give up. Remember, you can't do this until Chris leaves the estate, because otherwise your father will know he's alive. Now that Chris realizes you've been kidnapped, you can guide him to you."

"How?" she asked, feeling like the word "how" was becoming her new mantra.

Tara listened for Rhea to continue. The German accent she once feared and now trusted was silent. Tara was alone again, yet she knew she was going to be okay and free soon. She understood what she had to do.

CHAPTER ELEVEN

CHRIS HEARD WHISPERING IN his mind like the sound of a light breeze blowing across a live microphone. The breathless voice sounded like Tara's, but how could it be? Believing it was the stress of the moment, he closed his eyes and shook his head to clear this thoughts. But the whispering persisted, and suddenly, without explanation, he remembered that Tara had been kidnapped. An ugly vision of rumpled bloody sheets shattered his thoughts, burdening him with guilt for all of the time he'd wasted, thinking she'd run away. How could he have ever believed Tara had run away? What was wrong with him? As quickly as it had started, the whispering stopped.

George's lifeless eyes pulled Chris back to the current situation, gripping him with conviction. George had mentioned Wolf behaving very strange lately.

Chris knew that his memory had somehow been altered; nothing else could explain his belief that Tara had run away when he knew that she'd been kidnapped. He believed Wolf was behind the deception. From experience, Chris understood that memory modification was possible, but when ... Did Wolf have the ability, or had he hired someone? Either way, Chris was certain Wolf was behind the kidnapping of his own daughter. Why would he want her out of the way? There were too many questions, and no time to waste.

"I'll find her, old man," Chris whispered to George, placing his fingers on his dead colleague's eyelids, drawing them closed.

Chris hated to just leave George lying on the ground out in the open. Religion had never been a part of his life, so he just wished George a good journey as he covered him with his jacket.

Chris knew that whoever shot George was a trained marksman and after, seeing all of the guards' profiles, he didn't believe the sniper was one of them. Knowing Wolf was involved, he was even more certain that it wasn't one of the guards because Wolf wouldn't trust them to keep quiet. He would've hired an independent contractor.

The shooter was smart; he'd waited until Chris and George were standing in a spot that would keep George's body hidden from the guards' view when it fell. Judging by the angle of the bullet's exit wound, the rifle had to have been shot from a fair distance west along the ridge above.

Chris pulled himself in close to the stone barrier and peered upward, checking for the best vantage point that the shooter would have chosen along the cliff. Without binoculars, it took him a few seconds to zero in on the prime shooting location. It was where the cliff dipped in and immediately jutted out to the south creating a small peninsula shape, providing a platform to shoot from that pointed straight toward where George and Chris had been standing.

Chris didn't see any movement in that area to indicate that the shooter was still there. Then it happened—a flicker of light.

"Shooter," he shouted loud enough for the guards to hear him as he ducked behind the barrier; a bullet pinged off the stone above his head.

His plan worked, the guards starting firing in the direction of the sniper, keeping him pinned while Chris made his escape.

He bent low and ran in a zigzag toward the property's north gate. A bullet ripped through the grass just ahead of him. He jumped, landed on his hands, and flipped, landing on his feet just inside the property. He ran along the garden path, using the bushes and raised flower gardens as cover. He crouched below the hedges as he expertly weaved his way through the familiar twists and turns of the massive garden toward the exit closest to the garage. He looked around the edge of the ornamental post at the garden entrance to see the two closed-circuit cameras shielding the underground parking garage from intruders. The shooting had stopped, and Chris knew that the guards would now be looking for him. He needed a car, but he couldn't disable the cameras without setting off the alarm. If the alarm went off, Wolf's guards would immediately know where he was.

"Fuck it," he yelled and ran toward the garage.

Once inside the garage, Chris moved quickly. He lifted the keys for the blue 2003 E500 W Model Mercedes from its hook on the key rack. It was the newest of the five Mercedes and handled the best; it was also only about twenty feet away. He noticed the empty spot where the silver Mercedes always sat. Jake must have checked it out.

Jake was the chief guard and the only other person on staff besides himself and George allowed to drive any of the cars. Jake was also the only other man who could of have helped a kidnapper get Tara off the estate undetected.

Chris jumped into the car, engaged the ignition, and hit fourth gear as he squealed out of the parking lot. He sped through the gates of the estate to the public roadway. He no longer cared that his face was being recorded. If he hadn't been trained to control his emotions, he would have given the finger to his unseen watchers. He wasn't surprised when no one followed him, because Wolf didn't like drawing attention to himself and wouldn't risk a car chase in daylight, in case something went wrong. Wolf also knew where Chris was headed, and when Chris found Tara a deadly trap would be waiting for him.

He had been driving for about a half hour when strange thoughts entered his head accompanied once more by Tara's familiar whispering voice. There was a short, silent pause, and again his mind was pelted with random words. He thought he must've been going crazy.

Tara could hardly believe what had just happened. Was any of what Rhea had told her true or was it a stress-induced vision? She wanted it to be real, but she was afraid it was simply her mind's way of coping with the enormous pressure of her incarceration, giving her hope.

It's not possible. A soldier encountering an alien and being genetically mutated with such an unnerving power? Yet, for many years, she had repeatedly had the dream, and it was always so real. The voice in the dream had definitely sounded like Rhea's. There was only one way to determine the validity of what Rhea had told her; she had to go back into the trance.

Tara began to meditate. As she'd done before, she imagined herself lying naked in the stream, the cool water lapping against her skin. She focused for what seemed like minutes, and nothing happened. She was about to give up when she remembered the chant, "naked, water, stream," that she had repeated over and over. Slowly her body lightened, melting away the stress. Once again the cooling water swirled around her. The formidable energy coursed through her, jarring her back into the colourless world. Her psyche was instantly hammered with the thoughts and emotions of all people on earth. Tara struggled to ignore the crushing onslaught as she searched out Chris's mind.

A flash of what looked like a steering wheel briefly appeared, but the overwhelming tide of emotions once more diverted Tara's attention. She forced herself to concentrate. Her breathing gradually slowed as the cacophony of voices quieted, transforming into a rhythmic flow of energy. She soon realized that the jumbled thoughts and emotions belonged to the minds of individual people. Testing her theory, she singled out one of the minds. It seemed like she was becoming part of it. Suddenly, she was able to hear the person's thoughts. It was a woman named April who was contemplating suicide after her husband and only child were killed in a car accident. Not wanting to invade her privacy, Tara swiftly broke free from April's consciousness. She understood the reason that her father had to be stopped—this superior, influential ability should not be in the hands of someone so corrupt.

Tara once more searched out Chris. As Rhea had previously instructed, she envisioned him. It wasn't long before she found him, recalling her last memory of him kneeling beside the lifeless body of George Ferguson. Through his eyes, she could see that he was driving a car, and from the passing scenery, she reasoned that he must have left the estate. As Rhea had told her, Tara had to block Chris's mind. What had Rhea said to do? Oh yes, she was to encircle Chris's mind with nonsensical thoughts. A nonsensical thought …

Tara tried using childhood nursery rhymes. She rearranged the words and imagined placing each word around the periphery of Chris's mind. They quickly fizzled and disappeared. Concentrating harder, she tried again. Once more, they vanished, but more slowly this time.

It'll work this time, she thought. She imagined placing the letters of each word as if they were individually embossed. This time, they remained. Tara had succeeded in blocking Chris's mind from her father's manipulative grip.

Tara now had to guide Chris to her—a task much more difficult than she had first anticipated, complicated by her not knowing where she was. Maybe she could enter the mind of one of her abductors, and through his or her eyes, get a description of her location. She hoped she could then transfer the information to Chris.

This plan proved to be troublesome since she didn't know her abductors' names. *Rhea, I wish you were here*, Tara lamented. She was searching through the infinite collection of minds and was becoming overwhelmed when an idea came to her. She pressed her foot on the buzzer at the end of the bed, and within minutes, someone came through the door.

"What do you want, bitch?" bellowed the gruff male voice.

Just as Tara had guessed, she could directly enter his mind by being in close proximity.

"Sorry, sir. I pressed the button by mistake."

"It's about time you showed me some respect. You know, little girl, I could snap your spindly, little neck with one hand."

"Wow!" Tara exclaimed.

"Now that's what I like to hear: fearful respect. I'll let it go this time, but bother me again unnecessarily, and I'll break one of your fingers like a gingersnap."

"I'll be more careful, sir."

"Damn right you will, you little skank."

With that, the musk ox—as she began to think of him, mostly because of his hideous body odour—left the room with her in his head. Tara watched through his eyes as he walked the windowless hallway. He stopped in front of an elevator.

When he looked up, she could see the illuminated floor number—level B. She assumed she must be in a basement. The elevator door opened, and he pressed the first floor button. On the panel beside the door, she could see three floor numbers including the basement. There was a mirrored wall on one side of the elevator chamber.

As luck would have it, Tara saw his face while he admired himself, running a comb through his thick, black hair; she could later implant the image in Chris's mind. He was huge with a broad, round, fleshy face and a pug nose. He had a short, thick neck the diameter of the fence posts used for the horse paddock back home and a chest as big around as a rain barrel. He looked like he weighed about three hundred pounds. No wonder her shoulders still hurt from him slamming her into the steel platform. *He really is more musk ox than human*, she thought, grinning to herself.

The elevator stopped and the door opened to the first floor.

"What did that spoiled little brat want?" the woman shouted from another room.

Musk Ox didn't answer.

"Hey, you dumb brute, what did she want?" the woman yelled once more as she came through the doorway into the same room as Musk Ox.

"Nothing."

"What the fuck?"

"She kicked the buzzer by mistake, but I'm sure she won't do it again."

"You didn't harm her, did you, Tim?"

"No, Marta, just a slight threat."

The woman was closer now, and Tara could see her better. She was a short, thin woman about the size of Tara's mother, and her straight red hair hung below her shoulders. Her face had a grey pallor and tightly drawn cheeks—*too many cigarettes and late nights*, Tara supposed. There was no doubt that Marta was the one in charge. Now Tara knew her two abductors' names and what they looked like, but something was still very strange. They had travelled up three stories, and there were still no windows.

"I'm going up top for a smoke. I have to get out of this rat hole before I go fucking berserk. Keep an eye on things," Marta said.

"Sure."

Tara intuitively switched from Tim's mind to Marta's without much effort. She was getting the hang of this mind walking.

Marta opened a door to a set of metal stairs that looked like a fire escape and slowly ascended them until she got to a trapdoor with a combination lock on it. Tara watched as she pressed the numbers, committing them to memory. Once the woman was through the trapdoor and standing on flat ground again, Tara's excitement increased. Here, there were windows. The sun blazed into the room, exposing a thick buildup of grime on the glass. The woman glanced around as she moved toward another door. Tara could see that they were in an old abandoned warehouse; it was an open cavernous space with extremely high ceilings and steel support girders. Marta opened the second door and walked into what was once probably the front office. Tara panicked at the sight of overgrown bushes outside the office window, realizing they were on the ground floor. *Oh my god, I'm three stories underground! How the hell will Chris ever find me here?*

Even though Rhea was gone, Tara could hear the echo of her words telling her to remain calm. If she panicked, she would be of no help to Chris. Even though the outside area of the building was overgrown with weeds, there was a swath through the tall weeds—probably flattened by the locals—through which she could see a highway and a sign she couldn't read. With her power, she tried unsuccessfully to get Marta to move to the right so she could see the words on the sign. It was then that Tara realized her powers were not fully developed; manipulating minds would require a lot more practice and patience.

Rhea, why couldn't you have stayed longer? she thought.

Just as Marta snuffed out her cigarette and turned to leave, a deer wandered into the trampled pathway outside, causing her to turn back to the window. When the deer spotted her staring at it, it bolted, allowing Tara to see the writing on the road sign. It read, HASTINGS PARK 1 KM. Hastings Park—Tara remembered being there with her mother and father once. The park was in Vancouver.

She had enough information to guide Chris. She stayed with Marta until the woman unlocked the trapdoor to ensure that she had the combination for getting into hell.

CHAPTER TWELVE

CHRIS HAD BEEN DRIVING on the rippled, gravel road alongside overgrown ditches for twenty minutes and barely saw the little wooden sign that read BOB'S BAIT SHOP NEXT RIGHT, five feet before the turn. He skidded to a stop and made a sharp right turn onto an even rougher gravel road. The four wheels of the Mercedes took turns bounding through potholes as the car inched along. He swerved to miss low-hanging tree branches that had encroached onto the roadway over time.

He was beginning to wonder if Dak's place still existed when he saw a left turn sign. He turned the corner and was faced with the steepest hill he had ever driven down. He kept his foot solidly on the brakes as the car slowly crept downward. At the bottom, he drove straight for half a kilometre before rounding a short bend and driving straight into a weed patch that he guessed was once the parking lot of the old rundown, shack-like store. The slightly tilted, square building was covered with parched, grey wood siding with remnants of teal paint still clinging to it. A white sign with faded orange letters that read Bo 's BA T SHO hung tenaciously over the dilapidated wooden porch.

Chris had known about this place for three years, but he had never needed to visit it until now. This was where strung out field operatives and mercenaries came to either chill out or hide, depending on whether they were stressed or running from someone. Dak, the proprietor, never asked any questions.

The word was that Dak, a retired NSA analyst, almost swallowed the sporting end of his shotgun, but before pulling the trigger, he had thought better of it and come up to British Columbia, to get away from everything. He had found a fishing camp and liked it so much that he had bought the property from the old man who had owned it and had built a few more cottages. He had gradually let out the word that he had a place available for operatives needing to get away from the stress of fieldwork or for mercenaries wanting to hide from their enemies for a while. Everyone who came understood that they were on neutral ground and were not to harm anyone, even their worst enemy. It was a code that, as far as Chris knew, had never been broken.

The old wooden screen door hanging on the storefront screeched open and a young man about twenty-three emerged. He was at least six feet tall with a muscular build, military-style brown hair, and a thin moustache that blended with sideburns ending at the base of his chin. So much for retired NSA operative, Chris mused. Poor bastard, stuck back here in this desperate place, probably someone who wouldn't play the old boys' games. The young man cautiously ambled over to the car, probably wondering what the hell someone was doing driving a Mercedes into his shithole. Most people likely came in by helicopter or by four-by-four.

As he approached, Chris rolled down the window and hollered, "Hey, what's your name?"

"Dak. I'm the owner of this fine establishment. What brings you here in …"

"I know, you must think I'm an idiot driving down here, in a Mercedes no less. I thought Dak was an …"

"Older man," the young man said. "He was. He died two years ago, and I took over from him. I'm his son, Dak Junior."

"I'd like to ask you a few questions. Can we go inside?"

"Sure, Chris," Dak said, waving him out of the car.

"How did you know my name?" Chris asked.

"From the time you turned into pothole hell you've been under surveillance. The reason for the potholes and the steep hill is to slow down intruders—I mean potential guests—and give me enough time check them out. Chris Landry—spoiled rich kid who graduated with two PhDs from MIT and afterward joined the CIA. You vanished a year ago from the payroll to work as a babysitter for billionaire Wolf Ostermann's daughter here in British Columbia. How's that for a summary?"

"Other than the spoiled part, yes. How'd you get all that information so fast?"

"That's between me and the electronic cosmos."

"Okay, okay. Sorry I asked. Since you know all about me, what about you?"

"Not much to tell. My father—as you know—was an NSA analyst, and I, being the model son, followed in his footsteps. When Dad took sick, I came out here to look after him and got hooked on the great outdoors. I also came to believe in what my father was doing here and saw that many people had come to depend on this place. So, after he died, I decided to carry on."

"What's with the name Bob's Bait Shop?"

"That was the name of the business when Dad bought it. Out of respect for the old man, he kept it. And it makes for a great cover, don't you think?"

As they entered the shop, the old, spring-loaded screen door squawked and bounced against the doorjamb a few times before staying shut. Chris looked around and figured that the inside of the shop probably hadn't changed much since the original owner had left. There was a long counter with an antiquated hand crank cash register on it. All types of fishing bait and lures hung from the walls, and cobwebs spanned every corner of the ceiling. Chris liked the small plaque on the counter that read: "If you're still fishing, you're not dead. But then again, you could be in heaven."

"So, what can I do for you, Chris? To start, would you like a beer?"

"No, thanks. Some water or juice would be nice."

Dak reached into a small fridge behind him, the only modern piece in the place, pulled out a bottle of spring water, and handed it to Chris.

"Thanks," Chris said, opening the bottle and taking a long drink. "That babysitting job you mentioned ..."

"Yes."

"Well, the baby's gone missing."

"Run away or taken?"

"Taken."

"How can I help?"

"Since this place is not far from the Ostermann mansion, it's an ideal location for a kidnapper to stay while casing the estate."

"Do you think someone who stayed here kidnapped Ostermann's daughter?"

"Her name is Tara, and I don't think anything. My exhaustive search of the estate grounds and Tara's bedroom only uncovered circumstantial evidence that she was taken. So, I'm assuming it was a professional or someone with help from the inside. I'm looking for any leads I can get. If one of your more recent guests has been asking questions about the surrounding area, specifically about the Ostermann's, I'd really like to know."

"Since you know of this place, I also assume you know about its code. I'm forbidden to tell you anything that's said here by any guest."

"Yes, I know about the code, and I completely agree with it, but we're talking about a young civilian woman who's never harmed anyone. Tara's only stigma is being the heiress to a massive fortune. Whoever kidnapped her must be dealt with."

"You're right. If they've used this place to plan Tara's abduction, then they've broken the code already. You have to promise me, though, if you find them and they didn't kidnap Tara, you'll forget what I'm about to tell you."

"Promise."

"A man and a woman stayed here for the last couple of weeks, which is unusual in itself, since most people usually stay for at least a couple of months."

Dak stopped talking as if considering whether or not to continue.

"Go on, Dak," Chris urged him quietly.

"Well," he continued hesitantly, "they didn't openly say much but there are ways to hear private conversations. And based on what I heard and knowing what you've told me, I believe they were planning to kidnap someone. I can't tell you who because they were too smart to give that away."

"Do you have tapes of their conversations?"

"I've told you all I can."

"Do you have pictures of them?"

"Yes."

Impatiently, Chris asked, "Can I see them?"

Dak walked to a filing cabinet—another piece of modern furniture that Chris hadn't noticed before—punched in a key code, opened the drawer, and pulled out a file. He removed two photographs from the folder and brought them to Chris.

"Here."

Chris carefully scrutinized the pictures. He didn't recognize the man, but he did recognize the woman. She was an evil, Irish bitch named Marta Steinhouse, and she looked even more prunish than the last time they had met. Marta had been the secret weapon of the Irish Republican Army for years but no one had been able to take her out, including him. She had once nearly blown him away with a simple pipe bomb. Information flowing into his mind caused Chris to look more closely at the man's picture.

"Tim," he heard himself say.

"You know him?" Dak asked.

"No. Well, I've never met him, but I recall seeing his profile from one of my past missions," he answered, quickly covering up that he had no idea who the man was, yet somehow he suddenly knew his name and had a full description, including the size of his girth. Information continued to flow into Chris's mind—an image of a road sign and details about a warehouse and a trapdoor along with a lock's combination. He could envision it clearly. What was going on? Once more, a voice in his head sounded like Tara's. This time, he was sure it was her voice.

Chris recalled a quote from one of his trainers, "When logic stops making sense, go in the direction your instincts point you."

He didn't understand where the images were coming from, yet they were too real to ignore, especially since one of them was an exact description of the face in the photograph in his hand. And Dak had just confirmed that the man's name was Tim. Executing his plan would definitely require Dak's help.

"Chris. Chris!" Dak, shouted.

"Wha ... what?"

"You were standing there in a daze, man. What's wrong? Are you okay?"

"Yeah, I was just deep in thought. I have an idea where the two of them might be holding Tara hostage, and I'm going to need your help. Are you in?"

"Absolutely. If those two kidnapped Ostermann's daughter, I'll use them as an example to future guests thinking of breaching my trust."

Chris knew the Mercedes was equipped with a GPS tracking device. Time hadn't permitted him to remove it before leaving the mansion. Now he would have to leave it in place. If he removed it, Wolf's helicopters would quickly be sent to its last known location. If indeed Wolf was part of this, and he had to assume he was, he needed to keep him thinking that he was falling into his trap while he drove to the warehouse, the final details of which were being broadcast to his mind.

"Do you like the blue Mercedes I'm driving?"

"Yeah, but I don't have much use for it here. This is a long way from Vancouver."

"That's true, but I need your truck."

"It's yours," Dak said without hesitation, "I can always trade your fancy ride for another much better truck."

"The car is equipped with a GPS locater, and the man tracking it expects me to arrive at an old abandoned warehouse near Hastings Park," Chris said, weaving together partial truths.

"I know the warehouse. It's on Commissioner Street in Vancouver. It houses a three-story underground complex. A local mob family once owned it. The warehouse business was a front for their money-laundering operation. For ten years, the RCMP couldn't figure out where they hid their illegal enterprise until one of their own ratted the mob out."

"That's amazing," Chris said, knowing that he was headed in the right direction. "As I was saying, I will drive ahead of you in the truck. You follow me in the car, about one mile back at all times. When you get within a half-mile of the warehouse, pull over and wait one hour, then remove the GPS device and drive the car back here. That should give me enough time to rescue Tara and get out of there before the choppers arrive. I'm going to need some gear: night vision goggles, black clothing, and communication equipment for us to keep in touch. You know the drill."

"Yes, I do, and I have everything you need. Follow me," Dak said, as he headed for a black door in a recess to the left of the counter.

Dak and Chris descended the steps to the basement. It was very dry and had no windows, making it safe from curious onlookers. Chris was sure his eyes were bulging with excitement as he surveyed the impressive collection of high-tech spyware and weaponry. But he focused his attention and gathered up only the necessary items.

CHAPTER THIRTEEN

JAKE WATCHED AS THE headlights approached and the car eased over onto the shoulder of the road. Through his night scope he could see it was a Mercedes, but he couldn't tell the colour, because, of course, everything looked green. Wolf had called Jake earlier in the day to tell him that Chris might arrive there tonight, so he was watching for him.

He couldn't tell if it was Chris in the car. He hoped it was. Jake hated that son of a bitch. He had been elated when Wolf had said to do whatever it took to prevent Chris from getting into the warehouse. He could see that the driver of the car was talking to someone, but no one else was visible in the front or back seats. He thought the person listening must be very short, possibly a child, or was intentionally crouching below the windows. Maybe the driver was talking into a hands-free communication device to someone not in the car at all. *Perhaps it is just someone having car trouble calling roadside assistance,* he thought.

"Come in, Dak."

"Dak here."

"I'm in place. Give me one hour and then move out."

"Roger that."

"Oh, one more thing, Dak. When I was driving by the approximate spot where you would have pulled over, my headlights reflected off something in the trees. It might have been nothing, but stay alert."

"Will do. Over"

Chris had driven past the abandoned warehouse, and under the light of the full moon, he saw that the building had suffered much neglect. Large pieces of red brick were missing from the south wall, and strips of planking hung from the front window frames where boards had been forcibly removed and panes of glass had been smashed. Oversize weeds interspersed with hawthorn shrubs had overtaken the unkempt yard.

Mature maple trees grew along the side of each laneway. Chris continued past the second laneway and drove another kilometre up the road. After waiting two minutes, he turned around and headed back. The road had a slight downhill grade—just enough to make it possible to kill the truck's engine, turn the lights off, and coast to within five feet of the original transport entrance without being heard. He engaged the emergency brake and shoved the gearshift into first.

In order to blend in with the dark night, Chris had applied black paste to his face and put a black cap over his blond hair. He made sure that his MPK knife was securely strapped to his right leg and confirmed that his P226 Navy Seal pistol was loaded. He walked along the transport lane to where the growth of bushes and trees tapered off. Through night vision glasses, he scanned the perimeter of the building, first along the front and then along the west wall. There was no activity except for bits of paper and packing materials swirling along the ground, propelled by a light breeze.

Any other night, a full moon would seem romantic, but tonight, its brightness was a detriment. He could be easily seen by anyone watching if he attempted to cross between the laneway and the building. So, instead, he ventured into the brush and trees that lined the west side of the entrance. He circled around until he was north of the building. Thorn bushes clawed at his clothing, slowing his pace and causing him concern. He had given himself an hour, which should have been plenty of time to take care of unexpected eventualities, but he hadn't anticipated such thick groundcover. With his arms in front of his face, he rammed through.

He reached the edge of the brush and came to a small clearing that led east toward the building. He was thankful that the growth was high enough to keep him hidden and that there were no more thorn bushes. He lay facedown and simultaneously used his arms and legs to shimmy toward the warehouse. Partway there, he found a narrow path, along which he saw clothing strewn about: a ripped short skirt, a pair of faded red sneakers, grey matted socks, and a pair of pink bikini bottoms. The smell of the weathered clothing, combined with the damp night air, reminded him of the time he'd had to disguise himself as a homeless man in Los Angeles. At the time, he had been grateful that his bout with rock-bottom poverty was only temporary and fictitious.

Chris continued his crab-like crawl across the last small patch of grass between a half-dozen maple trees and the west wall of the warehouse. Crouching in the shadow of the building, Chris ambled toward a window that wasn't boarded up, being careful not to step on anything that might alert Marta or one of her accomplices. He didn't know how many people might be inside, and he wasn't about to find out the hard way. The discards of druggies, used needles, empty rolling paper packages, and a slew of cigarette butts littered the ground. As he passed by a weathered packing crate that had obviously been used as a makeshift toilet, the smell of human defecation assaulted his nose. This place was obviously a playground for the local bottom feeders.

When he reached the window, he checked the time. Twenty minutes had gone by. The window was the kind that pushed in from the bottom, and the latch was broken, so there'd be no problem entering. Before lifting himself onto the wide ledge, he reached up his hand to check for broken glass or other debris that would make a noise when disturbed. He cleared the ledge with meticulous care.

Chris didn't hear the gun but he heard glass break beside his head just as he was about to hoist himself onto the ledge. In a single, fluid motion, he leapt away from the window to the ground and launched himself toward a Dumpster to take cover as another bullet ripped up the grass where he had first landed.

"That was fucking close," he cursed under his breath. "That shooter's damn good."

The accuracy of the shot reminded Chris of Jake's expert marksmanship and brought him back to George Ferguson's death and the bullet that had ripped through almost the exact centre of his forehead. Chris couldn't help but think that Jake was George's killer and was now bearing down on him. He called Dak on the radio for help to corral the bastard. It didn't matter whether it was Jake or not, he was about to meet a superior combatant, Chris mused.

"Dak, are you there?"

"Yes, Dak here."

"I'm under fire. He must be using a rifle. He's far enough away that I can't get him in my sights. I need you to circle behind him. Be careful, he might have you lined up as well."

"Roger that."

Using the night-light on his watch, Dak searched for the fuse panel under the dashboard of the Mercedes and removed the fuse for the interior lights. Then he slid over to the passenger seat and exited the car. To avoid making unnecessary noise, he pushed the car door to the frame. He checked his pistol to make sure it was loaded with a full clip and confirmed that he had a spare in his jacket pocket. Dak was glad that he had worn black clothing in the event that Chris needed some covert help. In hopes that the shooter was busy watching for Chris to make a move, Dak rolled into the roadside ditch. A bullet pinged off the gravel shoulder at the back of the car.

"Son of a bitch," he muttered to himself. "Chris, are you there?"

"Yes."

"The bastard spotted me rolling into the ditch and took a shot at me."

"Can you see a place to take cover?"

"Yes, there's a line of oak trees about ten yards ahead of me."

"Good. I think I know who the shooter is. He's a trained marksman. I doubt he can easily hit a moving target. We'll run toward him, dodging back and forth, taking cover before he has a chance to get a lock on either of us."

"Ready when you are."

"Okay, when I say 'go,' run like hell…. Go," Chris commanded.

The two men launched into a sprint toward their respective covers. Chris barely avoided a bullet that ripped up the grass beside him before leaping behind a pile of wooden skids.

Jake was well positioned in the crotch of an oak tree to observe both men advancing toward him. Wolf had told him that Chris was coming alone. So who was this other prick coming up on his ass? He was getting anxious and frustrated. He hadn't hit either of them, not even a graze. He wished one of them would just stand still for a fucking second. How the hell could he lock his sight on that pair of frightened gazelles running and dodging across the field? Jake swore he'd give Wolf shit if he managed to get out of this mess alive.

Chris pulled the head-mounted night vision goggles from his pack. The special goggles doubled as binoculars with 5x magnification and a view range of 675 feet. Through the hands-free goggles, he could clearly see Jake positioned in a tree about thirty yards away.

"Dak."

"Yes."

"I can see the shooter, and it's who I thought it was. I can disable him from this range. I need to take him alive."

"Understood. I've got your back."

"Okay."

Chris had last taken cover behind a scorched stump that had obviously been struck by lightning. The remainder of the trunk, with its matching charred base, lay on the ground beside the stump. He shifted to the right, using the rest of the tree for cover. Chris steadied his gun. He could see that Jake was lining him up with his rifle, his fingers quivering. Jake's hair was flattened to his forehead—a sign he was sweating. Not a trained combatant like Chris and Dak, Jake was visibly shaken. Chris hoped that Jake was rattled enough for him to get his shot off first. He would only get one chance. If he missed, Jake would surely take him out. He aimed, squeezed the trigger, and watched with satisfaction as his bullet struck Jake's trigger hand. Jake jerked back, screaming in pain.

"You rotten bastard, Landry," Jake yelled, cradling his wounded hand.

Chris jumped up. With his gun pointed in Jake's direction, he cautiously walked toward him.

"Drop the rifle, Jake. Get down from the tree," Chris demanded, "or the next one will separate your skull from your brain."

"Yes," Chris heard Dak yell as he arrived on the scene, "and if he misses, I won't."

"Okay, okay. I'm getting down, you son of a bitch," Jake said, throwing the rifle at Chris.

"Make it quick," Chris shouted, dodging out of its path.

Chris smirked with malicious satisfaction as Jake struggled down the tree with one hand. Almost at the bottom, Jake's hand slipped, and he fell to the ground, landing on his back. Chris stepped over to him and forcibly pressed his foot across his upper chest.

"Okay, Jake, how many others are in that warehouse with Tara?"

"Tara? What the hell are you talking about?"

"You know exactly what I'm talking about," Chris snapped, moving his foot, letting it hover over Jake's shot-up hand. "You helped Marta and Tim kidnap Tara and she's being held captive in that warehouse."

"Marta? Tim? Who the fuck are they?"

Waving Dak over, Chris said, "Gag this piece of scum."

Dak dutifully took off his shirt, ripped off the sleeve, and wound it tightly around Jake's mouth.

"Thanks. Now, Jake, raise your good hand when you're ready to talk."

Chris slowly lowered his foot onto Jake's bloodied hand, gradually increasing the pressure until Jake's face went red and tears pooled in his eyes. His gagged mouth moved with muffled screams as Chris pressed harder. Jake finally raised his arm.

"That's better." Chris said, nodding for Dak to remove the gag.

As soon as the gag was removed, Jake yelled, "You rotten bastard. When I get a chance, I'll kill you."

"Sure, okay. Are you going to talk or do we have to have a repeat? Nothing would give me more pleasure."

"I don't know fuck all about that warehouse or who's in it. I didn't even know Tara was kidnapped."

Chris signalled Dak to put the gag back on.

"No!" Jake screamed.

"Why should I deprive myself?"

"Wolf!"

"What about Wolf?"

"He ordered me to come here and guard this place, but he didn't tell me why. He also phoned and told me you were coming and to do whatever it took to keep you out of the warehouse."

"And I bet you revelled in the thought of getting rid of me, didn't you?"

"I have to admit I didn't have any problem with the idea of killing you."

"So, Wolf is behind the kidnapping. Old George was right." Chris didn't say anything for a few seconds. Then he fixed Jake with a cold stare of death and asked, with his foot once more hovering over Jake's maimed hand, "Did you kill George Ferguson?"

"Yes. I killed the nosy, old prick."

"Why?"

"Because Wolf ordered me to. But believe me, I was delighted to comply. The old bugger reported me a couple of times for stupid stuff. Chickenshit."

Chris signalled Dak to again put the gag around Jake's mouth. He slammed his foot down on Jake's hand, crushing it into the earth with his heel until Jake passed out.

"You psychopathic asshole, you'll never shoot anyone else with that hand again," Chris said, grinding the bitter words between his teeth.

CHAPTER FOURTEEN

CHRIS AND DAK WORKED flawlessly together. They didn't say a word as they tied Jake's arms and legs securely and lifted him into the trunk of the Mercedes. With a solid clunk, the trunk lid closed like the door of a meat locker sealing in its icy chill.

Chris spoke first, "Dak, give me an hour. Then make sure you take him someplace very remote, and don't forget to remove the tracking device from the car before you leave here."

"Don't worry, Chris. I have an old hunting cabin so far off any known trail it'll take him a month to find his way home—that's if he's really good. The cabin is well stocked with food supplies, so he won't starve. And I'll be sure to remove the cabin's phone."

"Excellent."

Chris knew Wolf would send a helicopter the minute the tracking device was disconnected from the Mercedes. It would take at least forty-five minutes to arrive. By then, they'd be long gone.

The two men shook hands and gave each other a knowing look, accepting that they might never see each other again. If they did, it would most likely be under similar circumstances. They were not friends or acquaintances; they were compatriots in a dangerous way of life. Not wasting any more time, Chris turned and ran back to the warehouse.

Wolf observed the blip received from the Mercedes' GPS transponder moving along the video monitor in his office as the car arrived in the vicinity of the warehouse. Chris was being his usual stealthy self by not driving directly to the warehouse, Wolf mused. Chris's arrival at the right location meant that Tara's powers had manifested much faster than he had hoped.

Fortunately, Wolf had had the foresight to put Jake in place to guard the warehouse from intruders, specifically Chris. He was anxious to hear from Jake, but he didn't dare call his cell phone for fear of alerting Chris and giving away Jake's position. He'd agonized over whether to use Jake for this mission, and now he was concerned that his faith in him was unfounded. Chris had been there for more than an hour, and Wolf had yet to hear from Jake. If he didn't call in fifteen minutes, he'd phone the idiot.

Chris tried to open the warehouse window; it resisted. He got out the black grease he'd used on his face and applied a generous amount to the hinges to loosen them and keep them from squeaking. He pushed the window farther in; it made a very small noise. Had anyone heard it? Chris waited for thirty seconds. No movement inside. He rubbed more grease on the hinges. He pushed the window again, and this time it silently opened far enough for him to climb inside. He positioned himself so he could slide down past the window and remain in the dark shadow of the wall. To avoid detection, Chris always wore rubber-soled shoes. With the night vision goggles back on, he couldn't see anyone or anything in the vacated building except for a few broken skids, remnants of wooden packing crates, and of course, smashed liquor and wine bottles strewn about by vagrants.

Cautiously, he moved toward the centre of the warehouse, which was the location of the trap door, as he knew from the image that had been projected into his head. Stepping carefully around the rubbish, he couldn't see anything resembling the trap door image in his mind. He wondered if he had mistaken or misinterpreted the message he had received from Tara. Or was it Tara at all? Had he walked into a trap?

Then, he noticed a square, micro-thin crack in the floor about two feet away—a sliding panel. He walked over to it and examined the area for any traps or trip devices. Deciding the area was clear, he took his knife from its sheath and twisted the tip in the small crack; the panel moved. He pushed the panel all the way back into its recess, revealing the trap door with a digital panel under a protective Plexiglas cover. He lifted the cover and keyed in the numbers that streamed from his mind. As he pressed the last number, the lock released with a soft *whoosh*. With his gun in hand, Chris slowly lifted the door, listening for activity. He didn't hear any sounds, so he opened it the rest of the way.

Below him was a set of metal steps leading into the darkness. Chris shone his penlight into the hole and counted ten steps leading down to a closet-like space with a door that blocked the entrance to what he assumed would be the underground complex. His gun at the ready, he proceeded cautiously. Once at the door, he listened intently for any voices or movement on the other side.

"There goes that damn buzzer again," Chris heard a male voice bellow.

That must be Tim, he thought.

"If it's another false alarm, I'm going to strangle the bitch," Tim said.

"You won't do any such thing, you big shit. I'm not forfeiting my share of ten million dollars because of your short-fused stupidity," Marta said.

For the first time, Chris was thankful for that condescending wench, even though he might have to kill her.

"I'll check on her this time," Marta snapped.

Chris slid his single-lens spy tube under the door and positioned it until he could see Marta and Tim sitting at a small card table about ten feet away to the left of the door. Marta stood up and walked toward an elevator on the far wall.

Once the elevator closed behind her, Chris tried the doorknob. It was locked. He would have picked the lock, but he couldn't take the chance of being heard and having Tim shoot at him through the door. Quarters were too close to use even a small amount of the C4 he had brought with him. He needed the element of surprise.

Chris backed up and stood on the second step from the bottom of the iron stairs and placed one hand on each of the railings. From that position, with one swift motion he lifted himself into the air, and with the momentum of his powerful body and torpedo speed, he flung his legs toward the door, knocking it loose from its hinges. With a panther-like leap, he propelled his body through the door and crashed into the room, rolling along as bullets from Tim's gun lacerated the tile floor beside him. Slowing down, Chris raised his gun and fired, hitting Tim in the shoulder and jarring Tim's aim just as he fired another shot. It ricocheted off the elevator door, missing Chris by at least five feet. Chris's next shot blasted into Tim's neck. Tim ignored the blood spurting from his throat and continued shooting wildly. Lining up his gun once more, Chris pierced Tim's forehead with his third shot. Tim rocked backward, righted himself, and slammed face first into the card table, demolishing it with his massive, lifeless body.

Chris, figuring that Marta had heard the gunshots, propped himself up against the wall next to the elevator door to await her return. The elevator door opened, but it revealed no Marta. He knew she wouldn't be so stupid as to blindly walk out. Chris had to be patient.

"Tim, are you okay?" she yelled. "Tim, what the fuck's going on?"

After a long silence, the elevator door closed.

"Shit," Chris shouted.

Tara heard footsteps running toward her room. Then, suddenly, Marta threw open the door and rushed in. Tara knew it was Marta, because she had immediately entered her mind.

She heard her thinking that something had gone terribly wrong. There were gunshots, and Tim was either dead or unconscious—he hadn't answered her. Marta was planning to escape with Tara out the back way by a route that she hadn't even told Tim about for fear he would have bugged out on her and taken all the money.

Marta didn't know what was happening, but Tara did. She was sure Chris was here. As Marta attempted her escape, Tara would guide him to them. Tara transferred thoughts to Chris's mind. She told him that she and Marta were on the lowest level and rushing down a hallway. Tara sensed his frustration at not being able to retrieve the elevator because it was locked out. She would have to try to tell him the direction they were heading so he could cut them off.

Tara scanned Marta's thoughts, hoping to find out more about the escape route so she could better inform Chris. She discovered that the hallway led to a short tunnel, ending at a set of iron stairs. The stairs ascended the full three flights into a utility shed at the back of the property.

Just as Chris was contemplating scaling the elevator's shaft via the metal cable that drew it up and down, Tara's voice entered his mind, this time explaining exactly where he could head them off. He knew where the shed was because he had seen it when he had circled around the building. He looked at his watch. In fifteen minutes, Dak would leave, and the clock would start ticking—another forty-five minutes later, Wolf's minions would arrive.

The shed was about thirty yards away, but he had the advantage because Marta didn't know that he knew her escape plan. And she had to climb three flights of stairs with an uncooperative young woman while he only had to cross a small field. Nevertheless, Chris didn't waste any time.

Wolf tried calling Jake with no success; the phone just kept ringing. Something was wrong, and he couldn't wait any longer. He dispatched one of his helicopters with five of his best men to the warehouse. Their orders were to secure the area and shoot Chris Landry on sight.

"What the fuck?" He cursed when he saw the blip for the Mercedes disappear off the screen. The blips for Jake and Tara were still there. Jake's was quickly moving away from the warehouse.

Wolf wasn't going to take any chances. He would send a second helicopter after Jake and let the first one continue en route to secure the warehouse area.

Chris had not waited long before the trapdoor in the utility shed's floor began to open. He crouched in the shadow of the trapdoor where he couldn't be easily seen. Tara emerged first. Once she had placed her feet on the top rung of the stairs, she threw herself sideways, rolling onto the cement floor.

Marta raised her arm through the trapdoor firing a single wild shot that careened off a steel vise attached to a workbench; the bullet lodged in the ceiling. Before she had a chance to take a second shot, Chris slammed his foot into the wooden door, crashing it into Marta's body. At the same time, he rapid-fired his gun, splintering many holes through the trapdoor. He didn't stop firing until he emptied the clip. He popped out the empty clip and loaded a new one.

"That's for my five buddies who died by the pipe bomb that was meant for me ... you ..." He lifted the trapdoor and using his foot, he shoved her dangling corpse off the ladder and listened as it thudded on the steel steps. He closed the door and went to Tara.

Terrified by the violent gunfire, Tara was curled up on the floor in a shuddering ball of fear.

"Tara, are you okay? It's me, Chris"

Tara's throat tightened. She couldn't answer. She uncoiled herself and sat up so Chris could see her better, nodding her head to signal that she was okay. She heard him coming toward her and then felt his arms around her. Her arms lashed around him responsively. Sobbing uncontrollably, her body shook like an injured puppy. She felt compassion and an unaccustomed feeling of safety in his arms—not protection like behind the estate walls, more like a stronghold against the cyclonic winds of a raging storm. Chris was her refuge.

After a few seconds, Tara's voice returned, and she whispered, "Thank you, Chris"

"You're welcome."

Chris looked at his watch. There was no more time. In fact, he was five minutes over.

"Tara, we have to go," he told her, helping her to her feet while prying her arms from around his neck and removing her blindfold.

They were halfway to the truck when Tara stepped in a hole and fell, twisting her right ankle. She tried to stand but was unable to put any weight on her foot.

Chris lifted her into his arms and continued running. He could hear a helicopter in the distance. His time was up.

CHAPTER FIFTEEN

TARA HAD FALLEN ASLEEP, her head resting against the truck window. Her breathing was erratic; for seconds, she didn't seem to breathe at all, and then suddenly, a loud burst of air would erupt from her mouth followed by rattling snores.

They had barely escaped the warehouse before the helicopter landed. They were only about a half a mile away when Chris heard the props slow down—a signal that it was on the ground.

He looked at Tara as they passed under a street lamp. Her usual pink glow was reduced to a pale white. Her springy, curly, red hair was greasy and limp. She was the likeness of a young person one might find in a back alley with a needle in her arm. A good shower and some time in the sun would return her youthful beauty, but there were scars beneath the surface that would have to be dealt with. His only comfort was that she was still alive.

They were headed for downtown Vancouver, the opposite direction from her home. If he had his way, she would never go back there. Chris drove along Powell Street and was nearly at Gastown when Tara's body fell toward him. Her head jerked back spasmodically, waking her up. Her open eyes looked straight at him. Tara's once emerald eyes were now more of a mossy haze.

In a guttural sleepy tone, she said, "Did I thank you?"

"Yes, you did."

"Where did this truck come from? Are you taking me home? I hope not."

"Why?"

"My dad was behind my kidnapping."

Chris wondered how she knew about her father when he'd just found out, indirectly, from Jake. He was certain that Marta or Tim would not have told her.

Chris spotted a small, nondescript motel along the roadside and pulled in. The neon sign at the road read SECOND HOME MOTEL, ROOMS AVAILABLE $39.00 PER NIGHT. The parking lot was neat and tidy, and the building looked like it was in good repair except for needing a paint job. The price was right, because he hadn't brought much cash with him and didn't want to use his offshore debit card yet.

"Tara, why do you think your father was behind the kidnapping?"

"It's a long story, and I'm not sure you'll even believe me."

"After today, my mind is much more accepting. Does it have something to do with you being able to talk to me remotely?"

"Yes. It has a lot to do with that. Do you remember the dream I told you I was having?"

"Yes."

"Well, I don't have it anymore. But in place of the dream, I now have abilities that are beyond anything you can imagine, and I'm just beginning to discover them."

"If this is just the beginning, I can't imagine what you have to look forward to."

"Me neither. I'm afraid, Chris. I don't know what's going to happen to me."

"I'll stay with you, Tara. We'll get through this together, one day at a time."

"I feel a lot better knowing you'll be with me," she said, resting her hand on his shoulder.

"Tara, you need a good night's sleep and so do I. Let's stay here tonight, and we'll talk in the morning when our minds are clearer. Okay?"

Tara rubbed her eyes and looked out the window of the truck.

"Where are we?"

"Vancouver. You wait here while I check in."

"You're not going in there dressed like that, are you? With that black outfit on? You look like a cat burglar. They'll think you came to rob them."

"I have a change of clothes in the back."

Chris got out of the cab of the truck and pulled a knapsack from a box in the back. He had made sure to back into a parking space between a Greyhound bus and an extra long recreational vehicle, ensuring that his activities would be hidden from view. He opened the sack and removed a worn, navy blue cotton shirt, faded denim jeans, black sports socks, and a pair of running shoes. He quickly changed from his operations garb into street clothes. After looking in the side view mirror and making sure he'd removed all of the black paste from his face and neck, he opened the driver side door and looked in at Tara.

"Am I suitable for presentation now?" Chris was delighted to see a tenuous smile cross her lips.

"Yeah, you'll do. Get one room with two beds. I don't want to be alone right now."

"Sure thing."

He headed toward the motel. The black ops man had transformed into an average guy who could be seen in any town, on any street.

He thought about the plan he'd concocted while driving to Vancouver and wondered if he would be able to convince Tara to go to the United States with him.

"As you requested, my dear, I booked us in a room with two beds," Chris announced to Tara when he returned to the truck. "How's your ankle? Can you move it?"

Tara lifted her leg and moved her foot back and forth.

"It's a bit sore, but yes, I can move it."

"I've got a tensor bandage in my pack that I can wrap it with after you've showered."

Chris opened the truck door and offered Tara his arm. She leaned into him, using his body for support, and stepped down to the ground. He put his arm around her and held her up while they slowly made their way across the parking lot.

Chris panned the room. It was just big enough for two twin beds, with a foot of space between them, along with one small dresser to the right of the entrance door with a television on top of it. The washroom was on the left side of the room. The carpet was worn, but it looked clean, even though it smelled a bit musty—probably just age, he hoped. He pushed down on both beds to test the firmness of each mattress.

"Tara, which bed do you want?"

"The one by the bathroom. And, if you need to go to the washroom, you better go now, because I'm dying for a nice hot shower."

"I'm okay. Go for it."

Sitting on the edge of the bed, transfixed by the steam rolling out from under the door of the poorly ventilated bathroom, Chris pondered the months since Wolf had hired him, which was over a year ago. He wondered if there was something he'd missed—something he'd seen or heard that didn't seem relevant at the time but might have been a warning about recent events. Could he have prevented this horrible ordeal? He asked himself. He lingered on the conversations between him and Wolf, as well as others he'd overheard. There'd been nothing to indicate that Wolf had so little regard for his daughter. He knew that there had to have been something. How could someone with his training have missed it? He rebuked himself.

Chris picked up the remote control and flicked on the television, thinking some inane sitcom might take his mind off things for a little while.

A news anchor's urgent voice blared from the television, "If you're just joining us, there was an assassination attempt on Pope Benedict's life earlier today. Yes, the Holy Father of the Roman Catholic Church has been shot. Vatican City is a place of shock and solemn prayer. Thousands of Roman Catholic parishioners are amassed in St. Peter's Square. The Vatican secretary of state announced a few minutes ago that the pope is out of the operating room and in intensive care. He also said the Pope's injuries remain life-threatening, and he will be monitored around the clock. Details about this tragedy are still sketchy. It's suspected that terrorists were behind the shooting, but no group has assumed responsibility."

What the hell's happening to this world? Chris wondered if his former employer was involved. He shut the television off, not wanting to see or hear any more bad news.

Tara had been in the shower for over half an hour. Chris knew that she was trying to scour the wretched stench of the last few days from her body, attempting to erase it all. As if she could somehow purge the sediment of this horrible incident from her mind with soap and steaming hot water. From his own experience, he knew it was impossible.

The shower finally stopped running, and he could hear Tara crying. Cleansing tears would give her momentary relief, but it would take more than one bout of tears to wash away the pain of her father's betrayal.

She finally emerged from the bathroom wrapped in a towel. His thoughts were immediately suspended. His eyes were drawn to her glistening red hair, her pink rejuvenated flesh, and the tops of her firm, round breasts slightly showing above the white cotton towel. It was as if she had transmuted from that vagrant figure in the truck to some ethereal goddess, stepping through the misty gateway from her other world. Irrational lust inflamed him with unexpected sexual hunger. At that moment, all he wanted to do was caress the sensuous curves of her soft, tender flesh, feel her warm skin against his lips, and make love to her. Then he caught sight of her reddened eyes and chastised himself, knowing that his feelings were inappropriate.

"Chris, the bathroom's all yours," Tara said as she entered the room.
"What?"

She lowered her head and looked directly at him, "The bathroom. It's all yours."

"Good. Thanks. I can use a shower." *A cold one*, he thought.

Sheepishly, he got up from the bed afraid she would see shame in his eyes. He kept his head turned as he shuffled past her toward the bathroom.

When Chris returned to the bedroom, Tara was already asleep in bed. He turned out his bedside lamp and sat upright in the darkness with his head against the backboard, mentally reviewing the past few days.

A tapping sound startled him. He turned and saw that the phone Dak had given him had lit up and was gyrating across the surface of the nightstand. He reached over and grabbed it before it fell on the floor. Not wanting to wake Tara, he took the phone into the bathroom.

"Hello."

No response.

"Hello, hello! Who is this?"

"Chris. Is that you, Chris?"

"Yes. Dak?"

"It's Dak. I was ambushed. I haven't got much time before I'll be overheard. So just listen."

"Go ahead."

"After I arrived at my cottage, I heard the sound of a helicopter above the car, and the next thing I knew one landed in the field in front of the cabin. Then a voice through a megaphone shouted, 'Get out of the car. Come to the front and lie spread-eagle facedown.' I figured I'd better comply since it was dark and I couldn't see who I was dealing with. For all I knew, they could have had a bazooka aimed at me. As I was walking toward the front of the car some bastard fired, hitting me in the right shoulder, knocking me to the ground. I flipped over and scrambled to the side of the car before the next round of shots pocked the area where I'd been lying."

"What the fuck."

"What the fuck indeed. I escaped into the woods. Before going in too far, though, I watched two of them bust open the trunk and pull Jake out, while the third one came after me."

"Did you see them do anything to Jake?"

"They were untying him. It seemed like they were rescuing him."

"Didn't you take the transmitter off the car before leaving?"

"Yes, but there must have been another one."

"Impossible. I scanned the car thoroughly. Unless … ?" Chris panicked.

"Unless what?"

"I didn't check Jake for a transmitter. There must have been one on him. How could I have been so careless? I'm really sorry, Dak."

"I didn't think of it either. I'll have to cut you off soon. I can hear my pursuer getting closer. It doesn't appear that these guys are trained very well. Not by our standards, at least."

A loud explosion blasted through the forest.

"Dak, are you okay? What the hell happened?"

"I'm not sure. I think they blew up the car. Wait—my follower is leaving. I can hear him running away. It seems they're in a hurry to get out of here."

"Are you going to be okay, Dak?"

"Sure, I'm halfway down an underground bunker I built a few years ago just for this purpose. I have the medical supplies I need to patch myself up and a cot to lie on and rest overnight. Tomorrow, I'll head out of here."

"Okay, my friend, take care."

CHAPTER SIXTEEN

Chris stared expressionlessly at the bathroom door. If Jake had been planted with a GPS transmitter, had Tara been planted with one as well? Was it in the clothing or implanted under the skin? Knowing Wolf, Chris was certain he would find it under the skin. *How did Wolf get his hands on a transmitter small enough to go unnoticed under human skin?* He must have very high-level contacts in the military or some spy organization. Chris flicked the switch on the military-issued universal detection device that he'd gotten from Dak.

He walked over to Tara's bed. She had been sleeping fitfully. Her sporadic jerking and breathing had startled him more than once until it had evened out a few minutes ago. He observed her lying there—an innocent, a pawn in some mysterious plan that he didn't feel he was even close to unravelling. How and where did she fit in? Was Wolf associated with a secret sect? Was Tara to be sacrificed for a perceived greater purpose? Chris shook his head. He couldn't believe what was going through his head. He hadn't even watched much television as a child.

Chris ran the detector over Tara's body, starting at her feet. Halfway up her right leg it started to squeal. *Damn*, he nearly shouted before catching himself. He turned the volume down on the detector, so he wouldn't wake her and continued moving the wand. At her hip, the red light shone steady. He knew what he had to do next. He had to wake Tara. The two of them had to get out of there as fast as possible, but first, he needed to call Carl to secure their escape.

Carl was Chris's contact on his first assignment with the CIA; fortunately, the assignment had been in Vancouver. Chris and another agent had been assigned to monitor drug trafficking between British Columbia and the United States. The CIA had suspicions that terrorist cells might be funding their activities by supplying drugs to the United

States. Carl was the man who had prepared Chris to blend in with British Columbia's culture and had equipped him with a valid Canadian passport, driver's license, and health card. He had planned to call Carl before going to sleep to arrange a meeting for the next day, but it would have to be tonight.

The phone rang three times before a groggy voice said 'hello'; it sounded more like a growl than a greeting.

"Carl?"

"Who the fuck do you think it is? What fucking time is it anyway? Three o'clock in the morning! Who the hell is calling me at this hour?"

Chris remembered that Carl's language was a bit colourful because of his cover as a bouncer at a local rat hole called Hell Raisers, but he had never heard him swear like that before. Then again, he had never woken him in the middle of the night either.

"Carl, it's Chris …"

"Who the fuck is Chris?"

"Chris Landry. I worked on the operation between BC and the US with you and Jackson back in 1999 when I first joined the agency."

"Son, I don't know what agency you're talking about. You'd better be more specific."

"The agency that watches dogs as they sleep."

"What dogs?"

"The ones that would have you not see them," Chris said to finish the password.

Carl's tone changed instantly, as if someone had switched him to friendly mode.

"Well, Chris, it's been a long time. I'm surprised to hear from you. I heard that you'd left to do some private work. I probably shouldn't even be talking to you."

"That's true, Carl. I did. As for you talking to me, do you remember that night on Point Grey Road when I saved your ass from being shot off? If I hadn't come along, you'd have been playing dodge-the-fish in English Bay."

"Okay, Chris, you've made your point. What do you want?"

"I need a covert exit out of Canada and a safe place in the US to hide out for a while."

"Oh, is that all? Is it just yourself, or is this a family trip?"

"No. I have a woman with me too."

"Figures. How old is this woman?"

"Twenty-one. Carl, she's planted with a GPS tracker. I need you to arrange for a doctor to remove it."

"Would you like caviar and champagne waiting for you when you arrive as well? Who the fuck do you think I am, one-stop shopping for 'Spies R Us'? Anyway, what's to stop whoever put this tracker in the woman from using it to follow you right to me?"

"Nothing. That's why I need a GPS-blocking device. Stash it in a neutral location where I can pick it up before driving to your place, so I won't lead anyone there."

"Wow, this gets better all the time. Should I arrange for a private plane to fly you to the US as well?"

"Not necessary. A rental car will do."

"What?"

"Carl, what's your life worth?"

"Okay, but you're asking for a hell of a lot. We'd better be square after this, man."

"Absolutely."

"Chris, are you close to Gastown?"

"Yes."

"Good. It'll be there. You know the spot."

"I do."

"How long will you be?"

"Two hours."

"I don't know what doctor I'll find in two hours."

"I have complete confidence in you, Carl. See you then."

Chris clicked off the cell phone. The easy part was over. Now he had to convince Tara to go to the US with him. He sat on the edge of her bed and nudged her shoulder with his hand.

"Tara, wake up. Wake up, Tara."

Her hand thrust upward, knocking his arm away. She jolted upright and started pummelling him with both fists, yelling, "You bastard, you bastard, leave me alone."

Chris got hold of her arms as he tried to calm her.

"Tara, it's okay. It's Chris. I won't hurt you. You're safe."

Thrashing to free herself from his grip, Tara opened her eyes. The tautness in her face began to loosen when she recognized Chris beside her. Her arms relaxed, and he let go. Pulling the blanket up around her neck, she shimmied up onto the pillow. Chris handed her a couple of tissues to wipe perspiration from her face.

There was a tenuous silence between them. Chris knew what he had to say, but he didn't know how to begin until she questioned him.

"Why did you wake me? Was I having a nightmare?"

"No. In fact, you were sleeping quite peacefully until I woke you."

"Then why? I thought the idea was for us to get some rest."

"Yes … bear with me. I have a lot to explain and little time. Tara, do you know what the CIA is?"

"Yes, a geeky United States spy organization."

"Close enough. Before I came to work for your father, the CIA was my employer. My special training was the reason your father hired me. He wanted someone who could keep you safe under any circumstance."

"And you did."

"But I'm not sure how. I'd stopped looking for evidence of a kidnapping, because somehow, I no longer thought you'd been abducted. In fact, I believed you'd run away. I don't know how I could've forgotten such a thing. I've never forgotten anything in my life."

"You didn't forget, Chris. Your memory was blocked by my father."

"Huh?"

"The voice in my dream turned out to be a real person from the past. Her name was Rhea, and she still existed in a kind of holding state, waiting for me to become twenty-one. She introduced me to the power and informed me about my ancestry, including my father. She also told me that my father was the one who had had me kidnapped. Rhea showed me how to release blocked memories in people's minds—yours being my first."

Tara gave Chris the abridged version of how her family had received the power, how Rhea had first discovered its real potential, and then how the men through the generations abused it.

Chris tried to hide the disbelief he knew was cascading across his face. Suddenly, being an ex-CIA agent didn't seem like such a big deal.

"Figures," he finally responded, "give men power, and they always misuse it for greed. It's a good thing you were able to unblock my mind. Did you see any other blocked memories in there while you were poking around?" he asked, attempting humour but not sure he'd succeeded.

"I saw a couple of other ones but it's an involved process."

"Maybe later," Chris interrupted. "Right now, we have to get out of here."

"Why?"

He told her about the phone call from Dak and about how he'd discovered a GPS transmitter in her hip.

"Tara, do you trust me?"

"Of course, Chris."

"Good. We have to leave here, and a number of events are going to take place. I'll explain as we go along. In the end, we'll end up in the United States. Is that okay with you?"

"I don't care where we go, as long as it's far away from my father."

"I'm glad you feel that way, Tara, because we're being tracked, and I don't know what they'll do when they find us."

CHAPTER SEVENTEEN

WOLF'S FIRST PLAN HAD collapsed, but he quickly instituted his alternate. He was especially pleased with his ingenious use for Chris Landry. Now that Chris had screwed everything up, Wolf would use him as a babysitter. He never had planned on having Tara return to the estate. Once the baby was born, he would bring the infant to the estate and have Tara executed. In the meantime, he would let Chris watch over Tara until his grandson was born and then kidnap the baby and kill both Chris and Tara. All he would have to do is follow them wherever they went and, when the time was right, end their miserable existence.

"Pure genius. Perfect," he praised himself aloud.

His private cell phone rang.

"Yes?"

"It's me."

"Jake?"

"Yes. I'm parked up the road from the entrance to the motel where Chris and Tara are. What would you like me to do?"

"Jake, I want you to continue watching them, and if they leave the motel, follow them. And I want you to keep following them until they get to their destination, wherever that might be. Continue to watch them until I tell you otherwise. Is that clear, or did I use too many grade six words for you?"

"Will this assignment last much longer?"

"Until I tell you otherwise, it's indefinite. Just make sure you don't have any more surprises. If I have to send in the rescue squad again, believe me when I tell you … I'll break every finger on your other hand. And if I'm in a generous mood, I'll have you shot to put you out of your misery."

"Wolf, the GPS signal is moving outside. They must be leaving the motel. Why would they leave so early?"

"I don't know. Damn, unless Chris figured out …"

"What?"

"That Tara is implanted with a transmitter."

"Should I stop them?"

"No, you idiot. What did I just say? Just don't damn well lose them again, because he's probably planning to have the transmitter removed. They'll be a lot harder to track after that."

"They're about to pull out of the driveway."

"Before you go Jake, tell me what he's driving."

"It's a red half-ton truck with an open box. From this distance, I can't tell what make it is, but it's banged up quite a lot, as if it came from a construction site. Wait. On the tailgate, it says Ford in big block letters."

"Okay. Make sure you update me every half hour."

As he was pulling out of the driveway, Chris's eyes scanned the roadway up and down, looking for a tail. He spotted a navy blue, medium-size vehicle about two blocks up the street on the left side sitting below a streetlight. It hadn't been there when he had pulled into the motel. There was no house or office building within walking distance of the car, indicating that it was either abandoned or perhaps one of Wolf's men. If it was a tail, the driver wasn't very experienced. First of all, he should have parked in front of a house to look like he was visiting. Never, under any circumstances, should he have parked under a streetlight where he could be easily seen.

Seconds later another cell phone rang in a brown Chevy Impala a couple of blocks further up the street from the blue Toyota Camry. The Impala was backed into the driveway of an industrial complex and hidden from view.

"Raven here," was the terse response.

"They're driving a beat-up, red Ford, half-ton truck," Wolf told him.

"Good. Do you want me to take care of Jake?"

"Not yet. Wait till he outlives his usefulness. The kidnapper will concentrate on him, making him a decoy, drawing attention from you and your men. Right now the main objective is not to lose the kidnapper. I suspect he's headed to have the GPS transmitter removed from Tara, and then his next step will be to leave Canada."

"Where do you think he'll go?"

"Probably somewhere in the US."

"We won't lose him."

"You'd better not. I don't do failure well."

"We don't fail."

"I'm glad to hear that, but results speak louder."

Chris looked at Tara in the soiled, dishevelled clothes she'd been wearing when he had rescued her. He regretted that they hadn't had time to get her some clean ones. Her eyes were fixed ahead. Her hands were placed at least six inches away from her body, resting solidly on the truck seat, as if not wanting to touch her clothing in case the texture of the fabric alone could cement the horrific memories into her conscience.

"Sorry, we weren't able to get you a change of clothes, Tara."

"That's okay, I understand. We had to get out in a hurry," Her tightened lips parted long enough to respond.

Chris left her with her thoughts. She would talk more when she was ready.

They drove along in silence for a while longer until Chris pulled over to the side of the road.

"Where are we?" Tara's voice trembled with anxiety. "Why did you pull over?"

"We're in Gastown, and we won't stop long. I just have to pick something up. Remember, I told you there would be some odd events taking place."

"I'm going with you, Chris. I don't want to be left alone."

"It's okay. You'll be within my sight the whole time."

"No! I'm going with you. I won't be left alone again."

Against his better judgement, Chris reluctantly gave in.

"Okay, you can come but not all the way. When I tell you to stop and turn around, I must insist that you do so. Do we agree?"

"Alright, as long as you don't go too far from me."

"I won't."

The two of them stepped out of the truck and walked across the cobblestone sidewalk toward a statue of an old, rugged-looking man with a cowboy hat.

"Do you know who that man is, Chris?" Tara asked.

Encouraging the small talk, he answered, "Gassy Jack. He's considered to be the founder of Gastown."

"Thus the name Gastown," she echoed.

"You got it."

"Whew, what's that awful smell? It smells like someone threw up."

"In this place, anything's possible."

"Yuck, it's getting stronger."

"And for good reason. Keep looking straight ahead."

Tara looked down anyway, and what she saw made her turn away quickly. It was a pool of vomit with an empty wine bottle lying in the middle of it at the foot of the statue.

"Why would someone do such a thing?" she asked.

"Winos."

"Winos?"

"Yes, people who are addicted to alcohol often become winos because cheap wine costs less than hard liquor. It's kind of a bizarre homage that it would be lying at Gassy Jack's feet."

"What do you mean?"

"He established the first saloon in Gastown."

After they passed the statue, Chris turned to Tara.

"I need you to face the other direction and stay here while I pick up my parcel."

"Where are you going?"

"I'm going to see that old woman sitting on the sidewalk next to the building."

Tara looked at the building as if for the first time. It had many windows and was all lit up inside. A woman sitting on the sidewalk leaned against it. She was old and decrepit-looking. Her face was pockmarked, and her grey hair was long and greasy. She wore a ripped green coat with a red and grey plaid workman's jacket underneath. She had on at least two pairs of pants, and her dirty feet showed through the soles of her shoes. There was a brown paper bag sitting next to her. *What could this woman possibly have for Chris?* Tara wondered. She watched as he bent over and picked up the bag.

"Miss, do you have a light?"

Startled by the voice, Tara turned and looked into a mostly toothless smile, outlined by brown-stained lips. She figured he must have been one of those winos. He could have been the brother of the woman Chris was talking to. His hairline had receded halfway back from his forehead, and the remaining hair was sparse and long and rested limply on his shoulders. His face and clothing looked as if he'd been dragged behind a car over a muddy road.

"Do you mean a flashlight?" she responded. "If so, I don't have—"

The wino's brown lips and stubbled face twisted into an angry sneer. "Okay, bitch, enough of the sarcasm. Do you have a fucking light or not?"

"Thanks, Liz," Chris whispered to the old woman—who wasn't a day over thirty—as he bent over to pick up the paper bag. "Great disguise, by the way."

"Who's the hottie you brought with you?"

"She's a friend."

"Is she one of us?"

"Kind of."

"Kind of? What the hell do you mean kind of? Either she is or she isn't. And if she isn't, what the hell is she doing here?"

"Let's just say she's a very good friend, and in the last few days, she's suffered extreme duress, and I'm helping her escape."

"Look, Chris, I don't care if she's battled her way out of the bowels of hell and is being hunted by the devil himself, that's no reason to break protocol. What's happened to you? You were never the Good Samaritan type."

"I don't know, Liz, something inside of me is changing."

"I don't like it. You're losing your edge. That's the kind of thing that'll get you killed."

"Not going to happen."

"Sure, nobody thinks it will. You'd better get back to your girlfriend. It looks like buddy over there's taken a shine to her."

Chris turned to see the bum bothering Tara.

"Shit. See ya, Liz."

"Is this guy bothering you, dear?" Chris said to Tara, glaring at the bum with his best "Piss off" look. The bum snorted, raised his hands as if he'd meant no harm, turned, and shuffled away.

Once Chris and Tara were back in the truck, he opened the bag and pulled out a device on a plastic strap.

"What is this Chris? It looks like a wristwatch."

"It's supposed to look like a watch, but it's really a miniature GPS signal inhibitor."

"English, please."

"Basically, it'll block the signal that's being sent out from the transmitter imbedded in your hip, preventing anyone from tracing your whereabouts. Buckle it around your wrist," he said, handing it to her

He hadn't told her about the blue car that had been forced to pass them when he had pulled over. He had noticed that the driver was Jake. If

Jake was depending on Tara's little homing beacon to keep track of them, he was going to be very disappointed.

***

"Why the hell did you pass them?" Wolf yelled through the phone.

"I had to pass them. Chris pulled over to the side of the road and stopped, and now the damn signal's gone."

Clever, Wolf thought. *Chris got himself a GPS blocking device. He must be in contact with his old cronies.*

"Jake, if you hadn't been following so closely, you wouldn't have had to pass him."

"But Wolf, I'm not trained for this shit."

"You're damn right you're not!"

Wolf abruptly ended the conversation and placed another call.

"Raven, do you still have someone following the kidnapper."

"Yes. Do you think we're amateurs? It seems that Chris has gotten hold of a GPS signal inhibitor."

"Is that going to be a problem?"

"Of course not."

"Good. Keep me informed. Oh, one other thing: it's time to take care of Jake. I'd hoped he would last longer, but he's less useful than a stir stick."

"Understood."

***

Jake was bewildered. Why had Wolf ended the call so abruptly?

Someone suddenly rapped on his car window. Jake gave a startled jump and looked up. A middle-aged, medium-size guy stood there, smiling.

"Holy shit," Jake muttered and turned the key in the ignition. "Holy … holy, shit," he repeated. *If only I'd kept the car running.*

Just as the engine revved up, a gunshot sounded. Not loud. It was a low-calibre weapon: a .22 automatic pistol with a noise suppressor.

The first shot shattered the glass on Jake's driver side window. The bullet pierced Jake's jaw, veered off the steering wheel, and lodged somewhere in the car's interior. The shooter rammed his gun against Jake's head and fired a second shot. The bullet shattered Jake's skull and produced a gaping exit wound on the opposite side of his skull. His face slammed forward, cradling itself on the steering wheel. Blood from his crimson matted hair splashed against his ear and dripped onto his shoulder.

CHAPTER EIGHTEEN

RAVEN WAS THIRTY-SEVEN YEARS old and the leader of a troop of soldiers that consisted of some of the best technical minds in the US military. Those minds were responsible for assisting in global covert operations where highly sophisticated surveillance techniques were required. They were usually called upon to help capture global criminals and assist in political hostage situations. Their division was part of a larger group called the Special Forces Operational Detachment, Delta—commonly known as Delta Force.

Raven's real name was Blake Rosewell. He was born and bred military. He was a military prodigy, combining a sharp strategic mind and natural leadership abilities. He had a purposeful stride and calm demeanour that put men at ease in extremely stressful situations. Innovative solutions for demanding problems always seemed to be available when he needed them. All of the men in his family had been in the armed forces, starting with his great-great-grandfather who had fought in World War I. Blake's father had always told him, "You're only a leader if people follow you without question," and they did follow him.

Blake was six feet five with a solid, lean, muscular frame and olive skin. His hair was a glossy black—thus his code name Raven—even though, these days, it had a bit of salt sprinkled through it. Blake was not married and never had been. He had known many women but decided that, as long as he was in his demanding, violent career, he would never marry. He had met other older men who had been married, and the profession always took its toll, usually causing the relationship to end in divorce.

Raven's thoughts drifted back to how their mission had begun. It was at two in the afternoon, about thirteen hours ago. He and Teresa had been in the middle of full-throttle sex when the phone rang. It was Colonel

Samuels. He had commanded Raven to meet him in his office at 1430 hours.

He had knocked with authority on his commander's office door.

"Come in," Samuels had answered in an irritated tone.

You'd think that I was the one who'd pulled him from an afternoon tryst, Raven had thought. He marched into the office, saluted, and stood at attention.

"Sergeant Rosewell reporting for duty, Sir."

"At ease, Rosewell. Have a seat."

Raven knew this was going to be an extremely dangerous mission. The only other time he'd sat in the leather armchair—usually reserved for visiting generals and other dignitaries—was in 1989. At the time, he had been only twenty-one and had been on only two previous missions. Samuels had deployed him to Central America to assist the Drug Enforcement Agency in the capture of a drug boss by the name of Alfonso Rios. He had nearly been killed during that engagement. He was honoured that his commander held his abilities in such high regard, but he wondered if he wouldn't return this time.

Even though they didn't always agree, Raven had an impenetrable respect for Samuels, who was the personification of the word "soldier." For instance, he didn't bother with the short military haircut—he shaved it all off. Other than a few wrinkles etched into his forehead, he looked capable of running the complete twenty-six-mile Boston Marathon at the age of fifty. He still did his full workout every morning, including one hundred push-ups. Samuels' mind was as sharp as his physique. He had a knack for strategy, and generals continued to consult him from time to time.

Blake recalled being concerned. For the first time since he'd known the colonel, he'd detected a hint of indecisiveness in Samuels's usually rock-solid, chestnut eyes.

"Are you okay, sir?" Blake had asked, hesitantly.

"Yes. Why?" Samuels had answered with some doubt in his voice.

"You just seem a little off centre today. Not yourself."

"Very perceptive. You know me well. It's this mission."

"Mission?" Blake had been confused, because he didn't think the mission had been devised that could jar the unshakable Colonel Samuels.

Without entertaining Blake's lingering question, Samuels had gone directly into the mission parameters.

"Gather four of your best surveillance men for an operation in Canada. You'll be following a kidnapper and his victim. You won't be apprehending the kidnapper or rescuing the victim—a twenty-one year old girl—just following them. And here's the strangest part," Samuels said, as if what he'd already said wasn't strange enough. "You'll keep in contact with a man by the name of Wolf Ostermann—the girl's father. The number you can reach him at is in the file. The girl has a GPS transmitter embedded in her hip. You'll trace them to their location and begin the operation from there. You and your men will fly out at 1700 hours to a private landing strip in British Columbia. When you arrive, five cars will be waiting. The vehicles will be equipped with all you need to trace the GPS transmitter to its location."

"How long do we follow them, sir?"

"That's undefined."

Raven had watched the colonel's face, waiting for a smile to break through his veneer of forced composure, hoping this was a joke. But it never appeared as Samuels passed him the mission dossier. At that point, Raven knew that there was nothing more to be said—he had a job to do and would do it. He had stood abruptly, holding the file folder in one hand and saluting with the other. Then he had turned and marched out of the office.

The ring of his cell phone shook Raven from his thoughts.

"Hello."

"Phoenix here. Is everything okay?"

"Yes. Why do you ask?"

"You usually answer by the second ring, not the fourth."

"Sorry. I was deep in thought."

"Okay. It's done."

"Good."

Jake had been terminated. Why? Raven didn't know, but he was taking orders from Wolf, and it was made very clear from the beginning that Jake would have to be killed at some point.

Since they had lost the advantage of the GPS signal and could no longer follow the target from a safe distance, Raven ordered his men to switch to parallel tailing. Parallel tailing was difficult at the best of times, and it didn't help that this section of Vancouver was strewn with one-way streets. But Raven didn't know his adversary's level of expertise, so he couldn't take a chance that the kidnapper might detect that he was being followed, especially in the low traffic volume this early in the morning. Raven and his men would maintain a constant perimeter around the target vehicle, watching from parallel streets and keeping each other informed of the target's whereabouts through ongoing communication.

Colonel Geoffrey Allan Samuels wasn't known for being retrospective. He made decisions and moved on.

He couldn't help how proud he was of Rosewell as he recalled him marching out of his office thirteen hours before. He'd trained him well. Rosewell always obeyed orders; he was a team player. The colonel just wished he knew what kind of inferno he'd sent him into this time.

He wasn't able to tell Rosewell that the mission had spawned from a dream, because he wouldn't have understood. How could anybody understand? Samuels knew it had to be done. He knew that this was an important mission. Without it, something extremely vital would be put at risk. But the queerest part of all was that he had no idea what that was.

His desk phone rang. He grabbed the receiver.

"Samuels here."

"Raven reporting in."

"Go ahead."

"Everything's going as planned with one small hiccup. The kidnapper has disabled the transponder."

"Is everything under control?"

"Yes, sir."

"Good. Carry on, sergeant. Samuels out."

Chris knew that just because he'd lost Jake it didn't mean he was no longer being followed. He wasn't going to take any chances. He'd take the most circuitous route possible before arriving at Carl's safe house.

"Tara, don't be concerned if I do some strange driving. I just want to ensure that we're not being followed."

"Okay," she said dismissively, resigning herself to the fact that she was on the run.

Once Chris scanned the area and assured himself that there were no police cars in sight, he made a U-turn onto Carrall Street and an immediate left onto Water Street. He turned left on Cambie Street and left again onto Nelson. Then he drove to the Cambie Bridge, crossing over False Creek.

All this time, he kept his eye on the cars behind him and those that passed him, looking for patterns. Did any cars continue to follow him? Did anyone pass him while the car behind him continued to follow?

After crossing Cambie Bridge, he pulled over to the side of the road and put on his four-way flashers, waiting for the cars to pass. After five minutes, he turned off the four-ways and drove to Broadway Street and turned right. At Granville, he turned left and left again at Twelfth Avenue.

He slowed down and pulled into a driveway, waiting for the two cars behind him to pass. He watched as they drove by, and neither driver looked back—a good sign. He backed out of the driveway and continued in the same direction along Twelfth Avenue. When he reached Burrard Street, he turned right and drove until he crossed back over Burrard Bridge, heading back into downtown Vancouver. When he reached Davie Street, he turned right and drove until he passed through the intersection of Davie and Granville. He continued past Carl's safe house until he reached the underground parking lot a block away. As he turned into the underground parking garage, Chris was certain no one had followed him. He parked the truck in the designated spot in the back of the lot.

Chris looked over at Tara, wondering if it was fair to bring her into his world. *It's too late now*, he thought. He didn't have a choice; it was the only way to keep her safe. They couldn't go to the police or any other authority; who would believe a story about five-hundred-year-old powers delivered by an alien and about a family that has controlled the world through dreams since the fifteen hundreds?

"Tara, we're almost there."

Tara looked suspiciously around the sparsely populated underground parking garage.

"Almost where?"

"You'll see in a few minutes. First, we have to wipe down this truck, and then we'll say goodbye to it forever. Get out and leave your door open so I can clean it after doing my side."

Chris wiped down the inside of the truck's cab, and then he did both doors inside and out. When Chris was finished, he motioned for Tara to follow him. They walked in silence toward the exit door and climbed the stairs to ground level. When they reached the top, they emerged into a shaded area of the aboveground parking lot.

"Stay close," Chris whispered.

They proceeded across the lot. Chris tuned his ears to all of the natural noises surrounding them and listened warily for anything out of that spectrum. When they reached the safe house, he took another last look around and pointed for Tara to go down the stairs at the back of the building while he followed her. At the bottom of the stairs, there was a small intercom similar to any ordinary apartment building, except this one had an added feature. When pressing the intercom button, it made the usual buzzing sound while reading the person's fingerprint, checking it against a database for entry authorization. If matched, the door would unlock. Chris pressed the button, and in a couple of seconds, he heard the familiar *snap* of the lock releasing. Silently thanking Carl for adding him back to the database so quickly, Chris and Tara walked inside and were met by two armed men with their guns pointed directly at them.

Tara screamed at the sight.

Chris responsively put his arm around her.

"Tara, everything's fine. These guys are just making sure no one's following us. Right, guys?"

Seeing the terrified look on Tara's face, one guard responded quickly, "Yes. I take it no one is following you?"

"No." Chris said.

The other guard spoke to Tara.

"Sorry, miss. We didn't mean to scare you, but we can't take any chances."

"What kind of screwed-up world am I getting into?" Tara asked, not directing her question at anyone in particular.

Nobody answered. Tara released a deep breath. In the silence that followed her question, a truth she already knew resonated through her mind. She was running with a man she barely knew to save her life. She hoped she had made the right decision. What else could she have done? She couldn't go back home. She was trapped in a life out of her control.

Sensing Tara's apprehension, Chris gently placed his hand on her back, directing her toward the next door.

"Are you going to let us in, Chuck?" Chris asked the guard who had apologized to Tara.

"Sure, go ahead."

Chris watched Chuck's hand move in his pocket to press the button on the remote door opener. Tara's eyes widened as the wall slid away and a rectangular opening appeared where there hadn't been one seconds ago.

"Shall we?" Chris asked with his hand still on her back, urging her toward the opening.

They walked through, and the wall instantly closed behind them. They found themselves in a narrow hallway with sterile white walls, a grey concrete floor, and caged light bulbs hanging from the ceiling. There were no doors on either side. The only door was at the very end of the short hallway.

"This reminds me of a psych ward scene in a horror movie I saw on television a couple of years ago. Now I know why they call you guys spooks!"

"Calm down. It's not as bad as it seems."

"Easy for you to say ..."

CHAPTER NINETEEN

"CHRIS, MY MAN. HOW are you?"

Chris recognized the distinct bellowing voice. He turned his attention from Tara to see Carl swaying heavily down the hallway. Carl weighed about 250 pounds and had a small bar fridge for a chest, a large round head, long wavy, brown hair, and a full beard and moustache. He'd grown the beard and moustache to mask his soft facial features, because he certainly hadn't led the hard life he was pretending to have lived. With the pronounced swagger he'd mastered for his cover, he looked like a fierce gorilla approaching—John Wayne on steroids, as Carl always said. But in real life, he was as tame as a baby chimp.

Reaching out his hand even before Carl was close enough, Chris warned, "Don't dare hug me. The last time, I was in pain for two days. I swear you cracked a rib or two."

"Okay, okay," Carl chided, knocking Chris's hand aside and hugging him anyway, lifting him off his feet.

"Put me down, you overgrown musclehead." If the truth was known, Chris was more embarrassed than physically hurt when Carl hugged him, because in his mind, that wasn't how men behaved.

Carl dropped Chris, and he stumbled backward before regaining his balance.

"Hey, young lady. What's your name?" Carl asked, giving Tara a gentle smile.

Frightened that this giant of a man might hug her too, she backed defensively into the cement wall in an attempt to get as far away as possible.

"Don't worry, Tara. He won't hug you. He only does it to me, because he knows it pisses me off."

"Tara, that's a pretty name," Carl said.

He reached his hand toward her, as if toward a timid animal. She tentatively offered Carl the tips of her fingers.

"Okay, you big ape, are you going to invite us into your lair or keep us out in this hallway all night?" Chris jokingly snapped at Carl.

"Tara, see the ingratitude I have to put up with? I try to be friendly and warm, and His Ungratefulness calls me names. Maybe I should just let you in and send him on his way."

"Okay, Carl. You made your point."

Carl motioned for them to follow as he turned to walk away. "You too, Chris, before I change my mind!"

When they walked through the door at the end of the hallway, they were greeted by a skinny, green-haired, energy bar whose arms and legs never seemed to stop moving. Chris thought she looked like a strung out, punk rock, crackhead. Her dyed green hair sprouted in all directions like the top of a prized carrot. She had a metal loop through her pierced septum; the loop had a silver chain that ran from it to another metal loop in her earlobe. Chris figured she must be Carl's pretend girlfriend.

"Hi, my name's Mary-Lynn. You finally made it. You must be Chris. And you—what's your name, sweetie," she said, looking directly at Tara.

"Tara."

"Tara's a beautiful name. It means rocky tower," Mary-Lynn responded. "It reminds me of a painting that used to hang on the wall in our living room at home. It was of an old, abandoned, stone house on an Irish seashore with the waves crashing against it. I used to love that painting."

"How did you know the meaning of my name?" Tara asked.

"Because I have a photographic memory and I happen to like names and their meanings. It beats memorizing phone books."

"Is that something you have to do?" Tara asked with a pained look on her face.

"Well, not really. I just thought it sounded good. Tara, you could use some clean clothes, I see. Those threads are barely fit for the incinerator. Come with me, and I'll get you something decent to wear. We'll leave these two spooks to catch up with each other."

"Great," Tara said, looking at Chris as if requesting permission.

Before Chris could reply, Mary-Lynn said, "You don't need his permission. You're safe here."

"She's right. Go ahead."

The two women had barely turned to walk away when Mary-Lynn had engaged Tara in conversation; Chris noticed her responding.

"Carl, that Mary-Lynn is fantastic. She's just what Tara needs right now. How come you didn't tell me she was here?"

"She wasn't when you called, but when you told me you were bringing a young woman with you, I knew I wouldn't know how to deal with her, so I asked Mary-Lynn to come in from her current assignment for the evening. Would you like a drink? I have scotch, rum, or Southern Comfort. And beer, of course."

The mention of scotch brought the memory of Chris's first meeting with Wolf to mind.

"I want something from the U-S-of-A, Carl. Give me a triple Southern Comfort. No ice."

"Sounds good. I think I'll have the same. Two triple shots of Kentucky's finest, coming right up."

While Carl mixed the drinks, Chris contemplated what he would tell him. Considering everything Carl was doing for him, he owed him some kind of explanation, but Chris himself didn't even fully understand what was happening. And the stuff about Tara and Wolf's power—he wasn't sure how much of that was real or delusional. He didn't want to tell Carl some disconcerting story about mind control and aliens in a cave.

"Triple SC with no ice," Carl said, handing Chris his drink. Chris was lost in thought. "Now, let's you and I ... are you in there, man?" he asked, raising his voice a couple of decibels.

Chris abruptly turned around.

"Yes, yes, I heard you. This room hasn't changed since I was last here: the pool table in the right corner, the leather couch centred against the back wall with the smoky, glass-topped table in front, and the leather armchairs at each end. Keep things plain and simple—that's Carl."

"Damn right. My life's complicated enough."

"It brings back a lot of memories."

"Well, Mr. Sentimental, let's have a seat and talk about more recent events. First, I'd like to know how you got hooked up with Tara."

"Carl, it's a long story, and I don't fully understand what's happening yet myself, although I'll explain it the best I can. Do you know a man by the name of Wolf Ostermann?"

"Know him? Of course! He's a billionaire with a gargantuan estate northeast of Vancouver in the Fraser Valley area."

"I've been working for him over the last year, and that's his daughter who left with Mary-Lynn."

"What the hell are you doing, Chris? I knew you were crazy, but I didn't know you were out of your fucking mind. A billionaire's daughter? Are you trying to cause an international incident between Canada and the United States?"

"Whoa, Carl, let me explain."

"Explain what? You've kidnapped an heiress—a billionaire, no less!"

"Actually, it's the other way around. She was already kidnapped. I rescued her."

"So why don't you take her back to her parents where she belongs?"

"If you shut your mouth for five minutes, I'll explain."

"Alright, my ears are wide open, but this better jive with reason."

"Do you remember that sinister Irish bitch, Marta?"

"How could I forget her? She was the key organizer of most of the horror perpetrated by the IRA in the seventies."

"Right. She, and an accomplice named Tim, kidnapped Tara and held her captive in an old mafia hideout north of here."

"You mean, the old warehouse."

"That's correct. I have reason to believe that Wolf, Tara's father, hired them to kidnap her."

"That's preposterous. Why would you believe such a thing?"

Chris disclosed Jake's confession to him and the rescue of Jake from Dak and how Jake had been following them from the motel without making any move to help Tara, either by himself or by calling the police.

"Also, there was a chauffeur by the name of George Ferguson at the estate. He began telling me some suspicious things about Wolf Ostermann, which I had my doubts about until someone gave George a bloody third eye in the middle of his forehead," Chris emphasized the point by angrily thumping his index finger on his own forehead.

"George Ferguson … that name's familiar."

"You might have worked with him at some point. He was with Delta Force."

"It's not immediately coming to mind, but it will. It sounds like you're right, Chris, this guy Ostermann isn't interested in rescuing his daughter, especially since he knew you were at that motel with her and didn't do anything about it. Very strange."

"Strange doesn't even begin to …"

"I've arranged for a doctor to remove the chip from Tara's hip, but he won't be available until nine tomorrow morning. Sorry, it's the best I could do. You can stay here tonight, and I'll wake you when the doctor arrives. In the meantime, I'll prepare a United States passport and driver's license for Tara. I have a contact with a ranch just outside of Dallas. The ranch was left to him in his uncle's will, but he never goes there. He has agreed to let you stay there for as long as you need to. Does Tara know what you're planning?"

"Yes."

"Good, because I think I hear female chatter approaching at twelve o'clock."

No sooner had the words left Carl's mouth than Mary-Lynn and Tara emerged from the east hallway.

Chris was pleased to see Tara smiling brightly and walking with a more relaxed step. Her red hair glistened from obviously having showered again. She wore a yellow-print, short-sleeve, cotton blouse, tucked into loose-fitting, denim slacks, with a pair of navy blue sandals. Chris figured they must have been Mary-Lynn's clothes left over from her tamer days.

"Don't both of you offer at once!" Mary-Lynn said. "I'll have a Scotch, Carl. What would you like, Tara?"

"Do you have any pop or juice?"

"Pop or juice?" Mary-Lynn said. "She'll have a Scotch, too, Carl. Make hers a single and mine a double on the rocks, but keep the rocks minimal. Don't want to dilute the booze too much."

"I've never drank alcohol before," Tara said.

"Honey, after the little you shared with me in the bedroom, it's time you started. You should have at least a double, but we'll start you off easy. Anyway, it beats taking a sedative, which I'm sure you'll need if you're going to get any sleep tonight, considering what you've been through."

Tara didn't respond. She smiled uneasily at Chris. She hadn't expected Mary-Lynn to mention anything about their conversation. Chris could see that she was uncomfortable, so he returned her smile, nodding to let her know that everything was all right.

Mary-Lynn plopped herself into the armchair closest to the pool table, and Tara sat in the other one. Carl returned with their drinks.

"Just sip it until you get used to it," Mary-Lynn offered.

"Tara, Carl and I've been talking," Chris said, "we have a plan for you and I to get out of Canada."

"Where are we going?" Tara asked.

"First, we're getting some rest. There's a bedroom down that hallway for each of us. In the morning, a doctor will come to remove the GPS chip from your hip. Then we'll be off to the United States to a ranch outside of Dallas, Texas, where we'll stay for a while."

"How will I get into the United States? Don't I need a passport or something?"

"Don't worry," Chris said. "Carl will take care of everything."

CHAPTER TWENTY

CHRIS AWOKE TO A faint tapping at his bedroom door. When he opened it, he found Tara standing there, her face tense with fear and uncertainty.

"What's wrong? Why are you here? Are you not able to sleep?"

"What will happen to us?" she asked, entering Chris's bedroom.

"You really should go back to your own room and get some sleep."

"Just hold me. Make me feel safe, like you did back in the warehouse when you found me. I need to feel safe."

Tara's emotions had become erratic since Chris had rescued her. He was afraid that the alcohol might have contributed to her uncharacteristic behaviour. Seeing her in the clinging nightdress, caressing the sensuous curves of her fully blossomed womanhood, his last remnant of self-control was waning. Awkwardly, he opened his arms in an embracing motion and moved toward her. She fell into him, wrapping her arms around his waist.

"Thanks, Chris, for not taking advantage of me at the motel. I wasn't ready."

"We should stop now, Tara, before we do something we'll both regret."

"I noticed you staring at me back at the motel. I've been attracted to you ever since you arrived at the estate, but nothing could happen. We both know that my dad would've killed you if you came too close to me."

"But ..."

"You think I'm naive. I'm only inexperienced. What I don't have in experience, I make up for in education. My tutor, Miss Thompson, was brilliant and worldly. She started teaching me about my sexuality at the age of thirteen so I wouldn't be caught unaware. My mother definitely didn't discuss it with me. I want to do this, Chris. If we both end up dead, at least I'll have experienced the ultimate union between two people. So, let's stop yapping and get on with it," she demanded, pulling him closer.

Taken aback by Tara's forwardness, Chris didn't say another word. He slowly ran his fingers through her hair, caressing the back of her head while pulling her toward him. The raspberry-scented shampoo radiating from her shimmering strands teased his nose. His body relaxed, his arms drew her into a full embrace as if of their own accord; logic was no longer present, just raw emotion. He looked down at her snuggled against him. It felt right—her being there, the two of them sharing the same physical space.

He kissed the top of her head, burying his lips in her soft, loose curls. She tilted her head back. His lips caressed the cool skin of her forehead. Her small hands cradled his face; her tiny fingers spread open, holding his cheeks in her hands like a crystal chalice. They looked into each other's eyes. Hers were aglow with a turquoise sheen, and he knew his were glazed over with the heat of passion. They held each other, moving slowly together. Her perfect, full lips seared against his, melting away any inhibitions or reservations he had had about making love to this sensuous being.

Barely functional, he somehow noticed that the door was still open and turned his body to close it with his foot. They were now enveloped by the darkness of the room. While still locked in a ravenous kiss, his hand moved, intentionally tracing down the front of Tara's slim, fragile neck, gently caressing her right breast, kneading it slowly, and purposefully arousing its tensile nipple to full length.

Tara slipped the straps of her nightgown over her shoulders, letting it fall to the floor and signifying that she was completely his. With soft, gentle kisses, Chris traced a path down her neck to her right breast. His tongue circled the areola of her hardened nipple, feeling the firm but pliable texture of her unexplored flesh. He teased her nipple with his lips, and she pulled his head into her. His mouth was filled with her ample breast as he continued to lick and suck, as if trying to draw out some special, erotic juice. He devoured her left breast in the same way while continuing to knead her right.

He lightly traced the curves of her body with his fingertips through the thin layer of cool, damp perspiration that covered her skin, raising goose bumps on her arms. When he reached her firm round ass, he grasped it with both hands, feeling its tautness. He kissed between her breasts, flicking his tongue at her skin, tracing a path along her tight abdomen, working his way to her thighs. On his knees before her, he gently inserted his tongue into her womanly centre, flicking it up and down slowly at first, gradually increasing the speed. He manipulated her clitoris until her body wrenched out of control. She grasped his head as her legs weakened and she lost her balance. He continued, driving her to a frenzied orgasm.

"I want you inside me, Chris," she yelled. "I want you to be my first."

When Chris stood up, Tara ripped at his open robe, scratching his stomach. Stepping back from her clawing hands, he removed his robe, throwing it to the floor. He embraced her once more, lifting her into the air and lowering her onto his hardened state. Her body quivered as he probed her vagina.

"Fill me, Chris. Fill me—fill me with all of it," she screamed.

He eased himself into her. She yelped in pain; he stopped.

"Don't stop," she yelled, pushing down on him.

He held her even tighter, pushing into her and back out, working the natural juices. Before long, he was completely inside of her, sliding between the slick walls of her womanhood.

Their bodies moved in unison as he thrust his cock into her with every bit of energy he had left. Their bodies were drenched, and if she hadn't locked herself on to him with her legs and arms, he was sure she would have slipped right off. Chris began to lose his balance and moved backward toward the bed. With Tara still clinging to him, he put his arms back on the bed and lowered himself. She continued to ride him until he exploded inside her and was completely spent.

Tara collapsed on top of Chris. He wrapped his arms around her, and they kissed—a prolonged kiss that neither of them wanted to end.

"That was unbelievable," she whispered in his ear.

Raven's men surrounded the underground parking garage that they saw the kidnapper and Wolf's daughter go into. His cell phone rang.

"Yes," Raven answered.

"It's Wolf. What's the situation?"

"We've followed them to an underground parking garage at the corner of Davie and Granville. We have a man watching each exit, waiting for them to show themselves."

"Raven, I'm going to tell you something that you can't tell any of your men. You have to promise me that it'll be kept secret."

"If it's a secret, it won't pass my lips."

"Good. The man you're following is Chris Landry, an ex-CIA operative. He's probably resting in some safe house right now in the area you've followed him to. I would bet that when he leaves he won't be in the same vehicle he arrived in, and he and my daughter will be disguised."

"That certainly changes our surveillance approach. Why is it that you don't want us to apprehend this bastard and get your daughter back?"

"It's complicated. Once everything's finished, I'll explain it all—you certainly deserve to know. Why don't you get your men in position and catch a couple of hours sleep. You're going to need to have your wits about you when they surface."

"Okay."

Wolf placed the phone back on the cradle on his desk. He had only told Raven that he would explain everything to him once the operation was over to gain his trust. In fact, he wasn't going to tell him anything. It was none of his damn business. He knew it would be a few hours before Chris and Tara surfaced, because they had to get a doctor to remove the GPS chip and create documentation for Tara and maybe Chris. All of that required time. He hoped Raven would take his advice and get some sleep, because he needed to prepare him.

Before hiring Chris, Wolf had planted a request in Chris's mind requiring him to give Wolf the names and contact information of all of the people he had met during his life, particularly during his time with the CIA. From the list of names, Wolf had discovered that the only contact Chris had in Vancouver was Carl, who coincidentally ran the only CIA safe house in Vancouver. Wolf rightly figured that if Chris were going to try to get Tara out of the country, he would contact Carl and use his underground safe house located near the parking lot where they had abandoned the truck. Wolf also knew that they would leave from the underground parking lot of the Chateau Granville Hotel. What he didn't know is what he'd be driving or how they'd be disguised. He could only hope that Chris was getting some sleep tonight so he could command him to do something to alert Raven.

Wolf thought of Una—he had to do something about her as well. She was getting on his nerves, constantly yammering about Tara and asking when she would be home. She had to accept that Tara would never be returning, and tonight in the cave below his office, he would ensure that Una would stop pestering him.

Tara remained awake lying next to Chris while he slept. For the first time in her life, she felt like she belonged with someone, yet she was apprehensive and scared. Her virtue and innocence were gone. She had given herself over to one man—a man of secrets and lies, a man whom she really didn't know. Still somewhere deep inside, her intuition told her that he could be trusted, that he was a good and caring person. Relationships were very confusing. There was one constant she clung to: Chris had kept his word when he had said that he would protect her no matter what. She wasn't sure how or where this all might end, but right now, she could only live one day at a time. She cuddled closer to Chris's warm, muscular body.

Tara stirred at the sound of a voice entering the bedroom. Was she hearing things? No, there it was again. It seemed to be right in the bed with them, but that couldn't be. Chris was asleep, and anyway, it didn't sound like him. She decided that she must have been hearing things as she absentmindedly ran her fingers through Chris's hair.

She heard the voice again. It was clearer. It was her father. She knew what was happening. Her father was trying to reach Chris to plant a message in his head, but she had blocked Chris's mind. He would be unsuccessful. Tara whispered a silent thank you to Rhea.

Wolf's head jerked back, and his eyelids flew open. "What was that?" he shouted.

No sooner had he asked himself than he realized the answer. It was Tara. She must be close to Chris—probably sleeping with him, the little bitch.

But he hadn't been able to detect Chris. It was as if Chris no longer existed. Tara must have found a way to block access to his mind. Tara's mind walking ability was getting stronger than he had ever imagined at this early stage. Probably all of the stress had brought it to the surface, like a self-defence mechanism. He would have to rely on Raven and his men to recognize Chris and Tara leaving the safe house. He hoped they were as good as Raven had bragged.

Mary-Lynn knocked on Tara's bedroom door for the third time. Why wasn't she answering?

'Tara, Tara, are you in there?" she yelled. No response.

Mary-Lynn opened the door and turned on the light. The bed hadn't been slept in. She checked the washroom. Tara was not there either. Mary-Lynn surmised where Tara was, the only other place she could be. She walked across the hall to Chris's room.

Chris awoke to the sound of someone banging on his bedroom door. *There seems to be a pattern emerging*, he thought.

"Who's there?" Chris asked.

"It's Betty Boop. Who the fuck do you think it is? Come on, you two. The doctor's waiting."

"Alright, alright. Let us have a shower and get dressed first."

"Ohhh, the young couple want to have a shower first. Maybe they'd like room service too. Perhaps they think they're staying at the Ritz? Chris, you can shower, but the little miss who slipped into the man's room during the night better get her buns out here, because the doctor's leaving in two hours."

Chris shook Tara.

"Tara, wake up. Wake up, Tara."

She barely stirred.

"Come on, Tara, wake up," he urged.

She woke up and turned over to face Chris. Her eyes opened, and a calm, soft smile engulfed her face.

"Tara, you have to get up. Mary-Lynn is at the door."

"Why?"

"The doctor's here. You don't have time for a shower. He's only going to be here for two hours."

"Mary-Lynn, I'll be right there. Just give me five minutes."

"Okay, honey, but hurry."

"God, she talks to you like you'll break down if she speaks too harshly, and she talks to me like I'm yesterday's spittle."

"She's probably had some bad experiences with men. Once you get to know her, I'm sure she'll be fine."

"Well, I'm not planning to get to know her. Once we're out of here, I don't care if I ever see her again. I'm just glad she was here for you. You better get ready."

Tara threw back the blanket, crawled from the bed, and stumbled toward the bathroom as if she'd just come out of hibernation. Within five minutes, she emerged looking more alert and wearing the terry cloth robe that had been hanging on the back of the door.

"See you later, Chris," she said, blowing him a kiss before opening the door and leaving with Mary-Lynn.

Raven's ringing cell phone woke him from his sleep.

"Yes."

"It's Wolf. The phone rang a couple of more times than usual. Were you asleep?"

"Yeah. I managed to catch a couple of hours after making a phone call."

"A phone call?"

"Yeah, you're not the only one with contacts. I phoned a friend of mine inside the CIA to ask about this safe house and where the exits are, so we'll be certain not to miss our boy when he leaves."

"Well, Raven, you might prove useful after all. Good man! Keep up the great work. I'll be looking forward to your next report. By the way, there's something you won't know. They'll be disguised and driving a blue, Ford Taurus."

"How do you know … ?"

"The same as I know that Chris will have auburn hair with blonde highlights and Tara will have long, blonde, straight hair."

Raven's phone went dead.

He swallowed hard. He'd wanted to tell the arrogant, old prick to screw himself with a fence post, but he had held back. Delta Force training had taught him to be unshakable in all circumstances. If he could remain calm when taking out terrorists in a hostage situation, he certainly wasn't going to lose his cool because of that jerk.

CHAPTER TWENTY-ONE

"WELL, IF IT ISN'T the man of leisure," Mary-Lynn said when Chris entered the combination recreation and sitting room from the hallway.

"Don't be such a bitch, Mary-Lynn," Carl snapped. "Chris is helping Tara."

"Yeah, out of her clothes. Ask him. The two of them slept together last night."

"Is that true, Chris?"

"Yes. Tara was frightened. She needed comforting," he said, knowing he sounded like a teenager trying to make excuses to his girlfriend's dad.

"What dribble! And you decided you were just the man to take advantage of that naive, frightened, young woman," Mary-Lynn said.

"Look, I don't know what happened to you, but whatever it was, I pity you. It must have been horrible to cause you to be so bitter toward men. What goes on between Tara and me is none of your business. Our situation is not yours." Not giving her the benefit of a retaliatory response, Chris turned away from Mary-Lynn and addressed Carl, "There's something I've been meaning to ask you."

"What's that?"

"Did we have anything to do with the assassination attempt on the pope yesterday?'

"By 'we,' I'm assuming you mean the CIA. Not that I know of. As you're well aware, everything is on a need-to-know basis. Why are you asking?"

"I'm not sure. It smells like a setup—something we've perfected over the years. Never mind," Chris said, waving his hands, "I guess it's just my tightly wired, suspicious nature."

Carl nodded knowingly.

"How's the procedure to remove the tracking device from Tara's hip going?" Chris asked.

"The doctor should be finished soon, but Tara will sleep for half an hour until the sedative wears off. In the meantime, we can assemble your disguise and new documentation."

"My disguise?"

"Yes, your disguise," Mary-Lynn interjected, "that yellow blonde hair has to go. It stands out like a fog light."

Chris wondered if his face showed surprise when he realized Mary-Lynn was talking to him like a human being. He wasn't quite sure how to react.

He simply said, "You're right, Mary-Lynn."

"Good. I like cooperation. It saves a lot of time. Let's go to the lab to start the conversion."

Wolf was reading the morning newspaper and enjoying his first coffee of the day when the door to his reading room opened. It was Una.

"We need to talk."

"Can't it wait until I've had my coffee and finished reading the paper?"

"No."

"Alright, Una, what is it?"

"Why are you so sharp with me, Wolf? Is it because Tara's never coming back?"

"I apologize. I don't mean to be so harsh, but Tara's leaving has gotten me down—as it has you, love."

"We're never going to see her again, are we Wolf?"

"It doesn't seem like it."

"Why did she leave home?"

"I don't know. Maybe she didn't feel like she belonged here."

Wolf watched the tears well in Una's eyes, dripping over her lids like a slowly bursting riverbank. She cried uncontrollably, without emotion, as if all of her anger and hate had burned away and only tears remained.

For the first time since Tara's disappearance, Wolf felt pity for Una. He had used her like he used everyone else, and now she was like a granite fountain standing in the middle of the room. Attempting to show he cared, he wiped her tears and patted her face with his white linen handkerchief. She reached out for him, and he opened his arms to accept her.

"Am I the coolest, Carl?"

Carl turned to see Chris foolishly posing like a schoolgirl with her first hairdo. The black rim glasses and brown eyes were especially effective.

"Mary-Lynn, you've outdone yourself. I barely recognize him."

Bowing at the hip, as if humbling herself before an applauding audience, she responded, "Thank you, thank you."

Carl interrupted her basking, "Mary-Lynn, did you take the photograph?"

"Yes, without the blonde streaks and a different pair of glasses. We wouldn't want him to look too much like his passport photo. Customs might become suspicious."

"Good girl."

"You call me a good girl once more, and I'll crack your head open."

"Okay, okay. Good woman."

"Better," she said, with satisfaction.

"Is Tara awake yet, Carl?"

"Yes. She's in her room. She said something about having a proper shower."

"Good. I'll go and let her know I'm ready for her."

"I think she's warming up to me," Chris said to Carl once Mary-Lynn was out of earshot.

"You stood up to her. Most of the men in her life have deceived and taken advantage of her good nature, and as you can attest to, now she conceals very well. Every man she's met has initially come across as a nice guy, and in the end they've all hurt her. So now, she doesn't trust any man who seems nice at first. She always figures there's something lurking below the surface. She likes Tara and was genuinely concerned for her, especially because of her naivety. By the way, Chris, if you're getting involved with Tara, I hope you know what you're doing."

"So do I."

Tara stared at herself in the full-length mirror. She had been transformed into a different, more mature-looking woman. She no longer saw the younger girl image she had had of herself. In less than a week, she had been deceived, kidnapped, and rescued, and she was now on the run from her father. She recalled what the kidnappers had told her, that a baby—whose father was unknown—was growing inside her. Momentarily, she considered the possibility that they had lied to her.

"There was no reason for them to lie; they were only after the money," she said, clenching her fists. She was conflicted with having an abortion or carrying the child to term. How could she give birth to a baby that had been forced upon her? Would she always resent the child, causing its life to be painfully lonely?

It took all of Tara's strength to resist crying. She didn't want to ruin the mascara that Mary-Lynn had applied, prompting questions. Mary-Lynn's reflection appeared in the mirror as she entered the room.

"Now that you've had a chance to absorb it, what do you think, Tara? Do you like your disguise?"

"It's great."

"What's the matter?" Mary-Lynn asked, placing her hand on Tara's shoulder.

"I'm just feeling disconnected from myself, as if I'm two different people. I feel like I've travelled forward in time and I'm looking at myself in the future. I'm not sure which one is the real me anymore. Everything has flipped upside down. I've gone from a pampered life of daily routine and certainty to a chaotic life on the run."

"The truth is they're both the real you. Do you remember when you stopped being interested in the favourite toys you played with as a little girl?"

"Kind of ... it's a long time ago."

"Well, this is similar, except on a much larger scale. You're now becoming a woman. Speaking from experience, most women your age would have had more than one sexual experience by now, had their hearts broken, and been in many risky situations. You must be very overwhelmed, since you were so secluded growing up and are now being cast into adult life with additional unforeseen pitfalls. And, to make matters worse, you've entered into one of woman's most complex situations."

"What's that?"

"A relationship. Sex is one thing, but a relationship even scares me. Probably because I've had so many unsuccessful ones. I will say that Chris seems like the real thing—a nice guy. Not that I'd tell him ... wouldn't want to puff him up."

"Why are you so hard on him then?"

"That's a long story. Let's just say I haven't had much luck with so-called nice guys."

"Listen up men. Do you copy? Over." Raven transmitted to Phoenix, Alabaster, Tom Thumb, and Home Boy.

They responded in turn, "Copy that. Over."

"The kidnapper and the girl will leave through the underground parking lot by the Chateau Granville Hotel. Phoenix, face north and watch the east exit. Alabaster, face south and watch the east exit. Tom Thumb, face north and watch the west exit. Home Boy, face south and watch the west exit. Copy?"

"Copy, sir," each returned.

Raven continued describing the car and Chris and Tara's disguises. He was thankful for the chain of command and the trust he'd built up with his men. None of them questioned how he knew about the car and disguises. They just did their jobs.

"I have a driver's license, Chris. Isn't that great?" Tara bubbled with excitement.

"Yes, it is, as long as you remember it's only for show."

"And here, I was planning to drive the first leg of our journey."

"Yeah, right."

They both laughed.

Looking at Tara, Chris realized Mary-Lynn's level of expertise at creating disguises. Tara looked all of twenty-seven, wearing a strawberry blonde wig, pastel blue contact lenses, a little padding in the bust line, and—the finishing touch—a turquoise blue blouse, a pair of black spandex, straight leg pants, and multi-coloured sandals. She looked like a new bride right out of a fashion ad.

"Time to stop ogling the blond and get a move on," Mary-Lynn chided.

"She's right, Tara, we have to go. Shall we?" Chris said, offering his arm.

Playfully, she looped her arm into his.

"Tara, remember, since you and Chris are pretending to be husband and wife for the time being, you better be convincing in front of others. Customs officers are trained to detect behavioural inconsistencies," Carl admonished.

"Why I'm sure I'll behave just like a June bride," she said with a mocking southern drawl.

All four of them laughed as Chris and Tara headed to the parking garage.

"Chris, are you sure you don't want me to walk you to the car?" Carl shouted.

"No. You've risked enough. I know what I'm looking for: the navy blue Ford Taurus with Texas plates in the third parking spot to the right of the entrance door."

"Good luck, you two," Mary-Lynn and Carl called out in unison.

CHAPTER TWENTY-TWO

"HERE'S THE CAR, TARA. You get in, and I'll put the luggage in the trunk."

Chris closed the trunk and got in the driver side door. He put the key in the ignition, started the car, put it in gear, and slowly exited the parking space.

Tara's emotions were still quite close to the surface as she became overwhelmed with dread at the thought of the journey before them, uncertain about the days ahead. She knew that, if she had to, she could survive without Chris. But it was much more comforting knowing that he would be there to go through it with her. She hoped he would stand by her.

"Chris, I heard my father's voice last night in the room while you were sleeping."

"How is that possible?"

"Have you not listened to anything I've told you about the power my father and I possess?"

"Yes, but …"

"You don't believe me?"

"I believe you have some kind of ability to transport your thoughts, otherwise I wouldn't have been able to find you. But this whole thing about an ancient legacy and the woman from the past teaching you and … it's difficult."

"I guess if I put myself in your place I'd also find it hard to accept. Every word is true. I need you to believe me."

"Okay, Tara, I believe you," he assured her in his most convincing tone. "Go ahead. Tell me about last night."

"I suspect my father was trying to reach you to plant thoughts in your mind. But since I'd blocked your mind, he wasn't able to enter. I'm sure that would have frustrated the hell out of him," Tara said with a satisfied smirk on her face.

"I definitely didn't hear anything. It was one of the most restful nights I've had in a long time, especially after …"

"That was amazing."

"It sure was."

He reached over with his right hand, placing it on her leg, and she entwined her fingers with his.

Chris scanned the parked cars for anything out of the ordinary as he drove toward the parking lot exit. Everything seemed okay as he turned south onto Granville Street from the hotel's east exit. The atmosphere on the street was typical of lunch hour—cloistered groups of men and women or individuals dressed in suits and business casual clothing. Most of them were probably either on their on their way to their favourite lunchtime place or just walking, engrossed in conversation.

He glanced at Tara.

"Granville Street will take us right to Highway 99 and on to the US border and freedom."

Tara forced a smile.

"I'm not sure we'll ever be free."

"I certainly hope you're wrong," he said, fearing she might not be and knowing that she meant free of her father.

"So do I."

"Raven, Alabaster here. Do you copy? Over."

"Copy that. Over. Go ahead."

"Chris just pulled out of the parking lot driving the navy blue Ford Taurus just as you described."

"Copy that. Over. Did the rest of you hear that? Over."

"Copy. Over," all three said.

"Alabaster, you follow the target while Tom Thumb and Home Boy stay back in the traffic flow to switch with you. Phoenix and I will go ahead and cross the border to pick him up on the other side. Copy? Over."

"Roger that," they all responded.

Alabaster waited until Chris was well entrenched in the traffic ahead before he pulled out from behind a large produce truck he'd used for cover while waiting for Chris to emerge from the parking garage.

The phone in Wolf's office rang, but he let it ring a second time before picking it up.

"Hello."

"Is this Wolf?"

"Yes. Who's this?"

"Carl."

"Are you calling to confirm where Chris and Tara are going?"

"Yes, but I'm not sure why."

"Because you know it's necessary to keep Tara safe."

"Yeah."

Carl told Wolf everything, including detailed directions to the ranch in Dallas, Texas.

"I really appreciate this, Carl. You're a good man. There aren't many of us left in this world," Wolf reassured him. "By the way, thanks for the other information as well."

Mary-Lynn couldn't believe what she'd overheard. Carl, of all people, divulging everything—the complete plan, a plan he himself had orchestrated—to the man whom Chris and Tara were running from. What the fuck was happening? Not knowing Carl's motive, she didn't dare question him about his uncharacteristic behaviour. It was more important to warn Chris.

Chris had been driving for half an hour when his cell phone rang. *Who can be calling,* he wondered. Carl, Mary-Lynn, and Dak were the only ones who had his cell number. Why would any of them be calling? What could have gone wrong?

"Do you want me to answer that, Chris?" Tara asked.

"No. I'll get it."

Chris picked up the cell phone and pressed the send button.

"Yes."

"Chris, it's Mary-Lynn."

"Why are you calling me? What's wrong?"

"Change of plans, Chris."

"What do you mean?"

"Carl's betrayed you. I heard him talking to Wolf on the phone. Isn't he the man you're running from?

"Yes."

"He gave him complete directions to where you're going."

"Are you on drugs, Mary-Lynn? Carl wouldn't do that to me."

"Chris, normally I would agree with you, but this wasn't the Carl I know. He started out by telling the man on the other end of the phone that he wasn't sure why he was divulging the information but that he knew he had to. And he had a kind of resigned look on his face, as if he had no choice about what he was doing."

Damn it, Wolf strikes again. How did he know about Carl? How did he know who was telling the truth? Maybe it was Mary-Lynn who was programmed by Wolf, diverting him from his path right into Wolf's trap. One thing Chris knew for sure: given Wolf's ability, if he wanted to apprehend Tara and him, he could have done it anytime. There was obviously some reason he was just keeping tabs on them and not picking them up. Damned if he knew. In order to escape, Chris would have to go black—deep cover—avoiding contact with anyone from his past whom Wolf might be able to get to.

"Chris, Chris. Are you there?"

"Yes, Mary-Lynn. You said Carl's betrayed me. I still don't believe it, but I can't take any chances."

"I know. If you still want to go to Dallas, I can arrange for one of our men who's posing as a Canadian customs agent at the border to switch cars with you when you arrive there."

"Thanks, go ahead and do that," Chris told her, knowing full well he had no intention of showing up at the border. His new plan was to head for the nearest airport and get the hell out of North America.

After Chris ended the call, Tara bombarded him with questions.

"What do you mean Carl's betrayed us? Are we still going to Dallas? If not, where will we go?"

"One question at a time. I don't know who's betrayed us. All I know for sure is the only two people in the world I can trust right now are you and me. It seems that your father's tentacles reach into places I would never have imagined. Somehow, he has access to people from my past. We're going to have to leave North America and avoid contact with anyone from our past. That's the only way we'll be able to disappear."

Tara reached out to touch Chris to reassure him that she was with him all the way. She jerked back quickly, as if she'd been shocked by an electric cattle prod.

"What's wrong, Tara?"

"I don't know. When I touched you, images flooded my mind like a horrible nightmare. Images of death and killing ... lots of killing ... you with a knife and blood on your hands. You were dressed in an unusual, green outfit. You looked like a small bush."

"A ghillie suit."

"A what?"

"A ghillie suit. It's a camouflage suit that snipers wear. That's what I was in the CIA. A sniper."

"Why would I see those images, Chris?"

"I don't know. Maybe this power of yours is getting stronger."

"Chris, you're heading back toward Vancouver, aren't you? You're planning on flying to someplace called Bequia?"

"How do you know that, Tara?"

"I'm not sure. It all streamed into my head like a message board. What's happening to me? You must be right. It's probably another aspect of this power—the ability to read people's minds, past as well as present thoughts."

CHAPTER TWENTY-THREE

CHRIS HAD BEEN MONITORING the three cars that had followed them consistently from Vancouver, and knowing that he'd been betrayed, he recognized the pattern. Two of them had driven past, but the last car—a silver Ford Focus—was still tailing them from three cars back. He had no doubt that the driver's orders were to follow them to the border, and after he got through the border, there would be other cars to continue the tail.

"Tara, we're being followed."

Tara started to turn around.

"Don't look back. He'll know we're on to him. Use the vanity mirror in the sun visor. It's the silver Ford Focus three cars back. With that unique power of yours, do you think you can make us disappear?"

"Well, actually …"

"I was only kidding."

"I know. But maybe there is something I can do."

"You think so?"

"I can try."

"Go ahead."

Tara closed her eyes. She thought of her childhood pony, Coco, and started her mantra. She repeated it over and over again. Quicker than before, the clutter of images and thoughts from the past days were swept away with the repetition of Coco's name. Her other pair of eyes opened, apertures in her mind.

She was again transported to that other world that Rhea had introduced her to just days before. She saw the one-dimensional black and white shapes that varied from dark black to bright white, as if someone had decoloured the world. Again, the confusing overlapping thoughts and emotions—anger, hatred, love, joy, spite, jealously, mostly fear—washed over her. All of humanity's thoughts melded into one massive chaotic mind. She felt as if she was drowning in the throbbing, gyrating mass of that new place. However, she was able to pull herself out of it faster this time, by concentrating on her mantra, "Coco, Coco, Coco...."

Slowly, order emerged from the chaos, and she felt the familiar surge of power. The emotions and thoughts of each person separated, and she was able to recognize them as individuals. She could place them in time and space and physically locate them in the real world, hovering at the periphery of their minds. She couldn't see each person's surroundings, at least not until she honed in on an individual.

As she'd done with Chris, she mentally searched the core of humanity by thinking of the man who was following them. It had been easier to find Chris, because she knew his name and was familiar with his looks. For the man following them, all she had was a glimpse of his face in the mirror and no name. She imagined his vague features in her mind and first zeroed in on a man whose only thoughts were frustration with rush hour traffic in Toronto. After unsuccessfully hitting on four others, Tara knew she'd found him, because she could hear the order to follow them. She stepped into his mind as if walking through an archway and simply told him that he could no longer see their car—it had vanished, and he shouldn't panic. If he kept driving to the border, he would meet them there.

When Tara's eyes opened, Chris impatiently asked, "Well, what happened?"

Her lips moved without sound.

"Are you okay?"

"Yes, why?" she slurred.

"You look exhausted."

"I guess that experience depleted my energy."

"What happened while you were in that trance?"

"Before I say anything, let's find out if it worked. Pull off on Highway 91 up ahead, like you were planning to anyway, and see if he follows us."

"Like I was planning to anyway, and you call me a spook."

"Never mind," she said impatiently, "just pull over."

"Yes, ma'am."

Chris signalled for the Highway 99 off-ramp. He watched the silver Ford Focus intently for a few seconds, and it didn't signal. Maybe the driver was waiting until the last minute to signal so as not to appear suspicious, just another inconsiderate driver. Chris had driven three quarters of the ramp and was nearly at the stop sign, and he watched in disbelief as the car went right past the ramp, continuing south on

Highway 99. This man was either one of the best professionals Chris had ever encountered, or whatever Tara had done had worked. The driver didn't even glance sideways at Chris's car. Chris wondered if he was just being paranoid. Perhaps the guy wasn't actually following them.

"Believe me, Chris, that guy was following us, and he'd been ordered to by some guy named Raven. I heard those thoughts in his mind."

"Raven," Chris repeated.

Raven could only be one man, Blake Rosewell. They had worked together three years before on a deep cover mission in China, and somehow Chris had managed to impress him to the point where he had tried to recruit him for Delta Force. Why the hell is Raven involved in this mess? Obviously, Tara was right about her father's power, because there was no way Blake would play along unless his memory of Chris was blocked from his conscious mind.

"Tara, this power is really starting to frighten me."

"Do you still think we can be free of my father anywhere, Chris?"

"I'm willing to try. How about you?"

"Sure. Before we go any further, there's something else I need to tell you."

"What's that?"

"There's no way to cushion this, so I'll just say it. I'm pregnant."

"Pregnant!" Chris yelled, turning toward Tara, jerking the steering wheel. The car swerved, nearly crashing into the concrete median before he got it under control. "What do you mean pregnant? We had sex for the first time last night."

"It happened when I was being held captive."

"That bastard Tim raped you? If he wasn't already dead, I'd hunt him down and kill him again."

"No, Chris. It was the woman, Marta, she injected semen into me."

"Why the hell would she do that?"

"I'm beginning to understand something Rhea was explaining to me."

"And what's that? I'd sure like to understand too."

"She talked about the power being passed down to each successive generation. And since I rejected my father's legacy, he needs to find a way to create another heir to his insanity—my son."

"How do you know you'll have a boy? For that matter, how do you know the injection even took?"

"Except for Rhea and I, all the offspring have been boys. When I was just in the trance, I could sense my unborn son's presence."

"That explains why Wolf hasn't had us apprehended yet."

"Why?" Tara quizzed.

"He doesn't want to risk harming the child, especially if there's gunplay."

"Makes sense."

***

Home Boy's cell phone rang.

"Hello."

"Home Boy, it's Raven. Do you still have the target in sight?"

"Yes. They're just ahead of me."

"Okay. See you in a while. Raven out."

***

The rest of Highway 91 went by without a word spoken between Chris and Tara. They were each in their own worlds, filtering through recent events. Chris struggled with self-doubt as he worked methodically through the events of the past year. He wondered how much of what he had done was of his own free will and how much had been controlled by Wolf. He considered whether he should continue a relationship with Tara. Could he spend the rest of his life with someone who could read his every thought? Did he want to raise someone else's child?

Tara was overwhelmed by her recently discovered ability to read minds. How could she control the images of people's lives that were entering her head? Would she eventually hear and see everyone's thoughts? The horrible idea of an unrelenting din of people's thoughts and memories badgering her mind like a migraine headache caused her to close her eyes. She only heard Chris's thoughts when she touched him or when she went into her trance and specifically searched him out. Soon after releasing her hand from his, the stream of images and words had tapered off. That would be her defence; she would avoid physical contact with people as much as possible. How could she do that with Chris? She cared too much for him and wanted to be with him and be embraced by him. Tara resolved that she would have to risk it. Over time, she hoped that she could find a way to block others' thoughts from entering her head.

***

Raven watched from his position south of the Canadian-United States border as Home Boy, the last man tailing Chris and Tara, crossed over. But the navy blue Ford Taurus was nowhere in sight. Once Home Boy made it through customs, Raven immediately radioed him.

"Home Boy, it's Raven. Do you copy? Over."

"Copy. Over."

"Where's the car you were following?"

"I don't know. They should have been here."

"Damn it. What do you mean, 'they should have been here'? Weren't you following them?"

"Yes, but they disappeared, and I was assured they'd be here."

"Who fucking assured you, Mary Poppins?"

"No. I mean, I don't know. I was just assured."

"Sounds to me, Home Boy, like you're in need of some psychiatric help, which I'll recommend when we return to base."

"Men. Do you copy? Over."

"Roger. Over."

"Let's rendezvous at the Peace Arch in ten minutes."

"Roger that. Over."

The five cars arrived simultaneously, parking end to end along the roadside by the Peace Arch. The men got out of their cars and began to walk toward Raven's car. Before addressing them, he had to call Wolf.

"Hi, Wolf."

"Yes."

'It's Raven. I'm calling to report."

"Okay, so, report."

"We've lost Chris and Tara."

"I knew you idiots would botch it up. What the fuck happened?"

Raven hesitated.

"Tell me what happened," Wolf insisted with intense irritation.

"Somewhere on Highway 99 between the Highway 91 off ramp and the border crossing, they vanished. My man couldn't see them anymore."

"Incredible. You expect me to buy that load of crap? A car vanishing in the middle of the day on a major highway and nobody notices …" Then Wolf knew what had happened. Tara was becoming more powerful by the minute, more than he'd ever imagined possible. *This is a big problem*, he thought. Her power was already well beyond his.

"Yes, Wolf. I believe my man, if he says that's what happened."

"Okay, you're relieved of duty. I'll be talking to your commander. Leave the cars at the Seattle Airport."

Raven told the men that the assignment was over and for each of them to take twenty-four hour's of leave after returning to base.

They returned to their cars and drove toward Seattle.

CHAPTER TWENTY-FOUR

"WHEW! I'M GLAD THAT'S over," Tara said, loosening her grip on Chris's hand

"What's over?"

"We made it through security."

"Did you think we wouldn't?"

"It might sound silly to you, but I've only flown once before, when I was very young. I went with my mom and dad on one of his business trips to Paris. All I remember about the airport experience was the security man rifling through my parents' carry on bags. He pulled out the contents of each of their bags for everyone to see. My mom was so embarrassed. And I sure didn't want everyone seeing my change of underwear either."

"After everything you've been through, something like that bothers you?"

"I knew you'd think I was being silly."

"Not really. Actually, I think it's good that you still have some modesty," Chris smiled, putting his arm around Tara's waist as they walked toward the departure gate.

"Why are we going to Barbados? I thought we were going to Bequia."

"Bequia only has a small airport, so we have to fly into Barbados first and then get a connecting flight on a smaller plane to Bequia, probably Mustique Air. "

"Smaller! Just how small a plane are you talking about?"

"A twelve-seater."

"That's not a plane. It's a sausage with wings, and we'll be the scrambled eggs on the side, if it doesn't make it."

"Tara, I've made the trip many times. I assure you, it's perfectly safe."

"I guess I don't have a choice."

"Trust me, we'll be fine."

"By the way, isn't it risky to use a credit card?" Tara asked.

"It's an offshore debit card issued under a different name."

"Oh."

Wolf's cell phone buzzed in his inside pocket.

"Hello."

"It's Jocelyn at the Vancouver International Airport. The people you wanted to know about just left on a plane bound for Barbados."

"Was that their final destination?"

"Actually, they bought a return ticket to Vancouver."

"For when?"

"Three weeks from today."

"Thanks, Jocelyn. You've done me a great favour."

"You're welcome, sir. Glad I could help."

With her most recent experience of touching Chris still fresh in her memory, Tara cautiously slid her hand over his as the plane lifted off. This time the images came slower and more consistent—kind of like watching a movie. Tara saw him as a younger child, sitting in a limousine with his face pressed against the back window. His eyes were soaked with envy as he watched a group of boys playing basketball. Then she saw him at about age twelve, sitting alone in a private library at a wooden table covered with books and papers. He wasn't reading or writing; he was just staring at the ceiling with a smile on his face. She assumed he was imagining himself somewhere else—maybe where he could be the boy he wanted to be, she mused, like the boys in the park.

Gradually, the images began to fade, and she saw only the Chris she knew, sitting beside her. The man she was being drawn to, maybe even falling in love with—an elusive emotion that she'd lost faith in. The plane was airborne and she hadn't noticed or felt the ascent. Tara silently thanked Chris's childhood memories for distracting her. She moved toward him and kissed him on the cheek. He turned and their lips met, soft and moist. His arms slid under hers as they hugged. Their closed eyes made them oblivious to the surrounding holiday travellers.

Tara barely overheard a man whisper to his wife, "Honeymooners, you'd think they could wait till they got to their hotel."

"They might as well get as much as they can now before the spell wears off," she said.

"Touché, dear."

Suddenly, Tara broke free from Chris.

"Why did you lie to me, Chris?"

"What are you talking about, Tara? I didn't lie to you."

"You said we were going to the Barbados, and now I see we're going to Florida. Why didn't you tell me? Don't you trust me enough to tell me the truth?"

"Of course, I trust you, Tara. My mind was just working overtime, planning another sidestep to keep Wolf guessing. This plane has a stopover in Toronto, Ontario and I was thinking that, when we arrive there, we could get tickets to Florida on another flight. In Florida, we could charter a plane to St. Vincent and then fly from St. Vincent to Bequia or take the local ferry, completely bypassing Barbados. There was something very suspicious about how the ticket clerk in Vancouver looked at us, almost as if she was trying to match us to some mental image. Now that I know about the insidious nature of this power, I'm acutely aware of every nuance of every facial expression I encounter."

"So you bought a return ticket to Vancouver knowing you were never going to use it?"

"Yes."

"Now I know why you were such a good spy. Wait, did you say boat? A civilized means of transportation?"

"Yes, I did."

"That's the way I'm going to Bequia from St. Vincent."

"That's the way we'll go then," Chris said, shaking her hand.

Because of the many time zones, Wolf was preparing his mind through meditation. Having to enter peoples' minds while they were asleep would make the next twenty-four hours excruciating. He would have to enter many minds in every major country around the world. He no longer knew where Chris and Tara were. Jocelyn from the airport said they'd bought tickets to Barbados but that could just be another ruse on Chris's part. They could go anywhere. There was nothing stopping them from buying tickets to another location when the plane landed in Toronto.

Wolf was pissed. He had to do all of this extra work because those Delta Force jackoffs had failed to keep track of Chris and Tara. Once he got through this ordeal, he vowed to make sure they paid for their stupidity.

The four hours from Vancouver to Toronto passed quickly. Neither Chris nor Tara had had much sleep in the past forty-eight hours, so after they talked for a while, they both fell asleep. Neither of them woke up until the captain's voice came over the intercom announcing a local time of six o'clock AM and the prospect of a beautiful, sunny day. Fortunately, they were flying first class, so they didn't have to do the economy class shuffle to get off the plane. As soon as they disembarked, they hurried to the ticket counter.

Rushing to the ticket counter didn't make any difference. They were going to have to wait until the next morning for the United Airlines flight at eight forty-five with two empty seats to Florida. The lady at the ticket counter confirmed that their luggage would be rerouted, but Chris didn't hold out much hope. Not that he really cared; they could always buy more clothes.

"We'll have to get a hotel room for tonight and spend the day in Toronto. It's a good thing you brought a change of underwear."

Tara laughed and playfully slapped Chris on the arm with the back of her hand.

"I've never been to Toronto. My mother's from here."

"Neither have I."

"That seems odd but in a good way."

"What do you mean?"

"You not having been to Toronto. I had this feeling that there wasn't anyplace you hadn't been. We'll get to know the city for the first time together—as a newly married couple," she ribbed.

The words "newly married couple" seized Chris. He wondered if they would ever really be a couple, or if they were just clinging together because of their predicament. Once the danger subsided—if it ever did—would they still see each other the same way? Or would their common adversity bond them forever? Maybe that was the formula for a lasting relationship.

"Yes, we'll go into the city, but only because it'll be safer," Chris said.

"How's that?"

"It'll be a lot harder for someone to find us on the crowded streets of Toronto than out here by the airport."

After breakfast and booking a room at a hotel close to the airport, they grabbed a cab for town.

"Where to?" Asked the cab driver.

"Just drop us off in the centre of the city," Chris said.

"Sightseeing?"

"Yes," Tara answered.

"I'll drop you at Yonge and Bay. You can figure out where you want to go from there."

"That'll be fine. Thanks," Chris said.

"Tara, we have to keep our eyes open in the city. Anyone could be working for your father. Watch for people who take more than a casual interest in either of us. Tell me if you spot anybody following us for an unusual length of time. For example, if someone is staring at us while talking on a cell phone, he could be describing us for confirmation."

As they were walking up Yonge Street, Tara exclaimed, "The activity and the variety of people are amazing. This is the first time I've ever visited a city this size."

"What about Vancouver?" Chris asked, turning to look behind them.

"My first time in Vancouver was with you. I wouldn't exactly call that a visit. I guess what I mean is, I've never been on the street in the middle of the day before. This place has its own unique personality: all of the different restaurants, the shops, the many types of people, the languages, the sounds—buskers, horns, sirens, and street cars. It's all so fascinating. Now I know why Miss Thompson, my tutor, was really looking forward to going back home to London, England for a visit last year."

"Why would this make you think of Miss Thompson?"

"She made a comment about London being so much a part of her, and she was looking forward to returning to revisit her old haunts. I guess the place where you grow up becomes a friend—the streets, the parks, the out-of-way locations, your favourite restaurants, the smells and sounds. It etches itself into your psyche. Being here and taking in all the sights, smells, and sounds of this city, I can imagine how that could happen. This is a special experience for me, because my mother grew up here. Putting myself in her place, I can imagine how she might feel if she were here with me."

Tara felt sorry for the homeless people, and every time one approached begging for change, she asked Chris to give him some. Chris obliged, scanning them closely to ensure they weren't disguised and spying on them for Tara's father.

"It doesn't seem fair, Chris—my father with his billions of dollars and these people having to beg for money on the street. Are there people like this in Vancouver too?"

"Yes. People like this exist all over the world."

"That's terrible."

While Chris and Tara stood listening to a man play a Celtic folk song on an acoustic guitar, Chris turned and saw a man staring at Tara. He decided they'd better start walking to see if he was following them. Tara was so engrossed with the singer that she hadn't noticed the man.

"What kind of music do you like, Chris?"

"I am fan of the iconic iron men."

"I've never heard of that band before."

"That's because it's not a band; it's a generation. It's singers like Mick Jagger, David Bowie, Eric Clapton, Robert Plant, and Jimi Hendrix. We better keep moving, Tara," he said, urging her along.

"What's the matter? Nobody here knows us."

Once more Chris looked behind them.

"Stop being paranoid, Chris. No one's following us."

"Actually, Tara, someone is following us. And he's been watching you very closely."

"Tara, enter his mind and find out if he's working for your dad."

"Since I have to close my eyes, I'm not sure if I can do this while I'm walking. I'll try. Hold my arm, and guide me along."

Chris put his right arm around her and held her left arm with his left hand. Tara's pace slowed as she slipped into her trance, and Chris slowed with her. They passed a store window where Chris saw the reflection of their pursuer. He wasn't far behind. Tara's eyelids fluttered, and her pace slowed even more. They were nearly stopped when she opened her eyes.

"Well?" Chris asked.

"Ummmm, you understand, people mostly don't think in sentences, so it's kind of hard to translate what's going through his mind."

Chris nodded impatiently.

"I understand, but is he watching us?"

"Yes."

"Damn! Is he working for your father?"

"Ah, I don't think so. He's thinking something like, 'Man, look at the ass on that broad! Would I ever like a piece of that action.'" Tara blushed. "But like I said, it's not really in sentences. It's more like feelings and, well, images …"

"Right," Chris said, giving Tara's admirer a murderous glare.

Evidently, the man was a bit of a mind reader himself, because when he caught Chris's glare, he quickly slunk off into the crowd.

"Men think about sex a lot, don't they?"

"Yes."

They walked in silence for a bit.

Placing her hand on his shoulder, Tara made Chris pause as she leaned in closely. "Good," she whispered in his ear. "So just for today, why don't you spend a bit more time thinking about sex—with me, of course—and less time worrying about my father?"

"But ..." Chris began.

She nibbled his earlobe very gently.

"Okay, I give."

"And here I was hoping to twist your arm or something," Tara said with a sly smile.

Hand in hand, they made like tourists for the rest of the day. But Chris still gave the occasional glance over his shoulder.

Later in the afternoon, they were lucky enough to catch a baseball game between the Toronto Blue Jays and the Atlanta Braves at the Rogers Centre. Of course, Chris cheered for the Braves, and Tara cheered for the Jays. During the game, Tara heard a grinding noise. Looking up, she watched as the massive steel-panelled roof of the stadium slid open.

"Chris, that's amazing."

"What?"

"This stadium has a sunroof."

"Yeah, I remember hearing about it when they were building it. You really have been sheltered, haven't you?"

"I guess so."

In the evening they had dinner at an Italian restaurant on King Street. After stuffing themselves with bruschetta, mussels, fettuccine salmone, penne arrabbiate and a bottle of the restaurant's best red wine, Tara and Chris flagged a cab to return to the hotel.

They had barely done up their seat belts, when Tara said, "Chris, I feel kind of dizzy, and my stomach's ..."

"Damn!" Chris yelled as vomit spewed from Tara's mouth, covering the back of the seat.

"What the hell's going on?" The taxi driver shouted.

"Sorry, man. My wife's had a bit too much sun, food, and wine today."

"I hope you're planning to clean that mess up," the driver shouted back.

"Sure, I'll clean it up. Just get us to the hotel before it happens again."

"Did you say wife?" Tara asked.

"Yes, of course, I did. Have you already forgotten our wedding day?"

"Oh, yes," she said, remembering that they were posing as a married couple.

When they arrived at the hotel, the cab driver said, "Look, pal, I'm sorry I blew up back there. It's just that today is my first day on the job, and you are only the second fare in my new car. Don't worry about the mess. I'll clean it up."

"Are you sure? I can take the lady up to our room and come back to do it."

"Yes, I'm sure."

"Thanks a lot, buddy."

Chris gave the driver a twenty-dollar tip. After wiping Tara's face and hair with some paper towels he'd gotten from the driver, he propped her up beside him and walked her into the hotel.

CHAPTER TWENTY-FIVE

TARA HAD FALLEN ASLEEP. Instead of trying to get her into the shower, Chris laid her on the bed, undressed her, wiped her down with a soapy, wet facecloth, dried her off, and covered her up.

Chris was tired but unable to dose off, even briefly. The events of the last two days careened through his mind like a game of dodge ball. He had always been so proud of how quickly he could parse elements of rapidly changing events and glean key information to understand the root of a problem and know what to do next. All he knew right then was that he had to keep moving. He also knew that, after everything he'd seen and heard, Tara must be telling the truth about this fantastic power.

How can it be, generations of men from one family controlling people and events around the world, masterminding scenarios over the centuries to amass their fortune? Chris began to second-guess his whole past. How many things he had done that had been controlled by Wolf? Was it really his choice to join the CIA or had Wolf been moulding him right from the time when he was very young?

He walked to the hotel room window and watched the vehicles drive up and down Dixon Road. Because of that bastard, how many of those people had done things in their lives that they'd regretted? Then there was the big picture, all of the major events around the world over the last few centuries—how many were influenced by those self-serving pricks. His mind clogged with the horrific possibilities, as he thought of all the devastation he'd seen in his short stint with the CIA.

Chris couldn't think about it any longer, or he would jump on the next plane back to British Columbia and fill Wolf's head with lead. He had to put those nonproductive thoughts aside and address his first concern: Tara, pregnant Tara. He needed to get her someplace safe where she could have her child without worry. He wondered if there would ever be a place where Tara wouldn't worry as long as she knew her father was alive.

Wolf made one last attempt to enter Chris's mind and was convinced beyond any doubt that he would never again be able to. Tara must have blocked it, but how? Wolf's father had never taught him that skill. He continued mind walking, entering the minds of at least one hundred people. He had to stop for a few hours before exhaustion overtook him. He hoped one of those people would spot Chris and Tara and contact him.

Upon emerging from his secret place into his office, Wolf noticed the answering machine light flashing and pressed the play button.

The machine reeled off a message, "Hi. It's Linda from Pearson International Airport in Toronto. The two passengers you asked about, Greg and Laurie Morton are scheduled on a flight to Miami, Florida at 8:45 tomorrow morning. Hope this helps."

"Oh, it certainly will, Linda," Wolf said to himself, a sly smirk forming on his lips.

He would have returned to his cave and pushed past his exhaustion to enter the minds of some of his Miami contacts, but having anticipated Miami as one of Chris's possible destinations, he'd already done that.

At three thirty in the morning, Chris decided he'd better try and get at least a couple hours of sleep before Tara woke up and he had to deal with her first hangover.

He got into bed and kissed her on the back of the neck, spooning his body into hers and feeling her smooth, warm skin embrace his. To his surprise, she responded, resting her delicate hand on his side, caressing his hip. He pushed in closer to her, and she turned around. They kissed immediately, a passionate kiss—their tongues groping frantically in an attempt to vanquish a deep hunger. Tara pressed hard into Chris's body; her firm breasts against his chest filled him with electrifying sensations. Her legs and arms wrapped him in a wanton embrace. Chris was rigid with desire; his tip eased into her already moist opening. She pushed her body downward, taking all of him at once. They moved in rhythmic union. Taking control, Chris rolled her onto her back, thrusting into her with enflamed lust. Her lurching hips received him as an equal. They held each other desperately as they shuddered to a climax, and collapsed into cloistered exhaustion.

After a few minutes, Tara said, "Chris."

"Yes."

"I sensed my father again while I was sleeping. I could feel his presence. He was searching for you. I detected his disappointment when he couldn't find you."

"Good thing you blocked my mind. Now let's get some sleep, Tara."

"Okay."

Chris felt like he'd barely drifted off when the phone rang with their six thirty wake up call.

"Was that the phone?" Tara groaned.

"Yes. Our wake up call."

"Can we sleep a bit longer?" she asked, rolling over, gently kissing Chris on the forehead.

"I'm afraid not. Remember the plane leaves in a couple of hours."

"Okay, okay. But I'm going to have a hot shower to clear my head. It feels like a cement truck dumped a load of quick dry into it. Do you want to join me?"

Tara shrugged the blankets off and slowly emerged from the bed with one hand on her forehead and the other balancing herself against the nightstand to keep from falling over. "Guess I stood up too quickly. I feel like I'm going to pass out."

"Here, let me help you to the shower."

"No, I'll be okay," she said, starting to sidestep toward the bathroom, "Unless you're planning to join me."

"Not right now. I need to make a phone call."

"Who're you calling?"

"A pilot contact of mine. To arrange for our flight to St. Vincent from Miami."

Once Chris heard the shower, he picked up his cell phone from the bedside table and dialled Cap Jackson's number. He was breaking his own rule about calling people from his past, but he needed Cap's help, and anyway, he'd only met Cap briefly a couple of times.

"Yes."

"Cap?"

"Who's asking?"

"It's Chris Landry."

"Chris Landry?"

Chris could hear the uncertainty in Cap's voice.

"Colombia ..."

"Oh, yes. You're the young man I met a couple of times in Bogotá. How the hell are you?"

"Good. I need a favour."

"That's what I remember about you, Chris. You don't stand around kicking the curb. You get right to the point. What do you need?"

"I need you to fly a lady and myself to St. Vincent. We'll be landing at Miami International Airport between noon and one o'clock today."

"It'll cost you five thousand dollars."

"No problem. When I get to Florida, we'll make the transfer."

"Okay, I'll meet you at the airport," Cap said.

When Chris hung up he turned on the television to catch up on the news.

"Two high profile assassination attempts in nearly as many days," boomed the news anchor's voice, "David Lawson, the chairman and cofounder of ComputerLux Corporation, one of the largest computer software companies in the world, was shot while addressing a group of third-year business students at Harvard Business School in Boston, Massachusetts. Now we go live to Paula Lam, who's outside the Boston Medical Center."

"Paula, what's the status on Mr. Lawson?"

"The last we heard, Tom, was that he lost a lot of blood and was barely clinging to life."

"Do the doctors think he'll pull through?"

"They wouldn't speculate either way."

"Paula, have there been any reports from the police?"

"Tom, the FBI immediately moved in to take over the investigation of this case."

"Did they say why?"

"They said they're looking into possible links between this and the shooting of the pope two days ago."

"The bastards are laughing at us, aren't they?" a loud voice yelled from behind Chris.

Startled, Chris turned to see Tara. "Who's laughing at us, Tara?"

"The damn terrorists."

"What do you mean?"

"They're showing us they can shoot whoever they want, whenever they want, and there's nothing we can do to stop them."

"You could be right, but these could also be isolated incidents."

"Do you really believe these are isolated incidents?"

"I'm not sure what I believe anymore. For all I know, your father could be behind this."

"That's absurd. What could he possibly gain by getting someone to assassinate the pope and David Lawson?"

"Attempted assassination."

"Chris, the pope holds the highest seat of western religious ideology, and David Lawson represents free enterprise at its utmost. Other than the US president, these men are two of the foremost icons in western civilization. This has terrorism stamped all over it."

Noting her strong conviction, Chris realized that this was an argument he couldn't win.

He pointed to the clock on the bedside table and said, "You might be right, Tara, but we'll have to discuss this later. Right now, we need to leave for the airport, so you'd better get dressed."

CHAPTER TWENTY-SIX

CHRIS AND TARA MET up with Cap in Miami after a smooth flight from Toronto to Florida. They were in flight to St. Vincent in Cap's Lear Jet.

In the last few days, Tara had barely thought of her mother. She knew her mother loved her, but sometimes it was hard to tell, because of the way her mother sided with her father. Now Tara knew why her mother often agreed with her father. Two words: mind control. Her mother was obviously her father's puppet and always had been.

"Tara."

"Yes."

"What were you thinking about?"

"My mom. I was remembering one of the few times that she talked to me like a daughter."

"Nice."

"The more I learn about my dad, the more I hate him."

"I thought you were thinking of your mother."

"I was, and I realize that I don't really know her because my dad's been controlling her ever since he's known her. I should go into her mind and remove the planted memory of me running away …"

"Probably not a good idea."

"Why?"

"For the time being, what your mother doesn't know won't hurt her. If she finds out what's really happened and retaliates against Wolf, he might kill her."

"You're right. Am I ever glad you're here."

"When the time's right, we'll free her from your father's mental grip."

"Thanks, Chris," she said. She had a bright smile as she got up, pulled the magazine from his hands, and sat on his lap, curling into him.

"Tara, you said I had other mental blocks. Would you mind checking them out to see what memories they're inhibiting?"

As before, Tara wound her way through one of the knotted blocks in Chris's mind. She could read all the names from his past that he had relayed to her father during his first meeting with him. The meeting had been arranged as an interview, but it was really an interrogation in which Chris gave Wolf the names, addresses, and phone numbers for—or whatever he knew about—everyone from his past, including Cap, Carl, and Blake Rosewell. Chris only recalled a brief interview in which Wolf had been so impressed with his credentials that he had hired him immediately. Chris didn't remember being brainwashed into detailing his complete history.

Suddenly knowing the extent of betrayal he'd committed against men and women from his past, Chris was remorseful to the point of tears. His greed for the money Wolf had offered him to be Tara's bodyguard had endangered many lives. Now, Chris knew that with a simple twist of thought Wolf could have high-level, deep-cover operatives unveiled and killed by the governments and agencies they betrayed. Even though his transfer from the CIA to work for Wolf had been out of his control, he still blamed himself.

"I'm supposed to be a fucking super spy. Why the hell didn't I see this?" Chris shouted, slamming his fist into the wall of the plane. The noise jarred Tara from her trance-like state.

"Chris, what's the matter?"

"I fucking screwed up big time. I let them all down. Any one of them could be killed because of me."

She understood, but she knew that there was nothing she could say to settle Chris down. He was rightfully angry, but he was blaming the wrong person. Wolf, whom she swore she would never again call "Father," was the evil at the core of all the lies and deceit they'd both suffered. Tara would have to wait for Chris to calm down before reminding him that their battle was against Wolf—not themselves. She also realized the danger of unblocking some locked-away thoughts of actions taken without recollection. Actions that, if remembered, could pull the person into mental and emotional torment. Leaving Chris to work through his misplaced guilt, Tara sat back in her seat.

Tara squinted, using her hands to shield her eyes from the bright sunlight flooding through the window to her right. She must have fallen asleep. Chris was no longer in the seat across from her. He'd probably gone to the washroom.

Suddenly, she became aware of the total silence. She couldn't hear the familiar hum of the engines. She unclasped her seat belt, shifted to the window seat, and looked out. On the tarmac below were many other planes the size of Cap's as well as larger planes gathered around the airport hangars. They had landed.

"Thank God," she rejoiced. Knowing she'd missed the descent, she anxiously hoped that they were already in St. Vincent.

"Well, the little lady's finally awake. Welcome to E. T. Joshua Airport in St. Vincent." Tara heard Cap announce from close by.

Tara tried to stand up but felt a bit wobbly and fell back into the seat.

"Need a hand, little lady? Flying in a plane can sometimes be a bit disorienting, especially after a long beauty rest like you had."

"I'm not a little lady. I'll get up on my own when I'm damn good and ready." She wasn't going to tell Cap about being pregnant and have him feeling sorry for her. It was bad enough that he already treated her like a fifteen-year old.

"Whoa! The embers burn deep, and the fire rages high. Okay, suit yourself. We'll be outside waiting for you. I do love a girl with spunk," Cap said as he turned to leave.

"Condescending, chauvinistic prick," Tara said under her breath but loudly enough for him to hear, she hoped.

Placing her hands on the armrests, she slowly lifted herself to a full stance. Once she stood for a couple of minutes, took a few deep breaths, and the dizziness faded, she headed for the exit.

Outside, before Chris had a chance to relay the niceties of a proper farewell to Cap, Tara spit out a curt "thanks," turned, and headed straight for the terminal.

Seeing her sudden departure, Cap shouted loud enough for her to hear, "Well, Chris, it seems the little lady is as glad to be rid of me as she would be a flea-infested blanket."

"Sorry you two never hit it off, Cap."

"No worries, man, I have that affect on most women." Cap said in that deep voice of his, loud enough for Tara to hear, but she never even breached her hurried steps to feign acknowledgment.

"I appreciate all you've done, Cap," Chris said, extending his hand.

"All in a day's work, boy."

The two men shook hands, and Chris left.

Chris caught up to Tara about halfway between the plane and the terminal. "Well, here we are on the island of St. Vincent, Tara," he shouted, to get her attention. "The mainland, as the locals call it."

"The mainland of what?" she asked, without turning around.

"Actually, it's the main island of St. Vincent and the Grenadines—the jewels of the Caribbean, according to the marketing brochures. Can you believe it's only been three days since I rescued you from that warehouse?"

"Are you kidding? It feels like weeks have gone by," she said, turning to look at him beside her. Her eyes were suddenly distant as she pondered the last three days. During that time, she'd been to more places and experienced more than she had in her whole twenty-one years with her parents in that prison Wolf called "home."

"I know, Tara. A lot's happened. Before we head to Bequia on the ferry, let's browse around Kingstown for a while and catch our breath. We can pick up some fresh fruit for later."

"Wonderful idea, Chris. Actually, that reminds me, I've been meaning to ask you … where are we staying on Bequia?"

"That's my best kept secret. Two years ago, when I was here on vacation—one of my very few vacations—I bought a small cottage on a good-sized piece of property along the beachfront at Friendship Bay."

"Taxi, sir?" A tall, thin, smiling cab driver, shouted to Chris. He wore a bold yellow- and orange-striped, knitted hat and a bright yellow polo shirt with purple shorts.

Chris waved in acknowledgement as he and Tara headed for the cab.

"Where you headed, sir?"

"Kingstown. Do you know when the next ferry leaves for Bequia?" Chris asked the driver.

"Since it's Wednesday, the last Bequia Express leaves at seven o'clock this evening and arrives at the dock in Port Elizabeth about eight."

"Perfect." Chris looked at his watch and saw that it was only half past five. "In order to save some time, can you drop us right at the Kingstown Market Square."

"Sure, man. Do you want me to wait and drive you to the dock to catch the ferry?"

"No, that's fine. We'll have time to walk. It'll give us a chance to relax and unwind from the flight."

"All right, man."

Sitting beside Chris in the cab, Tara recalled what had happened before she had fallen asleep—the anger Chris had unleashed after realizing the kind of sensitive information he'd given to Wolf. Gently grasping his hand she asked, "Are you okay?"

"Not really, but I'm slowly reconciling my anger. I know that we have to stick together to fight this evil and not blame ourselves or each other."

"I'm glad, Chris."

"Are there any more blocks in my mind?"

After what Chris had just gone through, Tara hesitated.

"Tara, if I'm going to fight Wolf, I need to know what I've done and how he's manipulated me."

"Two more."

"Let's take care of them tonight."

"All right," she said, hoping she wasn't making a big mistake.

CHAPTER TWENTY-SEVEN

TARA WISHED SHE'D AGREED to charter a plane to Bequia. At least the suffering would have ended sooner. During the one-hour trip across the nine-mile expanse between St. Vincent and Bequia she threw up twice over the side of the ferry. And now, she was being jostled back and forth in a hell-bent-for-an-accident minivan named "Catch-Up." The locals called it a dollar bus or van—or something like that. Every two minutes, it stopped to pick up more passengers. Just when Tara thought it was already too full, a couple of small schoolgirls wriggled their little butts in between her and Chris, pushing her tighter against the window. Then, she was forced to watch the roadside pass by in a dizzying blur, which made her even more nauseous.

"Dollar van, my ass! Right now, I'd pay a hundred dollars to get out and walk," she said.

She was trying to put on a brave face but knew it wasn't difficult for everyone to see right through what she assumed was a green-grey pallor. The van stopped again.

"Not another damn person!" she yelled. But no one could hear her over the loud pop music pounding through the van's hidden speakers.

"Tara, come on. We're here."

"What?"

"We're here. You can get out now."

Tara almost felt the colour return to her face at the thought of getting out of the four-wheeled arcade. She was especially glad to see Chris standing outside on the road, waiting to help her down. Between her churning stomach and her spinning head, she wouldn't have made it off without his help.

"Tara, you look awful," Chris said, when he got a good look at her under the only street lamp.

"You do have a flair for the obvious," she said with a forced smile.

"Sorry."

"It's okay. Nothing a twenty-four hour coma won't fix." They both laughed. "Now I know why you bought that flashlight in St. Vincent—it's as dark here as that cave in my dream. Is this the only street light on the island?"

"No, but it's probably one of only a dozen on this side."

Tara grasped Chris's arm.

"Take me to your cottage, sir, before I fall down flat right here."

As they walked toward the other side of the road, Tara felt the tropical evening breeze swish around her. It was an odd combination. The air was still quite warm from the hot, daytime sun, but the breeze off the sea stirred it just enough to make it bearable, sweeping her flesh with tender brush strokes, slowly reviving her. There seemed to be a healing power in those gentle winds. The headache from the van's pop music slowly subsided along with the nausea in her stomach.

Tara was holding onto the arm of someone who cared about her, who maybe even loved her. No one had ever cared about her this much before.

"We're finally here."

"Where?" All Tara could see was a low wooden fence by the roadside. There was no cottage in sight. Chris raised the flashlight so Tara could see the gateway. "Where is the cottage? All I see is a fence with a gate."

Chris opened the gate. "Follow me and watch your step."

They walked through the gate with Chris leading the way, still holding onto Tara.

"Be careful, the stone steps are uneven."

Once they were settled on the first step, Chris shone the flashlight down the hill so they could see the rest of the stone passageway that led to a cottage on a flat piece of land halfway down the hill.

"Can we stand here for a few minutes, Chris? I want to absorb this view."

"Sure."

"Will this be our home, Chris?"

"If you want it to be."

"What are those tall flowers growing along the front of the veranda?"

"Hibiscus."

"I can't wait to see them in daylight. When you said it was a cottage,

I didn't imagine anything so charming. It doesn't look anything like a cottage back home. Chris, will I ever see my mom again?"

"I'll make sure you do, but it'll take time. Right now, I don't know how this situation is going to turn out."

"Promise me I'll see her again."

"I promise."

"Good. I'm ready to go to our new home now."

They descended in silence until they reached the wooden stairs to the veranda.

"Cool. The veranda goes all the way around the house," Tara said, as she headed toward the side of the cottage that faced the sea. She watched the waves lash against the beach, as if punishing it for being in the way. Palm branches flapped against each other in the wind, applauding the coming of night.

Tara felt Chris wrap his arms around her, his lips tenderly pecking at her neck. She reached her hands behind to take hold of his head. They stood there holding each other for a few minutes, listening to the nighttime sounds of Bequia. From somewhere down the beach, the sound of raw, sensuous music drifted their way.

"It's probably a jump-up. We'd call it a dance," Chris said.

"Now who's reading whose mind?"

Tara lifted her hands from Chris and removed the blonde wig from her head, turning to face him. She ran her fingers through her hair. It was no longer short-cropped as it had been before the kidnapping. It was good to feel her fingers slip through her own hair and not the synthetic strands of the wig.

They fell into each other's arms as if they'd been lovers forever. Their lips sealed their passion. Like a teenage couple unable to release each other while saying goodnight, they lowered themselves onto the wooden veranda swing. They were locked in an unrelenting embrace, absorbing each other's essence in the cool evening air. Tara wasn't sure how much time had passed, but she was feeling much better.

She reached down and cupped her hand over Chris's crotch, gently rubbing and caressing it. He reacted without hesitation to her touch. She undid his shorts and released his confined erection. Grasping it, she moved her hand up and down his rigid, throbbing shaft while gently taunting the sensitive underside. She leaned down and lightly licked along the tip of the crown, gradually consuming it with her whole mouth, still stroking the base with her hand.

Chris probed her vagina with his hand, teasing her clitoris, slowly entering her with one finger. As she moistened, his finger went deeper, making her wetter with each thrust. She stood up, shedding her already partially removed shorts and hungrily sat on his erect cock, taking him deep inside her in one gradual, enveloping motion. They rocked slowly on the swing, savouring every moment of their union—not rushing, just kissing, licking, touching, and then holding each other—even after climaxing.

Tara awoke and was surprised to find herself in a bed. The last thing she remembered was christening the swing on the porch with Chris. She must have fallen asleep, and Chris had carried her into the bedroom.

In her sleepy fog, she heard a loud screeching noise that sounded like an animal being strangled. *What was that?* she wondered. Then she heard it again and realized it was a rooster, which was not exactly a familiar sound to her, but she'd heard it before on a children's television show. It wasn't one rooster; it was many, crowing as if competing. The annoying crowing was coming from all directions. Local dogs barked incessantly, responding to the rude awakening.

We're obviously in the rural area of this island, she thought, wondering if the island was all rural. She threw back the sheets to soak herself in the heat of the morning sun, which was tempered by the constant sea breeze. Tara stretched luxuriously, feeling every muscle of her body pull into place. The smell of breakfast roused her from the bed; she slipped into one of Chris's shirts. The smell of food wafted into the bedroom, triggering her "ravenous nerve," as she liked to call it.

"Oh, my God, I'm starving, and he's making breakfast. What a wonderful guy."

She sauntered from the bedroom into the main living area, which she hadn't seen until then. It was a gorgeous open concept, combining the kitchen, the dining room and the living room. She was again greeted by the one constant on Bequia: the sea breeze. It wrapped around her, mixing delicious food smells with the hibiscus perfume drifting off the flowers along the front of the cottage; it provided what she could only describe as a plethora of aromas.

"Breakfast smells delicious, Chris. What are you making?"

"Papaya and banana pancakes with ham, toast, mango juice, and to top it off, some of those pineapple muffins we bought at the market yesterday."

"Where did you get all this stuff, Chris? Yesterday, we only bought some fruit and muffins and the flashlight."

"Tara, when you own a house on Bequia you never leave it unattended.

I have a local woman who comes by every week to do the housekeeping and check to make sure no one has broken in or done any damage. I called her from St. Vincent while you were still on the plane and asked her to pick up some food and drinks for us. It's the island way, Tara."

"This woman … what's her name?"

"Sandrina."

"Sandrina. Nice name. Will she still be doing the housekeeping while we're living here?"

"Only if you want her to."

"Do turtles lay eggs on the beach? Damn right, I do."

Tara devoured breakfast. The last full meal she'd had was at the Italian restaurant in Toronto, which she didn't remember too fondly; it was the reason she hadn't eaten much until now. Images of her vomit running down the back of the seat in the taxi almost destroyed her appetite again. She managed to overcome it by engaging Chris in conversation.

"Did you have something planned for today?"

"I have some ideas. Tell me what you think. We can go snorkelling—what I affectionately call Bequia T.V. There's a small reef on the far end of Friendship Bay that I like. Afterward, we can walk into town. I'll show you around Port Elizabeth. We'll have lunch at Mac's Pizzeria. You haven't had pizza until you've tasted their lobster pizza. Then we can go swimming at Lower Bay and lounge around for a while, drinking fancy drinks at De Reef. This evening we can get dressed up and go to the Plantation House for dinner."

"Whoa! That all sounds fantastic, Chris, but a bit ambitious for the first day. I think I'd like to work my way into this island life a little slower. I'd like to try snorkelling, but let's save that for another day. This morning, I'd like to relax and do some reading. As for the rest of the day, it sounds great. Except for the evening, once I get home I probably won't want to go back out."

"It's your choice. We'll take it slow. That's the great thing about island life—there's always tomorrow."

Tara smiled with appreciation.

"You're very special."

Having finished her breakfast, she stood up and headed for the open veranda doors.

Tara lowered herself into a white rattan lounge chair, stretching her legs flat out and reclining back into the thick cushions. She felt like a spoiled princess—a feeling she had almost forgotten. She hadn't experienced this since she was very young, when Wolf used to dote on her. Her eyes closed as her body relaxed. She immediately launched herself into that other world where she had power beyond even her own imagination.

"Hi Tara," a voice reverberated like a bad cell phone connection.

"Who is it?" Tara asked, knowing that the weak voice sounded familiar.

"It's Rhea," came the answer, stronger.

"It's amazing to hear your voice. I thought you were gone for good."

"So did I. Through some grace I was given this last chance to be with you, so we'd better make the best of it."

"There is something I'd like to know. Is there a way to see what will be unleashed from a memory block before destroying it?"

"Yes, but it's tricky."

"Tell me how."

"Before I do, there's something I need to share with you. I know this power you've been given can be very overwhelming at first, but give it a chance. Eventually, you'll come to see it as a special gift. It's an ability that, if used wisely, will allow you to make significant changes in the world—changes that can bring lasting peace. You must take it slowly, creating subtle shifts in the thoughts of world leaders that will eventually lead to new, more cohesive ideologies and peaceful ways of relating to each other."

"Are you kidding me? World peace is for beauty pageant contestants, not real, thinking people. Right now, I just want to know how to help Chris."

"Okay, someday I hope you remember what I've told you. To check a memory block, you have to merge with it, treating it like another mind, a separate creation from the person it belongs to."

"How do I do that?"

"Remember when I asked you to imagine yourself naked, lying in water, feeling it wash over you? The reason I told you to do that was to get you to completely relax. You have to relax totally and walk right into the mind knot as if you were walking into a separate individual's mind. If you are not relaxed enough, the charge from the block will rip through you like a raging lion—very painful. Too many of those vicious jolts, and I'm not sure what kind of damage will result to you or the other person."

Tara quieted herself by repeating her favourite mantra, "Coco …"

She felt herself drifting. She thought of Chris and walked into his mind. She could see the remaining two blocks. With fascination and fear, she watched the twisted, sparking knots undulate before her. She was glad that she had been able to distract Chris from remembering his request to destroy the blocks the night before, because she hoped to find a way to discover their secrets prior to unravelling them. She wanted to protect

Chris by not releasing any memories that would cause him anguish. Now she wasn't so sure. Did she have what it took to merge with those electrically charged lumps? It didn't matter if she did; she knew she had to try.

Tara followed Rhea's advice and imagined herself once more lying naked in a stream on a soft silt bed surrounded by smooth, round stones. The gentle curves of her body moulded to the sand as the clear, cool water flowed over and around her, gently plying her taut flesh. She closed her inner eyes. She walked toward the memory block, continuing to absorb the natural coolness of the soothing water. She could feel her muscles loosen from her head to her neck, her shoulders, her chest, her arms—all the way to her toenails. She was totally relaxed. When Tara entered the first memory block, she found that Wolf had manipulated Chris into joining the CIA rather than becoming an anthropologist as he had intended. This would bother him, but it wouldn't destroy him as much as finding out how he'd betrayed his friends and fellow operatives.

Tara moved easily into the second memory block. There was an image of Chris lying on a bed with a woman's hand wrapped around his cock, stimulating him. His mind was filled with images of Tara. She was naked, and he was on top of her, thrusting back and forth in heated passion, his erection sliding between her breasts. As quick as the sexual imagery came, it was gone, and Chris was ejaculating into a specimen bottle. The woman's fingers twisted the cap onto the bottle. When the woman stood up to leave, Tara saw her face. It was Marta.

The realization of what she had just seen snapped her out of her trance. Chris's semen had been injected into her. Chris was the father of her child. Why Chris? Why had Wolf picked Chris? Not that it upset her—she was glad to know that he was the father of her son.

Tara wanted to immediately tell Chris what she'd discovered. But how would he receive the news that he'd been manipulated into fatherhood? It wouldn't be fair to suddenly drop that on him without buffering it somehow. She'd have to keep it to herself until she could figure out how to introduce the topic. Tara hoped that Chris wouldn't ask her to unlock the two remaining memory blocks until she determined the best approach.

The ability she possessed was beyond her comprehension. Rhea had talked about changing the world. Right now, all she wanted to do was get through the day.

"Mr. Landry," Sandrina's voice chanted from the walkway as she approached the house.

Chris wondered what she was doing here. He was sure he'd remembered telling her that he didn't need her to clean today. Of course, she would say that she hadn't come to clean. She was just dropping by to say hello on her way into town. It was a good excuse to meet Tara. Bequia people were very friendly, and there wasn't much to do on this seven-square-mile island, so any chance to get first dibs on some ripe gossip was never passed up. By the time they arrived in town, everyone would know who Tara was because Sandrina would have told them.

He could hear it already—the buzz, like bees hovering around a jug of rum punch at a church fête—"Did you know that Chris Landry is shacked up with some redhead? She seems very nice, but they're not married, you know. Disgraceful, isn't it?"

Of course, no one would ever say it to his face. They'd more likely tell him what a sweet couple they were and, after a while, forget about them when another new piece of gossip became the trite of the week. Chris smiled to himself and just accepted it as part of the island's charm.

"Tara, that's Sandrina, and she's certainly coming to meet you. Go into the bedroom. I'll tell her you're not feeling well and that she'll have to see you another time. I'll entertain her for a few minutes and send her on her way."

"No. That's okay. Invite her in. I'll get changed."

"Are you sure?"

"Yes. I'm looking forward to meeting her. Like I said, I need to be around people."

Chris heard Sandrina's familiar knock—three quick taps with the knuckle of her index finger.

"Come in."

Sandrina hadn't changed a bit since the last time he had seen her. She was about forty-five years old. Of course, she'd never tell him her real age. Her above-average height and arresting smile gave her a strong presence when she entered a room. She wore a bright, multicoloured cotton dress, printed with island flowers, and her Sunday sandals. Today, Sandrina had obviously dressed in preparation for meeting someone new.

"Chris, where's that young lady you told me about yesterday?" she asked, without hesitation.

"She had to excuse herself for a minute, but she'll—"

"I'm right here, Chris," Tara said, as she came out of the bedroom.

"My, oh my, aren't you lovely, dear!" Sandrina exclaimed. "Welcome to Bequia."

"Thank you. You're very lovely yourself," Tara responded, offering

Sandrina her hand, "I'm glad you came by so we could meet, especially since you'll be working here."

"Thank you. I'm glad I still have my job."

Tara smiled, "For sure."

"Well, I'd better leave you two alone. You probably have plans for the day, and I'm delaying you."

"Nonsense. We have all day, don't we, Chris?"

"Yes, of course. And what we don't do today, we can do tomorrow. Right, Sandrina?"

"Yes. Island time is any time," Sandrina quipped, making the three of them laugh.

"Sandrina, sit for a few minutes and have a glass of juice while I finish getting ready," Tara said. "The three of us can walk into town together, if that's alright with you."

"Wonderful! I'd like that."

"Orange or pineapple?" Chris asked.

"Pineapple, thank you."

"Did you hear the most recent news, Chris?" Sandrina asked after Tara had left the room.

"You mean about the pope and David Lawson being shot?"

"Well, yes, but three more people were shot yesterday, three of those big action stars from Hollywood. I don't remember their names, but two of them are the owners of that popular new restaurant ... Planet something or other."

"Were they killed?"

"One of the restaurant partners was killed. I think he's also in politics. One of the other two was badly injured but was released from the hospital within twelve hours, and the other one is still under twenty-four-hour observation."

"What in the world is happening?" Chris shouted.

"I surely don't know. I surely don't know." Sandrina said, shaking her head.

"Sandrina, you have to promise me you won't say anything to Tara about this. She's had a lot to deal with lately, and this will just upset her."

"No problem."

The three of them strolled lazily along the road leading from Friendship Bay into Port Elizabeth. Sandrina singled out houses, telling Tara who now lived where and the history of each.

"See that point out there, Tara? It's called Saint Hilaire. Up on the top of it, a bunch of crazy Canadians tried to build a large hotel. They ran out of money before finishing and abandoned it partially finished. The local people ripped out anything of value that they could sell or use themselves, and the rest was left as a cenotaph to stupidity.

"That house over there belonged to a married clergy couple from Canada who started the Bequia Mission. They were good, caring people. They initiated a number of programs, some of which are still active today. One of the main ones is the educational sponsorship program for school children. Another one is the Sunshine School for children with special needs. Where are you from, Tara?"

"Canada."

"Where in Canada?"

"Toronto, Ontario."

"I have a sister who lives in Toronto. Her name is Cecilia White. I don't suppose you've ever met her."

"No. That name's not familiar. Toronto's a big city with millions of people."

"The founders of the Bequia Mission were from Toronto too. What church do you go to, Tara?"

"I've never been to church."

"You've never been to church! I suppose you're going to tell me that you've never been baptized either!"

"Not that I know of."

"I go to Holy Cross Anglican Church in Paget Farm. Would you like to join me this Sunday?"

Not knowing what to say, Tara looked at Chris, who answered for her. "Sure, we'll meet you at La Pompe and go together."

"Doesn't time slip by when you're spending it with quality people? Here we are at Port Elizabeth," Sandrina said as she started across the road. "I've a number of errands to run. See you tomorrow morning at eleven o'clock when I come to clean."

"See you," Tara said, with a wave.

Tara and Chris spent a couple of hours walking around town. He showed her where some of the essential places were—the bank, the drug store, the grocery store, Knight's Trading, and the Bequia Bookshop. Tara bought a t-shirt with the full chain of St. Vincent and the Grenadine Islands printed on the front of it from one of the vendor stalls set up on the north end of Front Street, the main road running north and south along the shore of Admiralty Bay.

As they were approaching the middle of town, Chris tapped Tara on the shoulder and pointed to a mature old tree on their right. "The local people call it the 'Almond Tree.'"

"Why is there a stone bench around the bottom of it? Is there something special about that tree?"

"I don't know of any historical significance, but it's the main meeting place in town. It's where everyone sits to discuss the day's news or the latest gossip, rest their tired feet, or gather as a group when meeting to go somewhere."

"Charming." Tara caught sight of a boat in Admiralty Bay, "that's a beautiful boat."

"That's the *Friendship Rose*, an old sailing schooner that was built here. It used to be used as the ferry that went back and forth twice a day between St. Vincent and Bequia, but now it's been refitted as a charter boat."

"Can we go on it some time?"

"Have you already forgotten yesterday?"

"No, but if I'm going to live here, I'd better get used to boats."

"You're right. Though, we should start with renting a smaller boat and puttering around the bay at first."

When they got back to the south end of Front Street, Chris took Tara along the Belmont Walkway, a boardwalk wedged between the cement breakwater and shoreline leading past a number of small shops and restaurants. He pointed out the Whaleboner Restaurant, whose archway and bar stools were made out of dried whalebone; the Frangipani Hotel, a century-old, wood shingle-sided building, now a restaurant and guest house, mostly surrounded by flowering Frangipani trees; the Green Boley café; and Mac's Pizzeria. Chris intentionally kept the conversation at a touristy level so as not to resurrect any thoughts of the last few days.

"Are you hungry? Should we go for pizza now?" Chris asked her.

"I think I'd rather try something more West Indian. I noticed on the menu by the Whaleboner Inn something called callaloo soup. Is that traditional?"

"Absolutely."

"Then, that's what I want."

"Okay, soup it is. And you couldn't have picked a better place. The Whaleboner makes the best callaloo soup on the island."

As they walked toward the inn, Tara noticed a couple of mongrel dogs humping on the walkway ahead of them.

"What is it with these dogs? They all look the same. They're everywhere. It's like an infestation."

"Tara, it's the island way."

"What's the island way? Screwing?"

"Yes, and making babies. If you're around here long enough, you'll see."

"What kind of breed are they? I've never seen anything like them."

"West Indian or Indy dogs. They're locally referred to as rice eaters or banana retrievers."

"Yeah, right."

"This tastes great. Spicy hot, though!" Tara gasped after tasting a spoonful of soup and chugging a big gulp of water.

Chris didn't hear her because his attention was drawn to a guy sitting at the corner table across the room. He had positioned himself so that the sun coming through the window made it difficult to see what he looked like. He seemed to be watching them. Chris noticed him look at his table and then back at them, as if comparing them to something, perhaps a photograph. Chris decided he was going to face this guy down and find out what he was up to. He stood up and walked over to the table. As he got closer, Chris noticed that he was of East Indian descent. He was wearing a green, short-sleeve, silk shirt, a gold chain around his neck, an expensive-looking watch, and a gold ring on each hand; he was obviously somebody with money. His shiny, black hair was perfectly trimmed and combed back. The guy's eyes tightened with a quizzical look as he noticed Chris approaching.

"What are you doing?" Chris snapped.

"I'm having lunch as I assume you are," he replied calmly, turning his head toward a half eaten roti, as if to say can't you see …

Chris had to admit the guy was cool.

"No, I didn't mean that. You've been giving us more than the casual glance I'd expect from another patron."

"You have me all wrong, sir. I'm a sketch artist. I was looking in your direction only because you're sitting close to the bar. I find it rather unique—a bar carved completely from the jawbone of a giant whale—so I was sketching it on this piece of paper. See," the guy said, holding it up.

It was exactly as he had said—an excellent sketch of the bar behind where Chris and Tara were seated. Chris still wasn't convinced. For all he knew, the guy could have drawn that picture at any time. With his training, he knew the difference between a look in his general direction and a fixed stare. The guy had been looking directly at each of them, as if scrutinizing their features, possibly comparing them to a photograph. Chris couldn't prove anything right now, so it would be better to back off, apologize, and keep a close eye on him. If nothing else, Chris had let him know he was onto him.

"Sorry for bothering you man. My wife and I have had a rough couple of days and I'm a bit on edge. Let me pay for your lunch. It's the least I can do after being such an ass."

"That's okay. Don't sweat it. Just relax here on Bequia for a few days and you'll soon shed that dreadful stress."

In his most apologetic tone, Chris responded, "Thanks for being so understanding. At least, let me buy you a drink."

"Okay. I'll have a Rusty Nail."

"Great, a Rusty Nail it is." Chris said, as he turned to walk away.

Once Chris had ordered the drink and was seated back with Tara, the guy at the corner table pulled out a photograph of Chris and a blond-haired Tara from between the pages of his sketchbook, confirming it was them. He'd phone Wolf later.

CHAPTER TWENTY-EIGHT

"Wolf, it's John Borg."

"Have you found them?"

"Yes."

"Where are they?"

"On a small island called Bequia."

"In St. Vincent and the Grenadines?"

"That's the place."

"Wonderful. Stick close to them for the next few months and keep me posted."

Wolf hung up. This was good, he thought. He had done the right thing. He had tired of that bitch he used to consider his daughter eluding him, so he'd hired John Borg.

John came recommended by a man Wolf did business with from time to time. His associate had hired John to find his youngest son, whom he hadn't seen in twenty years. John had found him living in a commune in Central America. Although Borg didn't come cheap at five thousand US dollars a day, he had already earned his pay. *After all,* Wolf confirmed to himself, *this is an investment in the future of the Ostermann legacy.* Once he had possession of his grandson, he would raise him and teach him the way his father had taught him. Someday, his grandson would sit where he was sitting, controlling the destiny of mankind and benefiting handsomely from it.

"That's amazing, Chris. I've never seen a sun set so quickly," Tara said, as they clinked their glasses of rum punch together, toasting the finale of their first day on Bequia.

"Yes. As the expression goes, 'if you blink, you'll miss it.'"

"What?"

"I haven't pushed this because I know you've had a lot of adjusting to do over the last few days, but your father is still out there, and we have to assume he won't stop looking for us. I need you to remove the other two memory blocks so I can clearly see what lies I've been living and the extent to which I've been manipulated. The information might provide some clues to help combat your fa—sorry, Wolf. You don't have to remove them tonight but soon."

"You're right, Chris, it has been difficult. Sometimes, I think maybe I've had a bad accident, and I'm in a coma in some hospital, and I'll come to soon. I try not to think about it. He'll never stop until he takes my child, will he?"

"I'm positive he won't. But as long as I'm able to fight back …"

"I have to be honest with you, Chris, this morning when Rhea returned she showed me how to read memory blocks prior to removing them, so I read yours. I hope you're not angry with me."

"No, I'm not angry with you. In your position and given the way I reacted the last time, I would have done the same thing, if I were you. With my training, I might not have even told you that I had done it."

"I don't think there's anything in those memory blocks that will give you greater insight into Wolf's plans. It's also not fair for you to be in the dark about what's happened to you. If you wish, I'll release them now."

"Go ahead. I'm ready."

Tara considered forewarning him about what was to be revealed, especially the fact that he was the father of her child. She realized it wouldn't matter what she said. Chris would still want to see for himself, and it was only fair to let him. They would have to deal with the fallout together.

Tara closed her eyes and went through the usual transition of entering Chris's mind. She easily released the first memory block, but when it came to the second one she had doubts. She feared how he would react to becoming a father. Her nerves must have gotten the better of her because she approached the sparking, twisted mass tentatively and was zapped with an electric shock, causing her to almost pass out. When she regained her composure, she staid her doubts and moved quickly into the memory block before they returned. Tara opened her eyes and saw Chris leaning on the balcony railing, staring at the shore as if it was miles away. She knew what concerned him.

"Chris, it must be terrible to find out that everything you've done was manipulated and controlled by Wolf," she said, starting off easy.

"That is very troubling, but I already thought that was the case. It's the other that more concerns me."

"I know."

"How come you didn't tell me as soon as you knew?" he asked, his words punctuated with shame.

"I honestly didn't know how to approach it. I was trying to think of a way to buffer the news. When you asked me to release the memory blocks, I thought it was best to let you find out for yourself."

"You're right, Tara. I wouldn't have been satisfied until I saw everything myself. Where does this leave us?"

"For me, the only thing that's changed is I now know that someone I care for very much is the father of my child. That's the best!" Tara said, as she stood and wrapped her arms around Chris, leaning into him and kissing him on the back of his neck. "How do you feel about being my child's father?" she asked.

"It's all backward. Not that I wouldn't want you to have our child … except I'd prefer it to be the result of our union, not this back-alley way."

"I can have an abortion, Chris."

"No way. He'll be born, and he'll be perfect, because he's our son."

"Chris, he'll be better than perfect," she said, a tear cresting from her right eye as she pulled closer to him and kissed him again on the nape of his neck. "I wouldn't have an abortion. I just needed to know that you felt the same way."

Chris turned and held her close. She could see that his eyes were a bit watery. They embraced each other tightly as their lips met.

"Are you positive there are no more memory blocks?"

"Positive."

Father Rudi was a thin man, about six feet four inches tall, with sinewy muscles like a long-distance runner. Each time he smiled, his small chin seemed to disperse into his jaw. That first Sunday, Tara thought his sermon was directed right at her. She glanced at Sandrina, sitting beside her. Tara could see by the look on her face that she was absolutely enthralled by the charismatic priest.

Father Rudi talked about material things not being the sustenance of life. Without the support of a loving, caring family and faith in something beyond earthly trappings, our life becomes one-dimensional. She knew what he meant because she had lived it. Tara knew her mother loved her, but she had never really showed affection in a maternal way. She was always very rigid and reserved. Over the last months, her father's intentions had also become painfully obvious as his true nature was revealed.

After the service, Tara left the church thinking about the child inside her and how she and Chris would have to wholeheartedly love him without reservation. They would teach him about the true priorities in life, the importance of family and friends and how to love them, the importance of honesty in his dealings with other people, and the need to respect the opinions and individuality of others.

Over the next three months, Tara attended church services with Sandrina every Sunday. Chris didn't always go, but Tara needed to hear Father Rudi's weekly sermon. She was beginning to find herself, discovering her inner being—or, as Father Rudi called it, her soul. Tara was mesmerized by his manner of speaking; his long, narrow fingers accentuated and wove each word into a pattern for life.

His sermon that Sunday transitioned, as it often did, into relationships between men and women—and for good reason, Tara well knew. The island was burdened with single mothers and children who didn't know their fathers. This really resounded with her because of her own pregnancy and the fact that she and Chris were not married. Tara had broached the subject, but he didn't think it was necessary. Chris had said that he would marry her if she really wanted him to. She wondered if she was too hung up about it. However, after listening to Father Rudi, she began to understand the importance of publicly committing themselves to one another. It told the rest of the world that they were officially a couple and no one should interfere with their relationship.

Chris's argument echoed in her mind: "What about the ones who make that commitment and divorce a few years later?"

The more she thought about it, she realized that Chris and Father Rudi were both right. Father Rudi was talking about a lifelong commitment. Wasn't Chris committed to her already? Hadn't he told her over and over again? For them, their binding love was enough to keep them together. If not, a legally signed piece of paper certainly wouldn't make the difference.

Like every other day, the lineup at Barclays Bank was moving on DCT—delayed Caribbean time. As he did every Monday morning, Chris had come to withdraw money for the week.

"Hi there!"

Chris turned to see the man he had accused of spying on Tara and himself at the Whaleboner their first day on Bequia.

"Do you remember me?" the man asked as he approached Chris.

"Of course, my wife and I met you at the Whaleboner our first day here. I guess, accosted you is more like it. My name is Chris. Nice to see you again." Chris said, offering his hand.

"I'm John," the man said, shaking Chris's hand. "Are you going to be visiting the island for much longer?"

"Actually, I live here."

"Yeah, what part of the island?"

"I have a cottage at Friendship Bay. And what about you? Do you live here?"

"Yes, at Spring."

"That's on the northeast side of the island. Nice area."

"I like it. By the way, I saw your wife the other day. She looked pregnant."

"She is."

"How far along?"

"Three months."

"That's wonderful. Congratulations."

"Thanks," Chris said, turning away to avoid any further conversation.

Chris knew that John—probably not his real name—was spying on him and Tara. It was fairly common for a resident of Bequia to ask what part of the island you lived on, because each area was geographically unique and had a different social stratum. It was usually a good way to initiate small talk or avoid it. But a perfect stranger, especially a man, would not ask about the pregnancy of another man's wife.

Chris could've asked Tara to go into John's head and find out what he was up to, but she was just beginning to relax and enjoy herself. The last thing a pregnant woman needed was to be stressed out. It would be best if he handled this himself. Chris would have to do some spying of his own without the benefit of Tara's mind power.

Briefly remembering his past employer, a smile creased his face at the realization of what the CIA would have offered to have someone with Tara's ability on their side.

Chris sat at an outdoor table by the Porthole restaurant waiting for his mango juice while watching for John to exit from the bank. Someone had left behind a copy of the Vincentian National newspaper, and on the front page, the headline read "Assassination Attempts Prompt High Cost Protection." While continuing to keep an eye on the front door of the bank, he scanned the article. According to the article, there had been at least five more assassination attempts and two killings that he hadn't heard about. One of the killings had been the son of an oil-rich Saudi.

The article continued talking about a company called Nano Securities Technology Corp. (NSTC). It seemed that NSTC was introducing a new product they claimed to be many times stronger than Kevlar and that could be woven into protective clothing to keep the wearer safe from gunshots. Before production even began, VIPs from all over the globe ordered hundreds of shirts for themselves and their family members. At five hundred dollars a gram, this material was only for the mega wealthy and the very powerful. Chris had seen the name of that company before, but he wasn't sure where.

"Your juice, sir," the waiter said, placing the glass in front of Chris.

"Thank you."

"You're welcome," the waiter said with a broad smile.

Chris was halfway through his drink when he saw John leave the bank. He waited for him to round the corner before following him.

After tailing him for half an hour, he stood behind a palm tree about twenty yards away and watched John enter the Spring-on-Bequia Hotel. *So much for permanent residency*, Chris thought. He moved quickly, shortening the distance between him and John. He looked around the thick, green bushes that surrounded the entrance to the hotel's walkway and saw John enter a room on the lower level. Chris waited a few seconds while John closed the door.

Unlike hotels in other parts of the world, the doors to hotel rooms in Bequia don't lock automatically, and Chris guessed that John was relaxed enough that he wouldn't think to lock his door. Through the hollow door, Chris listened to John talking to someone. He knew he had to be talking to Wolf on the phone because John was telling the person on the other end that he'd confirmed Tara's pregnancy and that she was three months along.

Chris heard the cell phone snap closed. He opened the door and wrapped his arm around John's throat before he could set the phone down. He wanted to kill the son of a bitch right then, but disposing of the body would be risky. Leaving it in the room would raise too many questions, and Wolf would read about the murder in the newspaper. It wasn't often that a white man was killed on the small island of Bequia.

"Don't kill me," John pleaded breathlessly.

"I won't. Not yet anyway, you slimy prick," Chris yelled, slightly releasing his grip to prevent rendering John unconscious.

"Why are you doing this, Chris?"

"You damn well know why I'm doing this."

"I don't."

"You're fucking right you do. You've been spying on Tara and me for her father. I just overheard you telling him that she's three months pregnant."

"Okay, okay, you're right! But no harm was going to come to either of you. He just wanted me to keep tabs on you for the next few months. And he's paying me a hell of a price to do so."

"How much?"

"Five thousand a day for the next nine months."

"I should kill you, but instead I'll make you an offer."

"What kind?"

"The million-dollar kind."

"I'm listening."

"You just have to agree to do what I tell you. As of this minute, you no longer take orders from Wolf Ostermann."

"Why should I take orders from you for a half a million less?"

"Because I'm here and Wolf's not, and I'll kill you." Chris said, ratchetting his grip on John's neck for emphasis.

John forced out the words, "I don't think so. It's too risky."

"You're right but the pleasure of draining the life from your body will be worth the risk," Chris said, further tightening his grip.

"Al … righ … t."

"Good. Nothing like near-zero oxygen to garner cooperation."

Chris released his chokehold and pushed John toward the bed with disgust. John gasped heavily for a few seconds, replenishing his body with air.

"How often do you have to report to Wolf?"

"Every Friday morning, unless something urgent happens between reports."

"What happens if you don't call in?"

"He never said, and I never asked."

"You said he was going to pay you for another nine months. How come nine months?"

"He never …"

"And you didn't ask. Well, John, you just won the lottery. I'll pay you a million dollars as promised, and you'll continue to check in with Wolf every week as if nothing's wrong, reporting the progress of Tara's pregnancy. Shortly after the baby's born, Tara and I will leave, but you just keep on reporting to Wolf for the remaining months." Chris locked an icy stare on John with his crystal blue eyes, "I'll give you two hundred thousand today and the balance will be transferred to your account after we're safely off the island and I'm certain that you haven't told Wolf anything. After three months, if I don't see any sign that Wolf has found us, I will transfer the balance to your account."

"You didn't say anything about only giving me two hundred thousand today."

"Oh, you're right, I didn't tell you everything up front did I? A concept you're not familiar with."

"In that case, I want five-hundred thousand now," John demanded.

"You'll take two hundred thousand and thank me for sparing your life."

"How do I know you'll pay me the balance?"

"Look into these trusting, sensitive eyes. Don't I look like a man of my word? Believe me, if you do everything I ask you'll get your money. But if you don't, you won't have a chance to spend any of it, including the money from Wolf. Now, open up your notebook computer over there, so we can make the transfer and I can get out of here."

Chris knew that John's greed would get the better of him; John would eventually betray him. But Chris believed John's will to live was stronger than his greed, and he wouldn't report any of this to Wolf until Chris and Tara had left the island.

Chris and Tara were relaxing at Basil's Bar on the shore of Britannia Bay in Mustique, having dinner and waiting for the sunset, when she got the shock of her life. Chris proposed marriage to her.

Tara wasn't sure if the hot equatorial sun had made him delirious or if their five-day romantic excursion visiting the other Grenadine Islands had wooed him, but either way, she was delighted.

"Chris, don't get me wrong, but what about all the arguments against marriage that you've repeatedly made over the past few months?"

"With baby Connor due in two months, I've been doing a lot of thinking."

"Chris, do you want to marry me because I'm having our child or because you want to spend the rest of your life with me?"

"Actually, it's both."

Chris could see the look of bewilderment on Tara's face. He knew that he needed to explain.

"My ideas about marriage haven't changed. I don't believe a piece of paper determines how you feel about each other. I accept that it's important for a child to see that there is a strong commitment between his parents. Recently, I've realized even more that there is no one else I'd rather spend the rest of my life with."

"This sounds familiar."

"I know everything I'm saying is mostly a repeat of what you've been telling me all along, but it hadn't jelled with me until last night. I was awake half the night thinking about it when I suddenly realized that I was being hypocritical. I was telling you that we didn't need marriage to make a commitment when, deep down, I was afraid of marriage because of the commitment. Does this make any sense?"

"No, but it does sound like a male explanation. Chris, of course, I'll marry you."

"Amazing."

"What?"

"Only a few months ago, I was just your bodyguard, and here we are now engaged and having a child together."

"I have to marry you," Tara said seriously.

"Why?"

"I still need a bodyguard, don't I?"

"Damn right. In fact, you deserve the best," he said, slapping his hand against his chest.

Tara laughed boisterously, making Chris laugh too.

John did not believe that Chris would pay him the balance of the million dollars. In fact, it was irrelevant. He had contracted with Wolf, and he wasn't about to betray him. Not because of any moral reason, he just always believed that you should go with the client who had the biggest bank account, which Wolf seemed to have. He was concerned for his life, but he figured that if he planned things well, he could be off the island and hidden in some remote part of the world before Chris knew anything.

Wolf wasn't surprised when John told him that Chris was going to leave the island within a week of his son's birth. He had already initiated the second phase of his plan.

CHAPTER TWENTY-NINE

THIS WAS NOT THE first time that Raven and his fellow combatant, Phoenix, had dared the imminent threat of a watery grave. Unexpectedly high winds flogged the Caribbean waters, violently pitching the black dinghy as it skirted the waves. With the fluidity of a champion skier negotiating moguls, Raven expertly kept them on course for the Friendship Bay shoreline. The plan was to make landfall on the southernmost part of the Bay's southern horn, keeping their landing out of view from Chris and Tara's cottage.

Raven saw this operation as a chance to redeem himself after he and his team had lost Chris the last time. He found this mission to be even more disturbing than the last one. He wasn't to return Wolf's daughter alive. In fact, he had been ordered to terminate Chris and the daughter and return with the baby only. He didn't understand Wolf. How could a father hate his daughter so much that he wanted her dead? When he questioned Wolf about it, he had simply replied that it must be done, and regrettably, Raven knew it to be true. Commander Samuels had ordered him to follow Wolf's commands, and that's what he would do. He wasn't just following his commander's orders blindly either. In his own mind, he too knew that this must be done for an important reason.

Raven had barely lifted the motor out of the water when a sudden lurch of the waves slammed the dinghy into the mud-soaked shore. The two men worked quickly, pulling the dinghy further up onto the beach so it wouldn't be pulled back out to sea by the strong undertow of the waves. They kept the black wet suits on to allow them to blend with the dark night. This was also a quick extraction operation, and they needed every second for escape.

According to local intelligence, Chris's cottage was small. The main part was all one room, and there was a single bedroom for Chris, Tara, and the baby on the north side of the cottage.

Both men knew what they had to do. Raven would take out Chris and Tara while Phoenix grabbed the child. They would meet back at the dinghy and return to the yacht anchored two miles off shore. Raven checked their location with the GPS. They were ten yards south of their intended landing spot. He looked at his watch. The time was 0315 hours—fifteen minutes behind schedule. They were to meet back at the yacht at 0430 hours.

"We've lost fifteen minutes. We better hurry," Raven whispered.

Phoenix nodded his understanding. Once they traversed the shoreline, both men, equipped with night vision goggles, moved diagonally up the hill along the ridge toward the cottage, knives and silenced guns ready at their sides. This operation was to be quick and silent—no waking up the neighbours as Raven had told Phoenix earlier.

Phoenix wore a special insulated carrier on his back for the baby, allowing him to keep his hands free for the escape.

They lay flat on the ground before surmounting the ridge at the edge of the cottage's backyard. Raven scanned the cottage, looking for any indication of movement. It was in total darkness and everything was still.

He signalled Phoenix to go through the sliding glass veranda door while he would enter the side door. Phoenix acknowledged. The two men, crouched and running, headed toward their points of entry.

The high winds off the sea drove the waves fiercely into shore as palm fronds clapped with noisy applause. With all of the loud, natural sounds, Chris shouldn't hear a slight scratching noise. Since he had become a CIA field operative, he never slept soundly. He was used to maintaining a state of sleep somewhere between resting and wakefulness. He called it limbo alertness. Before lying down, he always took the time to mentally register the sounds around him. While he rested, his brain was on constant guard for any deviation. If he heard something that didn't coincide with the norm, he was instantly on alert.

For Chris, that barely perceptible tick was louder than the crashing waves, because it didn't match. *It could have been a cat or another small animal,* he thought, but he wasn't taking any chances especially with Tara and Connor sleeping in the same room. He slipped out of bed, careful not to wake his family, and went to the closet. Chris retrieved his loaded revolver from behind the wooden panel on the top shelf.

Chris listened closely to the soft steps of an obvious professional as the intruder made his way across the living area toward the bedroom. Chris stood patiently waiting just inside the bedroom door. As the intruder stepped through the doorway, he looked toward the bed. Without hesitation, Chris delivered a crushing blow to the back of his neck, knocking him to the floor.

Because the unconscious assailant was wearing a pair of night vision goggles on his head, Chris was not able to see his face. He also heard another noise in the living area—a sudden shifting. *A person moving quickly for cover,* Chris assumed. He didn't know what was happening, but he didn't want his wife or infant son to be hit by a stray bullet. He figured that whoever was in the living area must be alone because a group would have attacked already, knowing that Chris was outnumbered. He would have at least thirty seconds while the other person assessed the situation and decided what his next step was. Chris would have to move fast.

He put one hand over Tara's mouth and shook her by the shoulder to awaken her. Her eyes opened with shock at the sight of the gun in his hand. She jerked her head and tried to pull his hand from her face. Chris held on with a tight grip. Using his free hand and placing one finger in front of his lips, he gestured for her to be quiet.

He bent down and whispered in her ear, "Don't be alarmed, there's someone in the cottage. I want you to get Connor and go into the bathroom and hide in the shower stall. Crouch down as low as you can get."

She nodded understanding. Chris lifted his hand from her mouth. Chris knew he was with the right woman as he watched her slip out of the bed without making a sound. She went straight to the crib, picked up the baby, placed her hand over his mouth, and carried him into the bathroom without saying a word. Even when she saw the body in the bedroom entranceway, which Chris hadn't had time to tell her about, she didn't flinch. In the meantime, Chris repositioned himself by the wall on the opposite side of the doorway, waiting and listening intently for the other predator to make a move.

Chris heard the sound of extra pressure on the wooden floor. He waited, poised and ready to shoot if necessary. These men had invaded his house, and he would defend his family with his last breath. He wondered if he had been hearing things and the only attacker was the man lying beside him. He crouched to the floor to steal a look into the living room, when he heard the windowpane break and the wooden doorframe splinter above his head. Whirling on the spot, Chris fired, hitting his would-be assassin in his night vision goggles, rendering him sightless. But that didn't stop the man from squeezing off another round. Chris heard the spit of the silenced gun a fraction of a second before the bullet whizzed past his head.

Leaning to the right and shooting again, Chris instinctively returned fire, and this time his ammo found the man's forehead.

He launched himself backward into the living room and to the right, away from the doorway. Gun poised and ready to shoot again, Chris walked out to the veranda and around the cottage to the window his attacker had tried to kill him through. Holding the gun out in front of him with both hands, he crossed the eight-foot distance between him and the crumpled body, watching for any slight movement that might indicate an ability to fire off one more shot.

Within a foot of the body, he saw the blood oozing down the side of the guy's head onto the wooden slats. He was certain that the man was dead, an assumption easily confirmed by a lack of pulse.

Chris pulled the dead man's night vision goggles off to see his face, but he didn't recognize him. He went back into the cottage to check the man he had rendered unconscious and removed his night vision goggles too. What Chris saw astounded him.

"Raven, goddamn it," he yelled. "What the fuck is going on?"

He dragged Raven's limp body into the living area and bound his legs and arms so he couldn't escape. Then he did some reconnaissance around the cottage before going back inside to tell Tara that she could come out of the bathroom.

Tara entered the bedroom with the wailing baby in her arms.

"Chris, what the hell's happening? I heard gunshots. What kind of violent world are we bringing our son into?" she yelled, loud enough to be heard over Connor's screaming.

"I don't know what's happening yet, Tara, but I'm about to find out. One of the two men who attacked us is still alive. If I don't get some answers soon, he'll be wishing he were dead. You stay in here with Connor and try to calm him and yourself while I question our attacker."

"Calm down? What the fuck do you mean, calm down? Men attacking us in the night, guns firing, and strange men invading our intimate privacy—it's insane. Our son could've been killed, taken from us by a stray bullet. And you want me to be calm?"

Chris grabbed Tara by the shoulders.

"I'm sorry. I didn't mean to minimize what happened here. But I have to interrogate the man in the other room to find out what's going on so we can put an end to this once and for all."

"I want to know what's going on too, but I'm scared," she said, her body still trembling. "Go and interview or interrogate that bastard—whatever you call it. I'll stay in here with Connor, but it will be a hell of a long time before I calm down."

Chris went into the other room where Raven now lay awake, struggling to free himself from his bonds.

"You're awake. I wish I could say the same for your partner. It'll take more than a kiss from some charming princess to wake him."

"You killed him, you bastard. When I get free of these ropes …"

"And I suppose if I hadn't stopped you and your now dead partner," Chris snapped, "you were planning to read me a bedtime story, because you knew I was having trouble sleeping. Funny, I don't remember you having any milk and cookies in your hand when you entered our bedroom."

"Fuck you!"

"No, fuck you, you son of a bitch. You talk like you don't even recognize me. What the hell's happened to you, Raven?" Chris noticed a slight movement in Raven's eyelids at the sound of his name. "What the hell's going on? How come you don't recognize me? Or has someone turned you against me?" Chris asked.

Chris heard a noise behind him and turned around quickly, his gun aimed, ready to kill. Just in time, he saw it was Tara.

"Shit. I just about shot you. Don't sneak up on me like that."

"It wasn't a problem before tonight."

"Yes, but things are very tense tonight."

"You're that man again, aren't you?"

"What are you talking about, Tara? What man?"

"The hunter, the killer, the man with blood on his hands—the man I saw in your memories when I touched you in the car."

"I never stopped being that man, and I always will be as long as scum like your father walk the earth." Chris yelled.

"I hate that man, and I don't want to spend my life with him. Will you ever be free of him? Will you ever be just Chris, the man I married?"

"I don't know, but there is one thing I do know: it will never happen without you and Connor in my life. And we have to put an end to this madness that your father's branding our lives with."

"Hey, you two, if you want to kiss and make up, just untie me and I'll get out of your way," Raven said.

Chris put his fingers to his lips as if he recalling something. "Tara, do you think you can check Raven's mind to see if a memory has been blocked? Wolf might have done that to him, and that's why he doesn't remember me."

"For sure," Tara said.

"Blocking memories? What kind of hocus-pocus are you two going on about?" Raven yelled.

Tara lay Connor in his carriage, settled into the white wicker armchair beside it, and closed her eyes.

It didn't take long to find Raven in the cacophony of minds. She began to read through his chronological history, starting about three years prior to when he had first met Chris. What she saw horrified her—the death, the killing, and the mental and physical abuse he had both endured and inflicted on others.

Just when she thought she could not continue, she found a memory block—that familiar electrically charged mass of tissue waiting to be obliterated. More experienced now, she quickly transitioned through the block, restoring the memory of Chris and Raven's first encounter.

CHAPTER THIRTY

"YOU BASTARD, UNTIE ..." CHRIS watched as Raven's eyes widened with disbelief when he recognized him, "Chris? Is that you? Chris Landry?"

"Yes, it is."

"What the hell are you doing here? And where are the two people I was sent to kill? Something very weird is going on here. Either that or I'm having some freaking major hallucinations."

"Well, that's the understatement of the century. I guess Tara was able to reach you."

"Tara. That's the name of the girl. Wait a minute, how do I know that you're really Chris. You could be an impostor."

"Believe me, I'm Chris Landry.'

"Prove it."

"Prove it, what the hell do you mean prove it? You break in trying to kill my fiancé and me, and you want me to prove who I am?"

"You sure sound like the Chris I remember. For all I know, you've somehow altered your appearance to look like Chris Landry. If you really are Chris, for my sanity, there must be something you remember about our past that no one else would know."

"Okay, but only because you weren't in control of your actions or you wouldn't have done any of this. I know that all too well. I bet I'm the only one who knows how you got that scar on the left side of your chest."

"Carry on," Raven said.

"If I hadn't walked into the room and caught that whore in the middle of cutting your nipple off while you lay there passed-out drunk, there might have been a few other body parts lopped off as well. As we found out later—if you recall—she was apprehended a couple of days later for dismembering four other men. 'Her father must have deprived her of hugs and kisses when she was a child,' I think you said at the time."

"Damn, it is you, Chris. There's a baby as well," Raven said.

"My son, Connor. I don't suppose you were told to kill him. I suppose he was scheduled to be delivered to Wolf."

"That's right. How did you know?"

"Wolf is Tara's father. Well, at least biologically."

"I know. It didn't make any sense to me either that he wanted his daughter dead."

"Yes, it's hard to believe."

"There's just too much going on here that doesn't add up. First, her father didn't hire me. My commander ordered me on this mission. And now that I'm thinking clearer, that's really screwed. Why would my commander send me on mission for a Canadian citizen? Too many things don't make sense. I feel like I'm in this limbo world, as if I've just recovered from amnesia. And my fucking head hurts like hell. What time is it?"

"It's four thirty. And you're not far off on that amnesia idea."

"Our rendezvous time."

"What?" Chris asked.

"We were supposed to be back at the yacht by zero four thirty hours or the mission would be called in as a failure."

"What's the backup plan if you and your partner don't show?"

"I was never told of any backup plan. It's a damn shame Gary's dead. He was one of my best men. His full name was Gary Whiteman," Raven lamented with mellow regret, not shedding a tear.

Chris knew that too many years of watching friends die took the tears away. "If it's any consolation, he almost got the better of me."

"That's no consolation. I would have been just as upset if you'd been killed. What do you mean I wasn't far off with the amnesia concept?" Raven asked, jumping from one topic to another. His mind was obviously still wracked by the enormous emotional strain of the situation, Chris realized.

"I'll explain it as best as I can. Tara can fill in the gaps."

Chris and Tara updated Raven on events as they had unfolded so far, being careful not to mention any details about Tara's power. That was something they would have to keep between themselves for the time being. It would have to remain enigmatic for now.

Richard Bonner was a short, round, podgy man with pink, translucent skin and yellow eyes. An angry patron had once told him that he looked like a snow bank that two drunks had pissed on. He had done many of these night runs, and he had never gotten used to the stress of a guest not returning on time. He worried if they were caught they would give his name and location to their captors.

He liked to use the words "guest" and "patron," because the men and women he transported were not usually the paying client. They were often executing some kind of illegal activity for the client, and Richard was just the deliveryman. He was never told anything about the missions, and he preferred it that way. As far as his family and friends knew, he was in the travel business, taking wealthy men and women on very expensive, exotic adventures.

The man with the dark black hair, known to him only as Bill, had given Richard a phone number to call if he didn't return by 0430 hours. He was to inform the person who answered of the situation. He did as instructed and was ordered by a deep voice on the other end of the line—a voice he recognized as the man who had hired him—to wait for another half hour, at which time he was to call back and provide another update. Richard didn't like the idea of staying past the scheduled time, and he told the man so.

"It's too risky. Who knows what's happened to them. If I wait any longer, I could be apprehended."

Wolf ignored his plea.

"Will you wait another half hour if I sweeten your payday by another fifty thousand dollars?"

"Okay, I'll wait," Richard said hesitantly. "And I don't care if you lather the pot with liquid gold, I'm not staying past 0500 hours."

Richard wouldn't have stayed for the fifty thousand if he hadn't lost thirty grand at the racetrack yesterday. This time, his wife would leave him if she happened to check the bank balance before he had a chance to replenish it. He wasn't even sure why he went to the track, because he'd sworn off gambling and hadn't been there for over five years.

"It's 0500 hours and there's still no sign of them." Richard reported to his client on the other end of the phone.

What the hell happened? Wolf wondered. He knew it must have been Tara again, but how had she countered him this time? Damn her, she was getting too powerful. She had to be stopped.

"Sir, I've done what you asked, and now I'm getting out of here."

"Yes, you'd better leave," Wolf said and hung up.

Richard turned the key in the ignition. The boat's engines revved with a deep, gurgling throaty sound. He thrust the throttle forward, lifting the bow above the choppy waters and took off. The more distance Richard put between himself and the waters surrounding Bequia, the more relieved he felt.

He had travelled about twenty miles out to sea when he heard a tremendous explosion. In a fraction of a second, the hull of the magnificent yacht blasted in half. Richard was catapulted through the air toward the stern, where an upright fishing spear pierced his throat, silencing any cries for help. No one heard the loud blast or saw the fireball light the Caribbean darkness or watched as Richard slipped away into his watery grave.

Wolf smugly cleared the number from the phone he had used to set off the bomb and dropped it in the cradle.

"Chris, remind me never to get tied up by you again. These rope burns on my wrists will last a week."

"Oh, Raven, quit whining. You've been through a lot worse than that."

"I guess I should consider myself lucky. I could've ended up like my compatriot. By the way, we're going to have to get rid of his body."

"I have an idea. Let's carry it down to where you left the dinghy and leave it there—wet suit and all."

"But when they find the body, they'll interrogate everybody on the island, and it's so close to our place. We'll be suspects," Tara said.

"Of course we will, and we'll tell them what we heard last night: loud distant noises that we thought was a truck backfiring. The winds were quite high last, night making any noise barely distinguishable. And because of the nature of the situation, the wet suit, the dinghy … it'll be suspicious in another way as well."

"How's that?" Tara asked.

"With all of the terrorism happening around the world these days, the authorities will wonder what someone dressed like that, travelling in a dinghy and sporting a high-calibre hand gun is doing dead on the shores of Bequia. It could even get the attention of the national newspapers, which is exactly what I want because then your father will find out. My hope is that he'll get the message that it doesn't pay to screw with us."

"I hope it works. Life would be so much better if he would just leave us alone. But my instincts tell me he won't. Wolf's stubborn, and I'm a major threat to him. But as long as I'm still breathing, he's never going to have Connor to twist into his maniacal view of the world!" Tara shouted.

"He's going to have to kill us both. Remember, Connor's my son too. I just hope this incident will give him pause, allowing us a bit of breathing space to plan where we'll go from here and how we're going to get there. Right now, Raven and I have to get that body out of here before the police arrive."

"But Wolf found us here, and we were so cautious."

"We'll finish this conversation when Raven and I get back."

Chris and Raven adeptly lifted Gary's dead body and hung him between them, as if walking a drunken friend home after carousing all night. It was something the two of them had obviously practised over the years.

"Chris, there's so much I don't understand here. What did you mean when you said that Tara must have reached me?"

"It's a long story," Chris said, not wanting to say too much. He knew that he could not keep Raven completely in the dark for long, because he was a trained interrogator and would continue badgering him until he told him something. "I don't totally comprehend it all myself yet," he continued, hedging his words, "Tara and her father, Wolf, have a special kind of genetic ability that allows them to remotely manipulate people. They can plant thoughts in people's minds that they later act upon. It's kind of like putting someone into a hypnotic state." The two men instinctively shifted their bodies as they approached the steep embankment ahead.

"Let's say, for argument's sake, I believe what you just told me. How does Tara undo what her father's done?"

"Tara is more powerful than her father allowing her to counter his attacks."

Chris was reminded that he would have to ask Tara to block Raven's mind so Wolf could not manipulate him any further.

"That's one un-fucking-believable story. I hope I wake up soon."

"If you do, make sure you wake me as well."

"You didn't answer my original question. What did you mean when you said Tara must have reached me?"

"As I said, she is more powerful than her father. At first, you didn't recognize me, as if all thoughts of me had been removed from your brain.

I realized that Wolf had brainwashed you, so I asked Tara to remove the memory block he'd placed in your mind."

"Here we are. There's the dinghy," Raven interrupted, pointing up the beachfront.

They laid Gary half in and half out of the dinghy, as they had discussed earlier, to make it look as if he had been shot while exiting the craft.

Tara had just thrown a small rug over the bullet hole in the floor, cleaned up the wood chips where the would-be killer's bullet had grazed the doorframe, and finished tidying up the living area when she heard a knock at the cottage's side door.

"Just a minute. I'll be right there," she shouted, not wanting to appear too anxious.

She was heading toward the door when the veranda's sliding door opened and Chris and Raven entered. She quickly put her finger to her mouth motioning for them to be quiet. They looked quizzically at her. She pointed to the door. Understanding, Chris signalled Raven to leave. They didn't want to have to explain any more than necessary. If a police officer was at the door, Raven's presence would prompt questions. On a small island like Bequia, the residents of each house are known to almost everyone. Raven slipped out the back and disappeared into the darkness.

Another knock rapped on the door just as Tara opened it.

"Good evening, ma'am and sir," the police officer addressed them politely, as Chris walked into his view. "It's a bit late to be up isn't it?"

"Well, officer," Tara began without hesitation, "we have a three-month-old baby, and the high winds tonight have kept him awake, so guess who else hasn't had any sleep?"

"Believe me, ma'am, I know exactly what you mean. I have two kids of my own," the officer said with a bright smile. "I know this is probably nothing, but someone reported hearing gun shots coming from this direction. Did either of you hear anything unusual?" he asked, peering into the cottage, obviously looking for evidence of a disturbance. Chris was happy to see that Tara had cleaned up. He would have to commend her later for her foresight.

"No, I didn't hear anything other than the strong winds and Connor screaming. How about you, dear?" Tara asked, looking at Chris.

"Ditto for me, officer."

"Well, like I said, sorry to bother you this late at night, but we have to check these things out, you know."

"We understand," Chris and Tara said together.

Chris waited as the officer climbed the stone path and got into his car by the gate before signalling Raven to come back in. Once Raven was inside, Chris doused the lights so as not to arouse suspicion in case the officer made a drive-by to see if they were still up. Any sane couple would go back to bed and try to get some sleep once their child had finally settled.

The three of them sat in the living room debriefing.

"One thing that's obviously been bothering me," Chris started, "is how Wolf knew we were here, and I think I've figured it out."

"How?" Tara asked.

"Remember that man we met the first day on the island, the one at the Green Boley …"

"You said he was only sketching a picture of the bar."

"That's true. But when I think about it, other times when I met him in town he was much too interested in your pregnancy, supposedly innocently asking how far along you were and how you were doing. Why would a stranger be so interested in the pregnancy of a woman he doesn't even know? It could've been completely innocent, but my instincts tell me differently, and over the years, I've learned to trust my instincts." Chris said, completely leaving out the fact that he had already confronted John.

"Damn," Tara cried out, "my father's reach is too widespread. We'll never escape him."

"Yes, we will Tara, and I want to congratulate you for having the sense to clean up the cottage after we left and on how well you handled the cop."

Raven gently placed his hand on Tara's shoulder, and with a sincere look of determination, he said, "After what Wolf did to me, you have my full support and that of anyone else I can get to help. We'll beat him if it costs me my last heartbeat."

"Thanks," Tara said with a forced smile.

"Tara, before you go to sleep, you'll need to block Raven's mind."

"I already did it. Meditating helped me relax after you left."

"That's great, Tara, but there's one other person you should block as well: Raven's commanding officer."

"What's his name?" she asked Raven.

"Colonel Geoffrey Allan Samuels."

"Consider it done."

CHAPTER THIRTY-ONE

"IT'S A SHAME YOU won't be able to stay in this little paradise of yours," Raven shouted from the veranda as he breathed the scent of a fresh, morning sea breeze.

"It really is," Chris said, greeting him with a fresh cup of coffee. "Did you talk to your commander yet?"

"Yes. And after Tara finished working her magic, he told me that he woke up in a cold sweat last night, realizing what he had ordered me to do. He was really glad to hear from me and even more glad that I understood why he had given me those psychotic orders, as he put it."

"What about Whiteman?"

"Well, that's where we were extremely lucky. Whiteman doesn't have any family so the colonel said to let him be buried here, and I must say I couldn't think of a nicer final resting place."

"How's the colonel going to explain this situation to his superiors?" Chris asked.

"He has to cover it up. He can't go to his commander and tell him that some guy he's never met gave him orders in his sleep. And that he gave me orders to execute a contract for a private citizen—a Canadian citizen, no less. In his own words, he would be immediately suspended with pay, pending a complete psychological evaluation. What he told me, though, is that you can depend on him to help in any way possible, even if it means being court-martialled. It goes without saying that any word of the colonel's involvement can't go beyond you and I—not even Tara can know."

"Of course."

Chris refrained from telling Raven the details of Tara's mind reading ability. *Why complicate things,* he thought.

"I appreciate you letting us use your mother's apartment in New York."

"She died six months ago, Chris. I went to the funeral, but at the time, I didn't have the emotional fortitude to go to her apartment, and I still haven't been there. I know I'll have to eventually empty it out and sell everything off. Having you live there allows me to put if off a bit longer, and for that, I'm grateful."

"Sounds like your mother and you were very close."

"She's the only one who understood me. This career sucks the life out of you, as you know, and she was the only one I could talk to during times of crisis. Obviously, the nature of my work precluded me from telling her everything, but she knew me so well she could read between the lines and always knew what to say to get me through."

"You were very lucky to have her. I wish I'd had someone like her."

"You do now: Tara. Don't let this crap blind her to you."

"You're right, Raven. I've been thinking about how we're going to get to New York without Wolf finding out, and the only idea I can come up with is military transport. Can you arrange it?"

"The colonel did say "anything" so let's put him to the test."

"Great. I'll make breakfast while you call the colonel."

"Deal. I'm starving."

"Raven, I've been meaning to ask you something."

"Yes."

"What do you think of all of the assassinations and attempted assassinations happening recently?"

"Well, at first it appeared to be some kind of terrorist plot. But then this company, NSTC—Nano Securities—suddenly started cashing in on people's fears. I'm beginning to think they might be behind it in someway. Maybe they're financing the whole thing to sell their armoured shirts."

"Who could pull off such an elaborate plan without the NSA or other worldwide security agencies finding out about it?"

"A ghost," Raven said.

A ghost, Chris thought, and then it came to him. He remembered the document he'd seen months before on Wolf's desk, the prospectus for NSTC. "The ghost idea isn't far off Raven, but this ghost has a name."

"Pardon me?"

"His name is Wolf Ostermann. Before I left the Ostermann Estate, I had a meeting with Wolf regarding how to find Tara and on his desk was a prospectus document for NSTC. I believe that Wolf decided to invest in the company. But, being an impatient man, he decided to ramp sales up by creating a fear of assassination within the assembly of the rich and powerful around the globe."

"Before yesterday, I would have said you were losing it. Now it seems like a plausible explanation," Raven said.

"Don't say anything to Tara about this," Chris said. "I'd like to talk to her about it myself."

Raven nodded acknowledgment.

"Good morning," Tara greeted Chris when he stepped back into the cottage.

Seeing her standing there holding baby Connor in his soft, blue blanket, Chris felt disjointed. This was his family, but his mind was divided into two worlds: a world of death and chaos—a world where trust is a bond earned in battle, where the political climate is your master bending you at will—and this new world of sincere compassion, union of love, and family values. It was a world he longed to give himself to fully, but he knew he couldn't as long as Wolf was out there manipulating people to track them down. Someday he would have to kill Wolf, but he contemplated whether he could kill the father of the woman he loved—even after everything he'd done to them.

"Chris, have you and Raven come up with a plan to get us out of here without Wolf tracking us?"

"Yes, I think so. Raven is just finalizing the details. Once he's off his cell phone, we'll know for sure."

"Good."

"How's Connor doing this morning?" Chris asked, changing the subject.

"He seems fine."

"I was just going to start breakfast. Would you like eggs and bacon, or are you going to have cereal this morning?"

"I'd love eggs and bacon, thanks."

For the fourth time that day, Wolf read the Reuters bulletin. It was mid-afternoon and he still had not heard from Raven.

Suspicious death reported. A man with no identification was found on a beach on the small Eastern Caribbean island of Bequia, the second largest island in the St. Vincent and Grenadine chain of islands. A local official was quoted as saying, "It's hard to believe, but by the way he was dressed, the military-style black dinghy he was found in, and the silencer-equipped gun found on his person, you'd think he was some kind of a spy or an assassin."

178

Wolf knew that man had to be either Raven or one of his men. Son of a bitch, those idiots had screwed up again. Wolf had been holding onto a filament of hope since he had not been able to reach Raven last night. He was optimistic that Raven and his man had completed the mission even though they had not returned to the yacht. He assumed that they would find another means of escape and bring him his grandson—the rightful heir to his throne. Now he doubted their success. If Raven or his man had his grandson, one of them would have called him by now. His only desire was that both were dead, saving him the trouble of having them killed.

Wolf's desk phone rang, and he quickly plucked the receiver from its cradle, anxious for good news—God knows, he needed some right then.

"Hello."

"Is this Mr. Ostermann?"

"Yes." Wolf knew by the West Indian accent that it was probably Sandrina from Bequia—the housekeeper that John Borg had told him about.

"You wanted me to call if anything happened with Chris and Tara. Well, they've left."

"Left? Where have they gone?"

"There was a note saying they would be gone for a few months, asking me to keep an eye on the house."

"Sandrina," Wolf said calmly, not to alarm the woman, "was there anyone else around the cottage lately?"

"Now that you mention it, yes. There was a tall, rugged-looking man with thick, black hair. Very handsome."

"Thank you, Sandrina, you've been a great help. Call me if you see anyone else around there."

"I will," she said, hanging up the phone.

Wolf knew the tall so-called handsome son of a bitch was Raven. Worse yet, his suspicion had been confirmed that his daughter was somehow blocking him from accessing people's minds.

"How the fuck does she to do it?" he cursed.

It didn't matter. She couldn't block everybody's mind at once. Eventually, one of the people he had looking for them would spot them. It was just a matter of time.

Tara awoke to the constant hum of a giant plane's engines as it ploughed through the atmosphere forty thousand feet above the earth, as Raven told her. Remembering Tara's fear of flying, Chris had given her a motion sickness pill that had put her to sleep. She glanced at Chris and saw that he and Connor were sleeping soundly.

"I feel like an important diplomat on such a big plane. What is it, and how did we end up on it?" Tara asked Raven.

"It's a C-17 Globemaster III."

"Oookay?"

"It's a US Air Force cargo and troop transport plane. We were just fortunate that someone underestimated the fuel requirement, and it had to land in Barbados to refuel, allowing us to hitch a ride."

"Wonderful. Will it be long before we get to New York?"

"In a couple of hours we'll land at McGuire Air Force Base in New Jersey where a military car will be waiting to take you to Manhattan."

"Can you give me the names of the crew members, so I can block their minds, just in case one of them happens to see us and reports back to Wolf?"

"Sure …"

Tara knew the plane was starting its descent when she began to feel the unbearable familiar pain, like her eardrums were being systematically stretched. She was suddenly more appreciative of commercial airlines. At least they warned her when the plane would be landing, giving her a chance to mentally brace herself. She watched Connor wriggle in Chris's arms; both of them remained fast asleep, seemingly unaware of the change in air pressure, for which she was grateful. She raised her arms in a quiet cheer at the sound of the plane's wheels hitting the tarmac.

They had barely taxied to a stop when Raven roused Chris and quickly escorted the three of them to a nearby limousine. Raven shook Chris's hand, kissed Connor's forehead, and hugged Tara. This was something new for Tara, a man other than Chris hugging her, and she liked it. It wasn't a hug of passion but a hug of friendship, something that had been lacking in her life. It was a friendship she was thankful for.

"Hurry. Get into the limo," Raven said urgently to Chris and Tara, holding the door open and ushering them forward, "before someone sees you."

"Thank you, Raven, for all you've done," Chris said before shutting the door.

"Tara, the limo driver's name is Barry Dunford. You'll probably want to block his mind too," Raven said.

"Yes, I will."

As the limousine pulled away, Tara spoke, "Raven lied to me, Chris, about the plane. It was actually arranged by his commander."

"Yes, it was, but you can never tell anyone."

"Of course, I won't. There's something I've decided about this power of mine. I'm going to have to deal with people not telling me the truth at times. I have to learn to let it go until they themselves are ready to tell me. That includes you, Chris," she said, her eyebrows raised with that whenever-you're-ready-to-confess look a mother gives when she's caught a child fibbing.

Chris knew what Tara was referring to.

"I didn't tell you about John Borg, because I didn't want to worry you."

"I was worried, but what made it worse was I couldn't talk to you about it, because I was trying to respect your privacy. I figured you would tell me soon, but you didn't. Aren't we in this together?"

"Yes, we are. However, I have to admit that your ability to read my mind is quite disturbing. I will do my best not to keep anything from you. You're going to have to be patient with me, though. If there is something that I haven't told you and you think it's important for us to talk about it, tell me. Do you agree?"

"Agreed."

Tara held Chris's hand as they traveled without talking the rest of the way to Manhattan.

"This apartment is gorgeous, Chris, with its exquisite antique furniture and those beautiful, gold brocade drapes and colourful, Persian wool carpets. It reminds me of the rooms described in the stories of kings and queens that my parents used to read to me," Tara exclaimed as she twirled in the middle of the floor, holding Connor in her arms.

She drew open the heavy living room drapes and was awestruck by the panoramic view of New York Harbor and the Statue of Liberty. "Fantastic! How long can we stay here, Chris?"

"Raven said we can stay as long as we want."

"Alright!"

"Suddenly, you're very happy. What's changed?"

"I didn't realize New York was so big. Surely we can get lost in this place—just another face in a crowded city. My father will never find us here."

Chris hadn't seen her like this for a while, and he didn't want to destroy the moment, so he just held her close. "My thoughts exactly," he said, forcing a smile.

"What is the name of that small island by the Statue of Liberty?"

"Ellis Island."

"What part of New York are we in?"

"Battery Park City in lower Manhattan."

CHAPTER THIRTY-TWO

WOLF WAS NOT A patient man. A month had passed without any phone calls. Where the hell could Chris and Tara have gone that they could evade everyone he had looking for them? It was time to call John Borg again.

John's cell phone rang four times before he found it on the front entrance hall table under the daily newspaper. "Hello."

"John."

The voice sounded familiar, but static on the line made him uncertain.

"Who's this?" John asked.

"It's Wolf. After all of our conversations, you don't recognize my voice?"

"Of course, I recognized your voice, but in my business, it's best to be sure."

"Are you available?"

John could tell by Wolf's tone that he was desperate, so he would twist every dime he could out of the miserable old bastard, "Well, actually, I've got this job I'm supposed to start next week that'll probably require about three months of my time."

"Bullshit. Last time, I paid you five thousand a day. This time I'll make it seven thousand. Do you still have a contract next week?"

John had never heard Wolf so desperate before and was enjoying it immensely.

"Your offer is tempting, Wolf, but I'd hate to go back on my word. After all, I am a man of honour."

"Cut the crap. Ten thousand a day, plus expenses—that's my final offer. But you only get paid if you succeed."

John knew he could get a couple of more thousand out of him but he didn't think it was worth the loss of future work.

"You push pretty hard. I guess my honour can be bought after all. And as far as me succeeding goes, you shouldn't have any doubts. What's the job?"

"That's what I like, a man who can be coerced. I want you to find Chris and Tara again. They've left Bequia, and there's no trace of them."

"Is there anything else you can tell me besides the fact that they've left?"

"They might have had some help from a man named Blake Rosewell who also goes by the code name Raven."

"Code name Raven? That sounds like military."

"Yes, he's stationed at Fort Bragg in North Carolina."

"Whoa. You didn't tell me the US military was involved."

"Why do you care as long as you get paid?"

"The last time I had anything to do with those pricks, I ended up in jail for two years, and that's not a place I want to go back to."

"Okay, fifteen thousand a day."

"I don't like it, but for that kind of money I'd take on the president."

"Good. You better get started."

Wolf liked John because he was capable, and he didn't screw around. Everything came down to price versus risk. If the price was high enough, the risk was never too great.

John was scared purple when it came to dealing with the US military. *But fifteen thousand a day helps choke down a lot of fear,* he thought, as he jimmied the lock on Chris's cottage door in Bequia. He didn't expect to find anything in the cottage that would lead him directly to Chris and Tara, but he hoped to uncover some less obvious clues, at least giving him some direction. After all, that was his business; painstakingly gathering one small lead after another and gradually building a map to the person he was searching for. The first thing he did was press redial on the phone to see where Chris last called.

The operator on the other end of the line responded with a friendly West Indian greeting, "Mustique Air. Josephine speaking. I hope you're having a fine day. What can I do for you?"

"Hi Josephine, it's Chris Landry calling. I chartered a plane with your company about a month ago for my wife and I, but at the last minute I wasn't able to go and my wife had to go without me. I know this is a bit unusual, but I was wondering if I could get some kind of credit or discount on a future flight."

"We don't usually offer credit, Mr. Landry, but let me check the flight. What was your destination, sir?"

John wondered if Chris would have gone down island to one of the smaller islands or if he would have left the Grenadines for another country. If he had left for another country, he would have had to stop at Barbados to catch an international flight.

"Sir?"

"Sorry, Josephine, I got distracted. What was your question?"

"Your destination, sir?"

"Oh yes, of course, it was Barbados," John said, fairly certain he'd guessed correctly.

"Thank you, sir. Here it is, Chris and Tara Landry. The records show that you and your wife both landed at Grantley Adams International Airport in Barbados on Thursday, May twelfth."

"There must be some kind of mistake, because I didn't go with her."

"Mr. Landry, it says right here …"

"That's impossible. I definitely never boarded that plane. Let me speak to your supervisor."

"No problem, sir. I'll get him on the line immediately."

John hung up the phone.

He continued searching the rest of the cottage. As he'd previously surmised, he found nothing except evidence of a gun battle: a bullet hole in the floor and minute traces of blood on the veranda. He hoped Raven was dead. That'd be one less grunt he'd have to worry about dealing with.

CHAPTER THIRTY-THREE

"WILL WE STAY IN New York and get our own apartment Chris?"

"Why do we need another place? Raven said we could stay here as long as we want."

"I really love this place, but it's not my own, and I can't do what I want with it."

"I think it's a bit early to think about settling down."

"Honey," she said, mockingly batting her eyes at him, "we've been here over a month, and there's been no contact from my father or anyone else. As long as we maintain our new looks, no one will recognize us, especially you with that cute, shaved head. Oh, how it shines."

"You might be right. Maybe we've finally found refuge from his grasp. If we're going to get a place of our own, I'd rather go some place more rural. I don't like living in New York City."

"I don't care where we live. At least here, we have anonymity."

Chris couldn't argue with her. If she felt safe here, this is where they should stay for now.

"Okay, we can stay in New York, at least until we're sure that your father has stopped looking for us. Why don't we start looking for a place tomorrow?" Not that he believed that Wolf had ...

"You're wonderful, Chris. I love you," she said, wrapping her arms around him as the two of them stretched out on the sofa. "When I run my hand over your scalp, it feels quite sexy, and I love the tickle of your little beard when we make love."

"You little minx," he teased, running his hand up her bare leg, squeezing her inner thigh.

From his table in the corner, John observed the men and women of McGuire Air Force Base at the bar drinking themselves into oblivion.

Knocking back a shot of whatever he was drinking, one of the soldiers shouted, "Let's drown another week from hell."

John had found out from one of his contacts at Grantley Adams that a US military cargo plane destined for New Jersey had made a stop for fuel at the Barbados airport. Because there was no record of anyone fitting Chris or Tara's description flying out of Barbados on a commercial airline, he assumed that Raven or Blake—or whatever the hell he called himself— had slipped them aboard the military plane bound for New Jersey, under the radar so to speak. Thus proving, much to his regret, that Raven was still alive. They could have gone anywhere from McGuire, and he needed to find out where that was. He stepped out from his table and, walking with the cautious swagger of an experienced drinker, made his way to the bar.

Standing just far enough away from the group of soldiers so they could hear him, he ordered a shot of Jack Daniels without ice.

"What's your name, young man?" John asked the bartender.

"Bill."

"Hey, Bill, give all my air force friends here whatever it is they're drinking—on me."

The tall, rusty-haired military man standing closest to him turned around when he overheard the generous offer, "Thanks mister, what's the occasion?"

John could see that the man was barely over twenty-one; he gave him a half smile while his deep, chestnut eyes transformed to sincerity, "I just wanted to thank all of you for helping to keep our country safe and secure. U-S-A the great. Cheers to the USA," John shouted, raising his glass and grabbing the bar at the same time, as if balancing himself.

"Cheers," the crowd repeated in unison, arms extended with glasses above their heads.

John began talking with the young rusty-haired soldier. He asked him where he was from, where he had gone to school, how he had ended up in the air force—all the usual friendly questions.

"You know, lad ..."

"Yes?"

"We've been talking for twenty minutes, and I don't even know your name."

"It's Rick Tomes, private first class. Nice to meet you," he said, jutting out his hand.

"My name's Sal Holburg, nice to meet you Rick," John said, firmly shaking the soldier's hand.

"Rick?"

"Yes."

"Never mind. I shouldn't bother you with my problems. You probably wouldn't know anyway."

"Know what?"

"I shouldn't ask, it could put you in a compromising position."

"Go ahead. Ask. I'll tell you if it's compromising," Rick said, by this time barely able to string together two syllables, never mind full words.

"Well, about a month ago, my cousin, his wife, and young child came here, and I've been looking for them. They arrived on a military cargo plane."

"Sal, between you and I, that's not permitted."

The soldier's hand jerked forward as if to make the point, spilling beer over the edge of his glass. "No civilians are allowed on military transport. But I do remember hearing about something like that. You didn't hear it from me, though."

"I didn't hear what."

"Good enough," his hand jerked for emphasis; more beer spilled. "My pal in the motor pool told me that a husband, wife, and child did arrive on one of our Globemasters about a month ago. It was totally against all regulations. Even worse, he was ordered to drive them to Manhattan and drop them off in Times Square. At first we figured they were some VIP family. But neither of us could figure out why a VIP family would be dropped off in Times Square. Seems odd, doesn't it?"

"Maybe they needed to do some shopping before going to their final destination. Your friend didn't happen to describe the people did he?"

"No, except to say that the child was very young."

"You've been a great help, Rick," John said, patting him on the shoulder.

"No problem, buddy. I hope you find your cousin."

"Can I buy you another drink?"

"No. Let me buy you one this time." Rick gestured, slopping more beer, just missing John.

"Okay, JD no ice," John said, stepping back to avoid future spillage.

John threw his keys on the nightstand beside the bed in his hotel room at the Marriott Marquis on Broadway. He had gotten a room at a hotel near Times Square in the centre of Manhattan, which was the last place Chris and Tara had been seen. Tomorrow, he would show the picture of Chris and Tara around, hoping to find someone who had seen them. Before going to sleep, he figured he had better give Wolf a call and update him. He picked up the phone and called him directly on his private number.

The phone rang three times before a brusque, tired voice boomed through the earpiece, "Hello!"

"Wolf, it's John."

"What the fuck are you doing calling me this time of night?"

"Sorry, I guess, I lost track of time," he said, a spiteful smile crossing his lips. "I have some good news."

"What is it?"

"I haven't found them yet, but I know that they came to New York and were last seen in Times Square. I've got a room on Broadway and will start showing their picture around tomorrow. Chances are someone saw them."

"That is good news. Keep me updated," Wolf ordered, hanging up.

John replaced the phone and muttered to himself, "At least the bastard could say goodbye for once. He's got the manners of a sea urchin."

"Who was that, Wolf?" Una asked sleepily.

"Someone who doesn't know enough to call at a decent time. Go back to sleep."

Wolf's eyes glazed over with heightened excitement at the prospect of his grandson once more being within his reach. He would soon be rearing him the way a firstborn Ostermann boy should be raised.

Tara got up just before sunrise and watched through the southwest window as morning light slowly lilted along the Hudson River, teasing another Saturday morning to life in lower Manhattan.

She thought about her life and all the events of the past year. She couldn't contain the tears that overwhelmed her—all the loss she had endured and all the blessings she had received collided in her mind. She loved Chris and her son, Connor, but she missed her mother and Miss Thompson, her tutor. Would she ever see them again? Chris had said that she would, but now she accepted what she knew to be true: he had told her that to keep her going, to fortify her resolve. Her fath—Wolf ... how could he hate her so much? How had he become so twisted by greed to continue amassing his wealth that even his own child was expendable?

She looked out the window at the sun's far-reaching rays. The overwhelming brightness of another day made her think of her power. She hadn't used it for weeks. She remembered what Rhea had told her to hone her skills and use her power to create a peaceful world. She laid her hands palm up on her legs and went into her meditative state. Tara entered her new world, letting her mind drift into the core of consciousness that surged with the energy of the world's emotion.

She passed from mind to mind, searching out world leaders, reading their thoughts. She was overcome by their diverse beliefs constructed out of misinterpretations of the past. All of them were driven by a hunger for power, and many were fuelled by a mixture of revenge and misguided fanaticism. On the outside, they displayed diplomatic tact, but internally, their hatred boiled for anyone who opposed their way. How could she ever bring peace to a world so philosophically opposed, she wondered—even with her powerful ability. Slowly she retreated from that melting pot of insanity, as she would come to call it.

Tara realized that her father was like those men and women of position and control. Now she understood him; he was defined by his greed and knew nothing else. She felt sorry for him, because his soul was a cancerous darkness rather than a place of solace and joy. She opened her eyes and saw Chris standing a few feet away with Connor in his arms. A delightful smile traced its way across her lips, and her eyes glistened with happiness.

"How long have you been standing there?"

"Ten minutes."

"Chris, I know we said we were going to look for an apartment today, but I'd rather go for a walk in the park and maybe even for a cruise up the Hudson. We haven't done anything touristy since we've been here."

"Fine with me. Anyway, it's Saturday. We can start looking for an apartment on Monday."

Tara stood up and stroked Connor's cheek, watching pure happiness gurgle to the surface as he smiled and fanned his chubby arms and legs.

Tara had never travelled by subway before and was extremely nervous, at first, about being trapped underground with no escape if something happened to the train. Chris assured her, in his usual calm manner, that the transit authority had many well-trained personnel who could handle any emergency. She listened to his words, but they did not bring much relief.

She was very pleased with the overall cleanliness and with the well-lit platform area, which helped allay her fear a bit, giving her a sense of hope that the system was well maintained.

Without any warning, a gust of wind swirled past her. The single headlight on the front of the train emerged from the tunnel as the train came to a screeching halt beside the platform. After boarding, Chris directed her to the seat at the front of the lead car so she could watch as the train travelled through the tunnel.

The novelty of watching the train's progress quickly wore off, and Tara turned toward Chris. She could see that he was deep in thought, which usually meant something was bothering him.

"What's all the deep thinking about, Chris?"

"Oh, I'm just being a bit nostalgic," he lied. He was actually concerned that they were getting a little too complacent about their situation. "I didn't know that they'd gotten rid of the Redbirds."

"What do you mean?"

"The old, red cars they replaced with these techno, stainless steel tubes that they call subway trains. The old Redbirds were so much more romantic and comfortable."

"There's something more going on than nostalgia, Chris."

"Damn, will I ever be able to get anything by you?"

"Doubtful."

"I'm worried that we're not taking the threat of your father seriously enough. All my instincts tell me we should be doing something more proactive, but I don't know what that something is. In the past I've always known what to do, but this situation has me stymied."

"Chris, let's not think about it. Today, I just want to enjoy our time together as a family."

"Okay."

Shortly after exiting subway line one, they were accosted by buskers selling every type of trinket imaginable, including fake Gucci watches. Tara was enjoying the fresh air scented by the vast number of trees and gardens as she and Chris walked along the esplanade in Battery Park. Chris carried Connor in an infant carrier in front of him. Connor began to stir after having fallen asleep on the subway ride. His fair skin, blond hair, and blue eyes reminded her of Chris as he woke from sleep, stretching out his small fists and twisting his tiny mouth into a yawn.

"Tara," Chris said, "why don't we take the ferry from the dock at

Castle Clinton over to the Statue of Liberty and Ellis Island? Would you like that?"

"Sounds interesting. Sure, let's do that."

***

Selwyn watched as John approached his cab. Selwyn Thorne was no ordinary New York hack. In his previous profession, he had worked for US Immigration at Kennedy Airport. He'd left that job after the tragic destruction of the World Trade Center, which had caused him to have a mental breakdown. As an immigration official, he had learned to identify faces and he had become one of the best at it. Things like hair colour and skin tone—the things that people could alter with makeup and wigs—didn't distract him. No, he looked at the shape of the face, the angles or lack thereof—features that people couldn't change without plastic surgery or a substantial shift in diet.

"Hey there," John said conversationally to the cab driver.

"Yes," Selwyn said.

"I'm trying to find a couple of people who recently came to New York and were last seen in Times Square. It's very important that I locate them."

"How important is it?" Selwyn said slyly, thinking he might be able to make a few bucks off this guy.

"It's worth fifty dollars, if you can lead me to them," he said, showing the photograph of Chris and Tara to the cab driver.

Selwyn eyed it closely, comparing the two faces in the photograph with the sea of facial shapes—round jaws, square jaws, close set eyes, bulbous noses—of his fares over the last few weeks, until a couple of images clicked in like the spinning fruit on a slot machine.

He turned to John with his best poker face, baiting him, not giving him anything, wondering how much his information was really worth. After a few seconds, he spoke.

"I think I have seen this couple, and they had a small child with them."

John's eyes lit up briefly. He regained his composure, but it was too late. Selwyn realized that his information was worth much more.

"Oh yes, that's right, they do have a child with them," John said, appearing nonchalant. "Where did you last see them?"

"I'd like to tell you, but somehow I think this info is worth more than fifty dollars.'

"Okay, if you can lead me to them, I'll give you one hundred dollars."

"Cut the bullshit. I've been reading people all of my adult life, and I'm certain I can convince you to pay me at least ten times that. But I'm not greedy. You give me five hundred bucks, and I'll drive you right to the place where I dropped them off. Do we have a deal or not?"

"That's a lot of money."

"Do you want to fucking find them or not? If you don't, I'll be on my way. I have to make a living, you know."

"Okay. You drive me to where you let them off, and I'll give you five hundred dollars after I confirm it's them."

"Nope. Pay me now, or no deal," Selwyn snapped.

John thought about it for a couple of seconds. This guy had mentioned the child and he hadn't said anything about the boy. He couldn't take the risk of letting this guy go if he really did know, and five hundred dollars was really a pittance to find out. He would have given him two thousand, if he'd pushed.

"Okay," John said, opening the back door of the cab. "Take me to where you dropped them off, and I'll give you the five hundred dollars when we get there."

"No way. The money now," Selwyn insisted.

John relented.

"I obviously don't carry that kind of cash on me. Take me to a bank machine, and I'll get it for you."

"I thought you'd see it my way."

CHAPTER THIRTY-FOUR

JOHN HID BEHIND A bulky old elm tree a few yards off the street, across the road from the building where the taxi driver said he had dropped Chris and Tara off. Patiently, he waited and watched the entranceway to the building, shifting his view between the avenues of approach. After two hours, he was rewarded as he saw Chris and Tara walking toward the building—Chris with Connor strapped to his body in a baby carrier. With their new disguises, he didn't recognize them at first, but the baby caused him to look closer, and he soon matched their facial features to his memory of them. He continued to watch as they opened the front door and entered the building. At least, the taxi driver hadn't lied. Not knowing which apartment they were in, he took cover behind the elm tree so they wouldn't see him through their window. He flipped opened his cell phone to call Wolf.

"Hi, Wolf."

"John. What's up? I hope you have more good news for me."

John couldn't believe it, the man actually sounded cheerful. *He must have gotten laid last night,* he thought, smiling to himself. "I have very good news—extraordinary news, in fact."

"Okay, okay. Don't keep me waiting. Have you found Chris and Tara and, most importantly, my grandson."

"Yes, yes, and yes."

"Where?"

"They're living in an apartment building in south Manhattan."

"John, I haven't said this to many people—honestly, I can't think of anyone—but you're the best. This is great news. I need you to find out what unit they're in and get me a list of all of the names of everyone in the building."

"The list of names shouldn't be difficult. There's probably a directory in the building's lobby. But as for which apartment they're occupying, that will take some time, because I doubt they're using a name I'll recognize."

"Forget their apartment number, just get me the complete list of names, and I'll do the rest."

"But how?"

"Don't worry about that, just get me the list."

"Okay." John said, finishing the conversation, abruptly flipping his cell phone shut. *Man, that felt good*, he thought, *hanging up on that pompous prick before he had the last word, for a change.*

John lowered himself to the ground, leaning his back against the tree. He would need to stay there until it got dark and he would be able to safely leave his hiding place without the risk of being seen.

Chris surveyed the street from their apartment through a slight parting in the drapes. Up and down and across the street, he saw no one suspicious. Maybe he was just being his usual paranoid self, but he had sensed someone watching them as they entered the building, and he was certain he'd seen the setting sun briefly reflect off something across the street by the old elm tree, possibly a watch or a camera lens. But now he saw nothing out of the ordinary.

He continued to observe for a few more minutes, hoping that if someone were out there he would think the coast was clear and emerge prematurely. But nothing happened; the sidewalk and roadway continued the flow of usual Saturday evening traffic. There was only one young couple holding hands as they strolled along the edge of the greenbelt area that ran along the Hudson. Chris left the window, but the image of the sun glinting off something still gnawed at him. He had to go across the street and check by the elm tree to make sure nobody was there. He wouldn't feel at ease until he did so.

He was about to leave when Tara's silky smooth arms wrapped around his waist and her moist cool lips massaged his tight neck muscles. Her right hand probed low, grasping his crotch. She undid his zipper and adeptly extracted his cock from its confines. *Okay*, he told himself, *I won't bother checking out the elm tree*. He was most likely over reacting anyway. It was probably just a cellophane candy wrapper that he saw the sun reflect off. Tara wrapped her hand around Chris's cock, stroking its complete length, easily drawing it to full attention. He turned and embraced her in a long, wet, passionate kiss. Their bodies squeezed together as if attempting to seal themselves to each other. His rigid shaft throbbed against her thighs, straining for release.

He lifted her body into the air with one arm and pulled her panties aside with the other. Slowly, teasingly, he moistened her by rubbing the head of his shaft along her vagina. Finally, she could take no more and pushed herself down onto his engorged cock, slowly taking him deep within her. Seizing him with her legs and arms, she rode him with wanton fervour. With adept agility, she lifted and lowered her body, at times nearly releasing his cock and then retrieving it again and again to fill her depths. Possessed by the heat of their sexual passion, she could no longer continue as she surrendered to blissful climax. Chris came at the same time, exploding inside her. Holding her close, he lowered the two of them to the loveseat, where they languished in each other's arms.

After a few minutes, Chris said, "Remind me to go with you for a walk more often."

Hoping that all was clear, John backed away from the elm tree. Using it for cover as long as he could, he made his way further into the post-dusk shadows of the surrounding trees. Sticking to the interior of the park, he methodically made his way around until he was directly across the road from the entrance to the apartment building. Lifting the hood of his light parka to hide his face from view, he crossed the road and entered the building. John had a photographic memory. All he needed was a good excuse to read the names on the buzzer panel in the building's entranceway. He saw that the security guard was quite young, probably just out of a local college. *That will make things a bit easier,* he thought.

"Hey, son."

"Yes, can I help you, sir?"

"I doubt it, unless, of course, you know the name of each resident in this building."

"I know a few of them by name but certainly not all of them. I'm fairly new on the job."

"That's okay. I'm looking for my Uncle George who just moved to New York and supposedly lives in this area. Wouldn't you know it, some bastard held me up at knifepoint no more than five blocks from here and took my wallet. I had a piece of paper in it with George's address and phone number. The old memory's failing me, and I can't remember any of the information, except that he lives on this street. If you don't mind, I'll just read the buzzer panel over here to see if his name is on it."

"Go ahead, take your time. Meanwhile, I'll call the police for you if you like, and you can give them a description of the man who robbed you."

"Don't bother. I'll wait until I get to my uncle's place and call them from there."

"Suit yourself. But I wouldn't wait. The longer you put off calling, the further away the thief will be."

"Believe me, the speed at which that jacked-up rabbit was running, I'm sure he's already long gone."

While continuing the conversation, John was able to read the complete panel and commit all one hundred and fifty names to memory.

"Sorry to bother you, but I don't see my Uncle George's name here. He must be in the building up the street. Thanks anyway," he said, with a cordial smile and a wave.

"Good luck finding your uncle and getting your wallet back. It can be a pain in the ass replacing all of those cards."

Reading over the list of names that John faxed him, Wolf couldn't believe his luck when he saw the name of Blake's mother, Mrs. Edith Rosewell. If Blake had helped them escape, it stood to reason that he would have put them up in his dead mother's apartment. *Damned idiot*, he cursed himself, *why didn't I think of this connection sooner*. It wasn't like him to overlook something so obvious. Putting his reprimand aside, he headed for his private cave. It was going to be another busy night. He would have to enter the mind of each person on that list. By tomorrow morning, there would be one hundred and forty-nine people looking for an opportunity to kidnap little Connor to get him to his grandfather, where he rightfully belonged and could begin to learn about his true heritage.

An intruder blatantly interrupted Tivona's dreams. It was as if the complete essence of another person had stepped into her mind. The shadowy embodiment held her mind captive. Unable to wake up, she was unnerved as her every thought and most guarded memories were scrutinized by the forceful presence. Every person she had ever known and everything she'd ever done flashed before her. Was she about to die? Had God come to take her from this world, she asked herself? A distinctly male voice began talking to her. It was much more than a random conjuring of her subconscious. He sounded as if he was seated right next to her. He told her of an infant boy who'd been kidnapped, stolen from his grandfather.

"You're the one," the voice said. He must have sensed Tivona's bewilderment, because he went on to say, "You were Edith Rosewell's best friend." The voice continued, telling her that she must rescue his grandson and return the boy to him.

"How can I do such a thing?" she said.

The voice said calmly, "You'll find a way. Once you have him, call me."

After planting a phone number in her mind, the intruder was gone.

Tivona Heber didn't sleep well at the best of times, especially since her husband, Josiah, died a year before last month, but last night she'd been especially restless. She regretted that she hadn't taken her own life at the same time that Josiah had died; they'd still be together. She also had one other regret. She had not been able to have children. Josiah had always said that it didn't matter, but she knew deep down that he had ached for a son.

Tivona—or Tiv, to her friends—hadn't thought of children for years, and that was why that night's dream was so disturbing. All she could remember was that she had to return Connor, a baby boy who was confined with his kidnappers in Edith Rosewell's apartment, to his grandfather. Why would anyone be living in Edith's place? As far as she knew, Blake hadn't even put it up for sale yet. She was supposed to retrieve the boy and turn him over to his grandfather. Why would she dream such a thing, and why would God place such an onerous responsibility on her at her age?

Still, she knew it was the right thing to do. But what if something went wrong? If the boy was injured, she agonized; she would never be able to forgive herself.

Tiv remembered the first time she had met Edith Rosewell in the elevator shortly after Edith and her husband, Paul, had moved into the building twenty-five years before. The two women had immediately connected. They had both enjoyed the arts, playing bridge, and going for long walks. Over the years the two couples had become very close friends, and that was why it was so heartbreaking now that they were all gone except for her. She would never have another friend like Edith she despaired. Tiv wasn't sure if she could deal with going into Edith's apartment and all of the memories it would resurrect. But she knew that she had to try for the grandfather's sake. Anger seized her as she wondered what kind of lowlife would steal another person's child.

A loud, church bell sound reverberated through the apartment and startled Tara from her ponderings, because it was the first time she had ever heard the doorbell. No one ever visited them. Her mind raced with the possibilities. Nobody had rung up from the lobby. *It must be Raven*, she thought. After all, he was the only person who knew they were there, and he should have a key. But then why would he ring the doorbell?

Her fear got the better of her. Had her father found them again and sent someone else to kill her and Chris and steal Connor? She was especially nervous because Chris had left to get a newspaper and probably wouldn't be back for at least another ten minutes. She felt vulnerable without him. She could fight with words, but she didn't have his physical prowess. If someone attacked her, she would be defenceless. Trying to calm down, she closed her eyes and told herself to get a grip. It was probably just a friendly neighbour paying a visit, and anyway, she could look through the peephole to see who was out there.

She forced herself from her chair and walked toward the door just as the doorbell rang again, further jarring her nerves.

Tara looked through the peephole and smiled to herself, realizing how silly she had been. It was an elderly woman, as she'd hoped—a friendly neighbour. She undid the inside latch and opened the door to see a well-groomed, white-haired woman with a large, round face like a pale moon. Each of her earlobes was adorned with dangling ruby-diamond, cluster earrings. She was a large woman, but she hid it well under an elegant, loose-fitting, floral-print, silk dress. She was obviously an affluent woman.

"Hello, I'm Tivona Heber from down the hall. I was very a close friend of Edith Rosewell, the previous owner of this apartment. I didn't realize that her son, Blake, had sold it until I saw you and your husband entering the other day."

"Well, actually, Blake hasn't sold it."

Looking quizzically at Tara, Tiv said in an accusing tone, "I don't understand."

"It's a long story, but Blake is an old friend of my husband, Chris, who should be returning soon," Tara said, glancing at her watch. "Chris and I decided to move to New York on fairly short notice, and Blake was very accommodating. He's letting us use his mother's apartment until we get settled and find a place of our own."

"Interesting. Since I'm here, do you mind if I come in for a few minutes?" Tiv said, walking into the living room like she had done many times when Edith was alive.

"Sure, no problem, come in. My name is Tara," she said, offering her hand. Tara felt that the woman must be legitimate, because she knew Blake's name as well as his mother's. She didn't seem to have much choice, since the woman was already halfway into the living room.

"You have a child, don't you?" Tiv asked as she sat down in the chair where Tara had been sitting when the doorbell rang. "At least, I saw your husband carrying a child yesterday when you entered the building. I just happened to be looking out the window when the three of you arrived."

"Of course, our son Connor."

"If it's not too much to ask, may I see him? I love children. I was never fortunate enough to have my own."

"I would be glad to let you see him, except I just got him to sleep and he's been a bit cranky today."

"I understand. Another time then. You haven't changed a thing in this apartment. Every thing is just as it was before Edith passed away. It all brings back so many memories."

Tara watched as Tivona's eyes glistened.

"Good memories, I hope."

"Mostly," she said, stifling her emotions, "at least, up until Edith became sick with cancer. We'd been friends for over twenty years. It was horrible watching her slow, painful death."

"I can't even imagine how that must have felt," Tara said with quiet respect.

Patting her eyes with a tissue Tara had given her, Tivona regained her composure.

"That was then, and this is now. How are you and Chris enjoying New York?"

"I love New York, but Chris would rather live somewhere more rural."

"So, are you planning on staying?"

"Yes, for a while, anyway."

"What is it that you like about New York?"

"There's so much to do here, and I like the anonymity of the big city. I come from a small town where everybody knows your business."

I bet you do, you child thief, Tivona thought. "Have you started to look for a place yet?"

"No, but we'll be looking this week."

"Well, I know that you hardly know me, and if you are wary, I would perfectly understand, but if you need someone to look after little Connor while you're apartment hunting, I would be glad to look after him."

"That's a very generous offer Tivona."

"Call me, Tiv."

"Okay, Tiv, but Chris will need to meet you as well, and he and I will have to discuss it. I hope you don't think I'm being overly cautious, but I've heard so many horror stories about terrible things happening to children these days."

"I understand, dear," she said, just as the apartment door opened and Chris walked in.

"Chris!" Tara rose to greet him, "we have a visitor."

"A visitor," Chris said, suspiciously.

"Yes. Tivona Heber, a lady from down the hall. She was a longtime friend of Mrs. Rosewell, Blake's mom."

Tivona stood with her hand out to greet Chris, "As I told your lovely wife, you can call me Tiv."

"It's a pleasure to meet you Tiv." Chris shook her hand. "I didn't know Edith Rosewell, except through childhood stories that Blake shared with me, but what I do know of her, she sounds like the kind of mother any young man would want. There is one particular story that I remember. Blake had taken a cigarette from his mother's purse and was in his bedroom smoking it, when she walked in and found him. She had not realized he was already home from school. He said she was so calm and cool, he couldn't believe it. She just said, 'Those things'll kill you son.'"

"Yes, I recall that story. A couple of days later, Edith told me about the incident. But she didn't mention cigarettes. She told me that it was one of Paul's cigars, and when she found Blake, he was coughing and hacking. And his face was a grey-green colour."

All three of them chuckled.

"You know, it was a cigar. I guess I've heard so many of these stories over the years, I'm getting them confused," Chris said.

Tivona looked at her watch. "Well, it's already noon. I'd better get home and have some lunch so I can take my pills. It was really nice meeting you both, and I hope to meet little Connor someday soon."

"Nice meeting you, too," Tara said as Tivona left.

When the apartment door closed, Tara said to Chris, "She offered to watch Connor while we go apartment hunting."

"Don't you think it's a bit premature to trust Connor with someone we've just met, especially after everything that's happened?"

"I agree. I'm not suggesting that we trust her immediately, but she does seem trustworthy."

"Tara, I believe she is. That story I told about Blake's mom finding him …"

"Yes."

"Well, it just happens that it was a cigar, and only one of Edith

Rosewell's closest friends would know that. But before we allow her to look after Connor, you're going to have to do some mind-probing to make sure your father hasn't reached her."

"You're right, Chris, and there's no time like the present."

CHAPTER THIRTY-FIVE

ONCE AGAIN TARA WAS faced with the evil, twisted persona of her father. She was astounded to see that he had gotten into Tivona's mind. Tara had entered Tivona's mind as a precaution and to pacify Chris, thinking that she wouldn't find anything. But there it was, a plan to kidnap Connor and turn him over to Wolf, along with a phone number that she didn't recognize, probably Wolf's private cell number that she assumed he used for these purposes. *That bastard doesn't fucking give up*, she thought. A deep sadness overtook her, and she longed for peace and a place where she could hide from the monster that she once called Dad. One more time, she would have to undo his treachery and block another mind from his access—hide another person from his probing deceit.

Tara opened her eyes, and staring blankly at Chris, blurted, "Will we ever be free of the son of a bitch?"

"He reached Tivona?" Chris asked.

"Of course. What do you think? It's my father, the human pathogen. His tentacles reach throughout the world, tapping in and manipulating people and sucking the life out of them as he pleases. Nowhere is safe, Chris, nowhere. The only way we will get any peace is if we ..."

Chris put his hand over her mouth.

"Don't say those words. There has to be another way. Once you start down the road of killing, you become part of a world that you don't want to live in. Believe me, I know. I live it everyday, and because of you, I'm slowly digging my way out. But it's a long, dark tunnel, and sometimes the loose soil falls back in."

Tara placed her hand on his and removed it from her mouth.

"You're right, Chris," she said despondently, her eyes half-closed. "I can't allow myself to be sucked into his heartlessness. I can't allow him to destroy my humanity. We have to find another way."

"We will," he assured her, although he was convinced that there was no other way.

"I hope so. I've removed my fa … I mean, Wolf's corruption from Tivona's mind and blocked her from further access. It doesn't seem to matter where we go; he finds us. Let's stay here in New York and make our stand. I'm more powerful than he is; I can defeat him. Tomorrow, we'll ask Tivona to babysit Connor while we go apartment hunting. We'll continue our life together in spite of him."

"Now that's the Tara I married," Chris said proudly. He knew that Tara was right. They had to get on with their lives. But he wasn't ready to leave his son alone without protection.

"Tara, we do need to try and live as normal a life as possible. But we can't underestimate your father. He's probably planted his thoughts into other people's minds in the building. After what happened on Bequia, I'm not prepared to trust Connor with anyone, especially a defenceless old woman. I think we should also employ bodyguards to watch our backs, men trained in the methods of counterespionage."

"I know it's probably the right thing to do, Chris, but I don't like the idea of someone always following us around. It gives me the creeps."

"It won't be forever, sweetheart."

"Who will we get?"

"I'm sure Blake can help us."

It was 0500 hours on Monday morning. Chris sat by himself at the dining room table reviewing the dossiers and photographs of the two highly skilled Delta Force operators that Blake had faxed to him. He was impressed with their credentials. The operator's names were William Janson and Marty Lockworth. Chris would never meet either man face to face. Instead, they would use a dead drop system, allowing them to trade information without raising suspicion. Chris also had an emergency cell phone number to contact either soldier in case of an emergency and vice versa. Janson and Lockworth were to arrive in New York that afternoon at 1300 hours.

Colleen closed her drapes after watching the young couple with the baby exit the building and immediately keyed Wolf's phone number.

"Hello," Wolf answered dryly.

"It's Colleen Ridley."

Wolf hurriedly scanned the list of names on his desk in front of him and spotted hers. *That was quick*, he thought.

"Yes, Colleen. How are you?"

"I'm well. I have good news for you. I just saw the young couple you asked about exit our building with your grandson."

"Do you know where they're headed?"

"North on West Street."

"Thanks for phoning Colleen, you've been helpful," he said as he hung up.

Wolf was going to make sure that he got his grandson this time, and no one was going to be left to talk about it. He picked up the phone and called the Carpenter. He mused to himself as to how a hired killer got a nickname like the Carpenter. Maybe because he always nailed his target, he thought, smiling at his own sick humour. The Carpenter had never let him down before, and as good fortune would have it, he lived in Brooklyn.

The phone rang the usual ten times before a voice answered, "Carpenter here."

"It's Wolf."

"Do you have some walls that need to be fixed?"

"Yes, two of them."

"Two. That's going to be expensive."

"How expensive?"

"One hundred dollars."

Wolf quickly translated—every fifty dollars was a million, "No problem. Just don't fail, not that I think you will of course. Do I deposit the money in the usual account once I receive the pictures of your finished work?"

"Yes. Where are they located?"

"Twenty-one West Street, south Manhattan. The apartment is number one thousand eleven. My tenants just left the building for a walk. If you hurry, you'll have time to do the repairs before they return. Phone my partner when you're finished, and he'll come by and pick up my grandson."

"Grandson! Whoa, what do you mean?"

"I want you to retrieve my grandson and deliver him to my partner. I guess I neglected to mention that part."

"Don't screw with me. If you want me to babysit your grandson, it'll cost you another hundred."

"Okay, agreed. Just make sure he's delivered safely. I'm faxing you the details now."

The Carpenter and Wolf had done business before, and every time Wolf called, it was urgent. The contract often had to be expedited—usually the same day. But the Carpenter wasn't complaining; Wolf always paid him well and on time, which was more than he could say for some of his clients, who sometimes needed a little convincing. The threatened death of a close family member—usually a child—rendered the quickest payment.

The Carpenter was a tall man with thin, sandy blond hair, a narrow face, and a long chin. His cheeks were slightly pockmarked from a severe case of acne when he was younger. He walked with a slight limp on his right side, because of a fall down a flight of stairs when he was fleeing the scene of one of his contracts five years before.

He prided himself in never having been caught and never having spent any time in jail. None of his clients had ever met him face-to-face, and he intended to keep it that way. That's why this contract had him worried. He would have to make contact to deliver the child.

After spending the latter part of the afternoon apartment hunting, Chris picked up a note from the second dead drop location. The note simply read, "No followers." It finished off with the time and location of the next dead drop.

"What does it say?" Tara asked.

"No one is following us, except one of Blake's men."

"That's good news, isn't it?"

"Yes, for now."

CHAPTER THIRTY-SIX

THE CARPENTER WAS HIDDEN out of sight in the upper foliage of one of the larger trees across the road from Chris and Tara's building. His position provided an unobstructed view of the apartment building's front entrance and the surrounding area. From the photographs and typewritten profiles Wolf had faxed him, which he'd committed to memory, he recognized Chris and Tara when they entered the building.

He wasn't about to move too quickly. He knew from Chris's profile and Wolf's summary of the last few months that Chris was no slouch and probably had some of his Delta Force friends working with him watching their rear ends. He continued to scan the area around the building for the next few minutes with his binoculars.

His patience was rewarded when an old seventies-style Ford van with no side windows pulled into the curb approximately two blocks east of the building on the north side of the street. It was a vantage point from which the driver could see all approaches to the building's front entrance. The Carpenter might not have thought much of it, except the driver didn't get out. He just sat there behind the steering wheel, watching the area. The Carpenter had also seen the van circle the block twice prior to parking. It was definitely one of Chris's bodyguards. There would certainly be another guard watching the rear entrance. If either of them saw anything suspicious, they would alert Chris and each other. The Carpenter scanned the back section of the building and nearby rooftops for the second guard, but he couldn't see him from his position. He would have to wait for the man in the van to contact his partner a couple of times to find out the length of time between checks before eliminating the guard. That would tell him how much time he had before Chris would be alerted.

Marty Lockworth only heard the split second sound of glass breaking before the bullet ripped into his skull and he fell dead against the driver's door—his blood smearing the van's window.

Having taken out the bodyguard, the Carpenter began to execute the rest of his plan. He had only fifteen minutes before the other guard tried to contact his partner again. He walked with confidence through the double doors of the River's Shore apartments.

"May I help you, sir?" the security guard's voice came through the speaker.

The Carpenter turned toward the guard and stared at him with his icy blue eyes for a measured ten seconds.

The young guard, unnerved by the tall, silent stranger staring at him, reached for the button to notify the alarm company.

"I wouldn't do that if I were you," the Carpenter said, pulling the silenced gun from inside his jacket and shoving it into the half-moon-shaped hole used to pass messages.

"What the fuck ..." the guard said, his red cheeks slowly turning ashen white. "What the fuck are you doing?"

"I'm going to kill you, son, if you don't do as I ask."

The Carpenter pulled a photograph from his inside jacket pocket and slid it to the guard. "I want you to phone Chris Landry's apartment and tell him that the man in the picture—his name is Wolf—is in the lobby, waiting to see him."

"Are you planning to kill Mr. Landry?"

"No, I just want to talk to him, but he won't come down if he knows it's me."

"If you just want to talk, why do you have a gun?"

"It's none of your business, and if you don't shut up and make the call, I'll blow a hole in your forehead right now," he said, pushing the gun toward the guard.

"Okay!"

His hand shaking, the guard pressed the buzzer for Chris's apartment.

"Yes," Chris said.

"Mr. Landry, there's someone here in the lobby to see you. He says his name is Wolf."

Stunned, Chris asked, "Describe him to me."

Trying to remain calm, the guard spoke slowly as he described the photograph held in front of him.

"Okay. Tell him I'll be down in a minute."

"I'll let him know, sir," the guard said, releasing the intercom button.

"He's on his way down?" The Carpenter asked.

"Yes."

"Great."

Instantly, the Carpenter pulled the revolver's trigger, opening a hole in the centre of the guard's forehead. The guard's upper body jerked back and then fell forward, his head slamming into the counter with a dull thud. The Carpenter reached through and pressed the button to release the security door.

Quickly, he entered the guard's area and pressed the red button under the counter to send a silent alarm to the security company, alerting them of a problem. They would call the guard's desk, and then, not getting an answer, they would call the police to check out the situation. Depending how close the police were, it would be about ten minutes before they arrived—plenty of time for what he had to do.

"Tara, you're not going to believe this, but the guard in the lobby just called. He says that Wolf is down there waiting to see me."

"I don't believe it."

"I didn't at first either, but he described him exactly. I'm going down to the lobby. In case this is a trap, which I think it is, I want you to go to Tivona's apartment. Get Connor, and I'll walk you over."

After leaving Tara and Connor at Tivona's, Chris pulled out his cell and immediately called Marty. He should have heard from Marty if someone resembling Wolf's description had approached the building. Marty didn't answer his phone; something was wrong. Chris hung up and tried to call William.

He picked up on the first ring.

"Yes."

"William, it's Chris. When was the last time you checked in with Marty?"

"Four minutes ago."

"Something's wrong. He's not picking up his phone."

"I'll go around and check on him."

"No, you stay where you are. It seems we've been compromised, and someone might try to come in the back way. I've left Tara and Connor with a neighbour. I'll go down and check the front. I'll call you once I know more."

"Okay."

Chris entered the elevator. As it approached the lobby, he crouched down, his gun at his side. If somebody was waiting for him, he wasn't going to have an upright target to shoot at. The shooter would have to lower his arm and re-aim. By the time he did, Chris would have taken him out.

The elevator door opened, and there was no shooter. He looked around the lobby and, as he had expected, there was also no Wolf. He walked over to the guard's station and had no sooner discovered the guard's body than the police arrived. Instantly, they levelled their guns at him while their eyes darted back and forth between him and the dead body. Chris knew what they were thinking. He had to come up with a good explanation quickly and get back to Tara before anything happened to her. How could he have been stupid enough to fall for such a ruse?

The Carpenter had reached the tenth floor before Chris went downstairs and hid in the stairwell just before Chris came out of his apartment with Tara and the baby. He held the stairwell door open slightly and watched Chris drop Tara and Connor off at the apartment next door on his way to the elevator.

The Carpenter waited a couple of minutes before going to the neighbour's apartment. He knocked on the door, standing away from the peephole to ensure that the person on the other side could not see him clearly. A voice came from behind the door.

"Did you forget something, Chris?" Tivona asked, starting to open the door.

"Tiv, don't open …" Tara said, but it was too late.

Once the door was partially open, the Carpenter raised his foot and kicked it in the rest of the way. Tiv flew back against the entertainment unit, slamming her head on the corner. The Carpenter strutted into the apartment, right arm extended, his gun aimed straight ahead. Tara was on her feet standing in front of the playpen, a protective mother guarding her son. He aimed his gun at the lady he had knocked to the floor and shot her in the forehead. Then he turned to find Tara careening toward him with a glass vase. He shot wildly, hitting her in the stomach. She reeled from the impact and fell backward, her neck crashing into the edge of the marble end table.

The Carpenter was out of time. He picked up the baby and left. He would call Wolf's partner once he was clear, and then return to finish the job. While the Carpenter slipped away down the building's back fire escape, the police would be busy with Chris in the lobby, thinking that he was the gunman.

Half an hour later, John Borg's cell phone rang, and he plucked it from the bedside stand. "Hello."

"I have Wolf's grandson, and I'm in the lobby of your hotel. What room are you in?"

"Five-oh-four."

"I'll knock four times in quick succession. You open the door and reach out your arms, and I'll hand you the baby around the corner of the doorway. Do not come out into the hallway or attempt to see me, or I'll kill you. Do you understand?"

"Yes."

"Good, I'll be there soon," the Carpenter said, closing his cell phone.

Fear penetrated John as he waited for the knock on the door. He stood a few feet away, his eyes fixed on the centre of the door. When he heard the four brisk knocks, he had to force himself to go and open it. As instructed, he held his arms out into the hallway, waiting for the baby to be placed into them. Once he had baby Connor, he pulled his arms in immediately and closed and locked the door.

Connor was asleep, but he had obviously been crying, his face was tearstained and his eyes were puffy and red.

"You'll soon be with your grandfather, little guy, and he'll take care of you," John whispered to him.

CHAPTER THIRTY-SEVEN

THE BASTARD DIDN'T EVEN come to pick up his own grandson, John cursed as he opened the rear door of the limousine and turned to watch the Learjet taxi toward the private runway located on the outskirts of New Jersey. No doubt the plane and runway were both owned by Wolf Ostermann.

John asked the driver to take him back to his hotel. He continued watching through the car's rear window as the plane jaunted down the runway, taking little Connor away to his new life. For the first time in John's life, he deeply regretted his actions. He knew that someone must have died for him to get Connor. Why else would the man who delivered him not want John to see his face? He was probably some kind of hit man, a paid killer.

He looked up at the sky. It was a sunny day—his last sunny day, because tonight he would party hard, and tomorrow, he would be in darkness, because he was going to kill himself. He wasn't sure why he was having such dark, depressing thoughts, but he knew it was time to leave the world before his ugly life brought any more pain into it. If there was a hell, he was sure he'd find himself there within the next few hours.

Once the plane reached altitude, Wolf engaged the autopilot and turned to take his grandson from his bodyguard. He cradled him in his arms and ran his fingers through his thick, curly, red hair. Wolf admired the boy's sparkling green eyes as the overhead lights skipped along their surface. Connor reminded him of his daughter the first time he had held her as a baby. *This time it will be different,* he resolved; this time, he would have a true heir. Little Armin—as he would be known, after Wolf's great-grandfather—smelled clean and fresh. Wolf had ordered his guard to bathe his grandson as soon as he came aboard.

"Yes, little man, someday, my empire will be all yours. But in the meantime, a lot of learning must happen. I'll teach you everything, just as my father taught me and his father taught him," Wolf said with pride, looking right into Armin's face as he lifted him into the air.

The thought of seeing her grandson provided a small measure of healing for the wound gouged into Una's soul after, Tara, had left home; she would never see her again. The final memory of her only child would be a box lowered into the ground—*the last funeral I will ever attend*, she thought.

It had all begun the evening before, when she had responded to the intercom from the estate's main gate.

"Yes."

"There's a RCMP officer here to see you and Mr. Ostermann."

"Did you check his ID?"

"Yes."

"Okay, send him up to the house."

What would bring a police officer to our place? Una wondered. *Has the silent perimeter alarm been tripped again by a deer?* That annoying alarm was tripped at least once a week. The police officers who responded never asked to see them unless they were rookies, and even then they were only supposed to ask for Wolf. *This one asked to see both of us. Very strange*, she thought. The doorbell rang, and she went to answer it. At the threshold of her door stood a very tall, solidly built, young officer. He was probably only about thirty years of age and extremely handsome. He reminded her of the first time she'd met Wolf at the grocery store in Toronto so many years ago.

"Ma'am, is your name Una Ostermann?" he asked with calm authority in his voice.

"Yes. What's this about?"

"My name is Officer Tomlin. Do you have a daughter named Tara?"

Perspiration beaded on Una's forehead as panic gripped her.

"Yes, why?"

"Mrs. Ostermann, do you know where your daughter is?"

"No, I don't. She left home over a year ago. Her father and I haven't seen or heard from her since. Why are you asking me all of these questions?

Have you found Tara? Has something happened to her? You're scaring me." Una babbled.

"Sorry ma'am, I apologize, but I need to be sure before I go any further. How old is your daughter now?"

"She's nearly twenty-two."

"We might have found her."

"What do you mean, you might have found her?" Una growled impatiently, as she felt Wolf's large hand gently grip her right shoulder.

"What's the matter, dear?" Wolf asked.

"He's asking about Tara, but he won't tell me what's happened to her."

"Do you know something about our daughter, sir?" Wolf asked.

"We're not one hundred percent certain. There was an apartment fire in New York's lower Manhattan area. One of the registered tenants—Tara Ostermann, a young woman—had a Canadian passport in her purse with this address on it. According to the report—"

"Is she alive?" Una interrupted.

"I'm sorry to say that she died on arrival at the New York Downtown Hospital. The New York City Police Department requires a relative to go to Manhattan to identify the body. I'm very sorry. I hope she's not your daughter."

"So do I," Wolf said, wrapping his arms around Una.

"Here's the address in New York City," the officer said, handing Wolf a piece of paper from the notebook in his jacket pocket.

"What do you mean, you hope it's not our daughter? The passport proves her identity, especially her picture. Why are you trying to give us false hope?" Una screamed at the officer, her face taut with anger.

"Mrs. Ostermann, it's not my intention to give you false hope, but it could have been another runaway who had stolen her passport."

———

As Wolf stared into his grandson's pink chubby face, he smiled. He had orchestrated everything perfectly, right down to the police officer.

"Wolf, you are brilliant," he congratulated himself aloud. When he had called Una to tell her that the body was Tara's, she had dropped the phone. He had continued to yell his wife's name until she had picked it up again.

"Una, I'll …" Wolf said, pausing for effect, " … have Tara's body flown to Canada, and we'll give her a funeral fit for a princess."

"Okay, Wolf," she said vacantly.

"There's one other thing. Una, are you listening?"

"Yes. What other horrible thing has happened?"

"It's not horrible, dear. You're a grandmother."

"What the hell did you say? You must be joking. A grandmother! This is no time to play games, Wolf. Are you saying that Tara had a child?"

"Yes, I am. They were able to rescue little Armin from the fire, but they couldn't get Tara out in time. Wait till you see him, Una. He has tight, curly, red hair and green eyes, just like your beloved daughter."

"You mean 'our beloved daughter.'"

"Yes, our beloved daughter. I didn't mean to imply that I didn't love her as well. It's just that you two were very close—closer than she and I."

"And whose fault was that?"

"Mine, of course."

"Did you say his name is Armin?"

"Yes, after my great grandfather."

"How did you know his name?"

"I didn't. I gave him that name because nobody knew his real name."

"It's a strong name. I like it. I'll see you when you return," Una had said as she had hung up.

Wolf was quite pleased with himself. All he had to do now was keep Una from wanting to see the body. That would be the easiest part. He didn't even need to have a burial service. He could just plant a memory of the service taking place in Una's mind, and she would never know any different.

Chris explained to the officers that he had returned from a walk down by the Hudson River and had just come across the body when they arrived.

"So, you being here is just a coincidence?" the taller officer asked.

"Yes."

"What's your name?"

"Chris Landry."

"There's no Landry on the directory, Rick," the shorter officer said.

"That's because I'm not registered here. My wife and I just arrived last month. A friend of mine, Blake Rosewell, let us use his mother, Edith Rosewell's apartment."

"There's an Edith Rosewell on the directory, Rick."

"Buzz the apartment and see if either Mrs. Rosewell or Mr. Landry's wife picks up."

"You won't get an answer," Chris said.

"Why's that?"

"Mrs. Rosewell died seven months ago, and my wife is in the neighbour's suite."

"Rick, I've tried buzzing a few times, and no one's answering."

"Well, Mr. Landry, what's the neighbour's name?"

"Tivona Heber."

"Did you get that, Jim?"

"Yes. There's no answer there either."

"Okay, we'll wait for SWAT to arrive, and then we'll sweep the building. In the meantime, Mr. Landry, we'll have to hold you on suspicion of at least one murder. Put your hands behind your back."

"That doesn't make any sense," Chris said. "Tara has to be there. Something's very wrong. We need to get up there right now. She might be injured and can't get to the phone."

Chris ran toward the stairwell.

"Stop, or I'll shoot," Rick yelled. His words were wasted. Before he could draw and aim his gun, Chris had passed through the door and was ascending the stairs two at a time.

As he crested the first flight of stairs, Chris heard the officers enter the stairwell. He knew that time was on his side. The officers would have to be cautious, not knowing what he might do. Pushed by fear of what might've happened to Tara and Connor, he reached the tenth floor landing without breaking a sweat and slammed through the door to the hallway.

"Son of a bitch," he yelled, when he saw Tivona's door open. On the way to Tara's body, he quickly checked on Tivona. She was dead. When he got to Tara, he found that she still had a pulse, but without medical help, she'd be dead in minutes.

"Get away from the woman," Rick called from the doorway, aiming his gun directly at Chris.

"Fuck you, this is my wife, and she needs medical help now, or she won't make it."

"Jim, radio down and ask EMS to get up here as fast as possible. Request a couple of SWAT officers to escort them."

Chris pulled one of Connor's blankets from the nearby diaper bag and held it against Tara's wound to stem the blood flow. He caressed her head with his other hand.

"Tara, you're going to live. You have to. I've never loved anyone before you."

Tara's eyes opened partially, and a slight smile adorned her face before her eyes closed once more.

CHAPTER THIRTY-EIGHT

CHRIS WAS AMAZED AT Colonel Samuels' ability. The story that Samuels told the precinct captain about Chris being a special forces operative whose name had been leaked to a terrorist cell in Los Angeles was frighteningly believable That was the reason Samuels had given for relocating Chris and his wife to New York under a new identity with the hope that they could start a new, and hopefully normal, life. Samuels continued to tell the captain that the terrorist group's reach must go deeper into their organization than they had realized, because Chris's new identity had also been compromised. But Samuels hadn't found out about the breach until after the attack on Chris and Tara in New York. And, he went on to say that it was all top secret. The captain could not tell his men why Chris was being released but Chris would be available for questioning if needed. Chris couldn't help thinking that if it hadn't been for the recent World Trade Center terrorist attacks in New York, the captain wouldn't have been quite so cooperative.

The sun was just beginning to set as Chris walked through the wooded area across from his apartment building. He remembered the flash of light behind the old tree and once more chastised himself for not following up on it. Looking toward the apartment building, he suddenly stopped, realizing that from where he stood the front entrance of the building could be easily seen through the trees. He looked up and saw that the trees were much taller in that area. He shimmied up the tallest of them. As he reached the top, he noticed that some branches were bent down, as if someone had already been there. Then he saw the Ford van being towed away and thought of Marty Lockworth—poor bastard didn't even have a chance.

Chris looked at his watch. He only had an hour before he had to meet with Blake and some other Delta Force operators to plan an assault on Wolf's estate to get Connor back.

He had just reached the bottom of the tree when a bullet zipped passed his head, ripping bark away. He threw himself down and whipped behind the tree. Wolf's assassin had returned to finish the job, Chris realized.

"This time you're not dealing with a defenceless old lady and a young woman. You're a dead man, you prick," Chris cursed under his breath.

Based on the trajectory and impact of the shot, Chris estimated the shooter's approximate location to be about fifty yards northwest.

Without showing himself, Chris worked his body into a crouched position with his back to the tree. He then duckwalked straight toward a larger clump of trees that would provide him more cover. Once he got to the clump of trees he worked his way toward the riverside, and then on his stomach, he shimmied along the shoreline until he thought he was past the shooter's location.

The Carpenter knew that he should split, because the kill had gone bad, but his pride had gotten the better of him. He was a professional, and being a perfectionist, he was angry with himself. As soon as that young bastard stuck his head out from behind that tree he was cowering behind, the Carpenter would blow it right off. Then he would finish off the girl.

He realized he'd waited too long. He had to get the hell out of there. He would just have to kill them later.

Just as he lowered his rifle, he felt the searing pain of a knife plunge into the base of his neck. With a short-circuited spark of energy, he whirled around, rifle raised. Before he could pull the trigger, his grip loosened, and he fell against the tree and slid to its base, streaking a morbid path of blood along its rough surface.

The Carpenter's lifeless eyes stared up at Chris, filling him with a strong sense of repulsion for what he'd just done—taken another man's life. Even though he knew that the man lying beneath him would have killed him without a thought, it didn't make it any better. Chris had not experienced this feeling for a long time, and he was afraid of it, because he knew the killing was not finished.

He knew that he had only been a killer because of Wolf, and now, ironically, his humanity was returning because of Wolf's daughter. But this was not the time to weaken, because he was certain that this was just the beginning of more death.

Chris hadn't had much sleep in the last twenty-four hours. He had been at the hospital, guarding Tara's unconscious body.

Blake and Chris had finally come up with what they thought would be the perfect plan to get Connor back from Wolf.

"Blake, I hate to leave Tara here unconscious, but I have to get our son back."

"Is it her safety you're worried about?"

"No. There will be a Delta Force operator both inside and outside the room guarding her. I just hate the thought of her waking up alone, without me here."

"Chris, why don't you stay here and let my men and I go in and get him? We're perfectly capable of doing the job."

"I know, but you're not as familiar with the Ostermann estate and Wolf's security protocols as I am."

"Not to mention you want to be the one to kill him," Blake said, bluntly.

"I hope it doesn't come to that, but I'm afraid it will be the only solution."

"Of course, it is! As long as he's alive, you and Tara will never be free."

"Spoken like a true soldier," Chris said.

"Isn't that what you are, Chris?"

"I'm not sure anymore."

"As long as who's alive?" A groggy Tara asked.

"Tara! You're awake," Chris shouted. He rang the bell for the nurse and then gave Tara a hug and kiss, holding onto her like he never wanted to let go.

"Yes, I am. As long as who's alive?" She asked again.

"Blake and I've been planning how we're going to get our Connor back. Now that you're conscious, you'll be a great help."

"How?"

"We'd like you to go into your trance state and persuade William Koch, the chief guard, to drug the food of the guards who will be on watch the night we go in to rescue Connor. It'll be easier than us trying to bribe him."

"What kind of drug? Not something that will kill them, I hope."

"No. It will be a time-released drug that will put them into a deep sleep for a couple of hours so we can slip in, retrieve our son, and slip out again."

"Sounds like a good humane plan. I like it."

"We're quite proud of it," Blake said.

"I don't want any more death. Please promise me that no one else will die," Tara pleaded.

"I promise," Chris, pledged without hesitation, knowing full well he would probably break his promise. He hoped he wouldn't.

CHAPTER THIRTY-NINE

FLAT OUT IN THE eight-inch deep grass five feet back from the tree line and covered in his ghillie suit, Chris was invisible to the searchlight that passed over him every fifteen seconds.

The night was filled with the nocturnal chant of the male cricket's love song. The earthy smell of wet grass mixed with the perfume of fir trees diffused through the cool air, creating Mother Nature's deodorizer. It was a stark contrast to the proverbial stench of evil that resided beyond the fifteen-foot high walls in the distance.

As a CIA sniper, there had been times when he wouldn't sleep for as long as five days, but he wasn't used to it anymore and was beginning to feel the effects of little sleep. Lying there motionless, he kept losing focus, but thinking of Tara in a hospital bed in New York and of his son behind those walls ahead of him was enough impetus to keep awake.

He had asked the doctor to be completely honest with him, and now he wished he hadn't. The doctor had said she might never walk again. She would be in a wheelchair for at least six months, possibly forever. The damage to her spine from the severe twist to her neck when she hit the end table, was worse than anyone had originally anticipated. Chris thought of their infant son—only three months old and torn from them by Wolf's goon, like some kind of invaluable commodity. Chris would make him pay! He knew he would have to kill Wolf. Blake was right: the constant terror would never end until Wolf was dead.

He could see Tara's pain-stricken eyes as she begged him not to let anyone die. Feelings that had been distilled out of him during the last five years through heartless training and discipline crashed like giant waves against the breakwaters in his mind.

Once more he thought about the career he'd chosen—or, to be more accurate, the career that Wolf had chosen for him. Chris was trained to kill; every muscle to the tiniest joint and thought was modulated for death. He'd learned to live with death like other people lived with a bad hair day. Having few social skills and no friends, he had grown up a loner. So, when recruited, he had instantly signed up with the CIA. After four years, he had become a killing marksman—one of their best snipers. He had engrossed himself in a life of black operations for the CIA. He ran the kind of missions that never make it into the history books, and if you didn't return, no one came looking for you; all ties were severed. During the past year with Tara, there had been an unsettling disturbance in his soul, and it grew more intense every day. He could no longer detach himself from the lives he had ended. He felt them tearing at his being for reprieve, demanding remembrance. He had promised Tara that he would not let anyone else die.

Through his night vision scope, the walled compound looked formidable in the green, clinical hue. Chris buried his head in the grass again as the searchlight passed over him. When he lifted his head, he saw the guard on the northeast corner fall. The guard's body slumped to the catwalk, slamming against the railing that ran along the top of the wall. Startled by the noise, the guard on the southeast corner aimed his M16 toward the tree line. He sidestepped his way over to his fellow guard, all the while watching for any sudden movement.

Just as Chris had him in the sights of his silenced Beretta 92 FS, the second guard wobbled and fell straight back, his head bouncing off of the grated catwalk. The sound created a dull echo. Chris hoped that the other guards were already down from the sleeping drug that had been in their evening meals. He clicked on his radio. "Blake. Nick. Are your guards down?"

"Nick here. Yes."

"Blake here. Yes."

"Did you hear that, Carl?"

There was no response.

"Carl, respond. All of the wall guards are down. Do you copy?"

"Yes, Chris. Sorry, I dropped my radio. I'll give you fifteen minutes, and then I'll break through that front gate as if it was made of cheese cloth."

"Good. And don't scare me like that again. Remember, this is my son were rescuing."

"Yes, Chris," Carl said soberly.

Chris could smell death in the air like a whitetail deer senses an oncoming storm. He wanted to keep his promise to Tara, but he knew he couldn't.

"Blake. Nick. I'm going to get Connor. Copy?"

"Copy," they both said.

Chris leapt to his feet, threw off his ghillie suit, and ran toward the wall. Without a covering, he felt the cool damp air against his face and hands. Adrenalin charged through him with a ferocity that woke up every operable sense. He was focused once again. There was no room for error.

At the wall, he removed his pack and pulled out the retractable grappling hook and its twenty-five-foot nylon rope. Chris pressed the button that catapulted it up toward the railing on top of the wall. It looped around the iron bars with a clang and hooked solidly on the first try. To be sure, he gave it a tug and then started scaling the wall. He was pumped. Hand over hand and foot above foot climbing like an opossum, stealing through the cover of night. He flipped over the railing and landed in a crouch on the balls of his feet, ready to pounce.

He checked the time. He still had thirteen minutes.

Chris pulled out his night vision scope and scanned the grounds. Starting at the south end by the swimming pool and working north toward the mansion, he saw movement.

"Damn it, a guard." Chris cursed under his breath. "What the hell went wrong? Why is he still standing?"

The guard looked confused. His head swivelled back and forth as he looked at the walls where he expected to see his fellow guards on watch. Regretfully, Chris knew what he had to do. He aimed his Beretta and was ready to shoot when the security alarm sounded. The bastard had pressed his remote alarm button.

Chris pulled the trigger. Through his scope, he watched the blood burst between the guard's fingers as he clutched his throat. With a look of disbelief on his face, he stumbled and fell backward, hitting the ground like a felled tree. Looking at the crumpled guard, all Chris could think was, "Sorry, Tara."

Now that the alarm was sounding, he knew where Wolf would go, and he had to get there first.

"Una, wake up. Can't you hear the alarm?"

"What? What? What's going on, Wolf?"

"Someone's breaking in, and we have to get the hell out of here quick. I'll get the baby. You get dressed. I'll meet you at the helicopter pad. If you're not there by the time I arrive, I'll leave without you."

Wolf didn't bother to get dressed. He just threw his robe over his pyjamas and grabbed a small suitcase he'd already packed for the next day's business trip.

As Wolf ran by the upstairs hall window, he could see out into the front yard. His backup guards were running from their quarters and scrambling for position, scanning the grounds for the enemy. He watched as one of them fell backward, blood spurting from his forehead. Wolf was sure that bastard Chris Landry was behind this.

"Why hasn't anyone been able to kill the son of a bitch?" he cursed.

Anxiety and sheer determination emulsified into sweat on Chris's face and hands, making it difficult for him to hold onto the rope as he climbed the mansion wall. He had to get to the helicopter pad before Wolf. He couldn't chance the pilot, like the guard he'd killed, not being tranquilized as well. He heard the backup guards' M16s firing in the direction of silenced Berettas that were picking the backup guards off at will.

It was a cacophony of death, as ricocheting bullets splintered shards of stone from the fortified wall and clanged against steel girders and railings. Nick and Blake's superior shooting skills continuously toppled guards.

Just as Chris landed onto the terrace, the sky lit up. The guards were aiming a floodlight at the north wall where Blake and Nick were positioned. Chris saw movement on the north wall—a shadow—an M16 fired. The shadow fell.

"Fuck," he said to himself.

Then he heard the sounds of a bullet and crashing glass—a second explosion. The light was out.

He had to keep going. He had to make it to the rooftop before Wolf.

"Shut up, you little brat," Wolf yelled in frustration at the screaming baby he held under one arm as he ran toward the three flights of stairs leading up to the helicopter pad and his escape. Wolf had phoned the pilot to make sure that he was up and ready to go.

There had been no answer, so he assumed he was on his way to the chopper. Halfway up the first flight of stairs, he stumbled. He let go of the suitcase and clutched the baby with both hands while resting his elbows on the stair. He watched the suitcase tumble to the bottom.

"Screw it," he said, getting back on his feet and continuing toward the top.

***

Chris saw Una standing by the helicopter, waiting for Wolf. He could tell she was very nervous and agitated, because she kept turning her head and moving her feet in jerking motions. Looking from side to side as if she might have heard something, Una walked toward the helicopter. She reached out for the helicopter door and started to open it slowly. With her back to him, Chris saw his chance.

She must have heard him approach, because she turned quickly, but it was too late. The last thing she saw was Chris Landry's face. She heard him utter the words, "Sorry, Una," before his hand connected with the side of her neck.

Careful not to hurt her any more than he already had, Chris lifted her gently but swiftly into the other side of the chopper.

He grimaced as Connor's resounding screams bounced off the walls in the stairwell, composing a symphony of horror for his ears. He wanted to charge down the stairs and grab the baby from Wolf's arms, but he knew that that would be a fatal mistake. If Wolf lost his balance and fell backward, his son could be severely injured or even worse—Chris didn't want to consider worse. Instead, he flattened himself against the wall to the left of the doorway and waited for Wolf to emerge.

Within seconds, Wolf burst through the door, charging toward the chopper. Suddenly, he realized that it wasn't running and there was no pilot. He stopped and yelled, "Where is that stupid, lazy bastard?"

A voice from behind him calmly answered, "I think he's still snoozing."

Wolf turned abruptly. He saw Chris standing with his handgun aimed.

"Wolf, give me my son, and I'll spare your life."

"Do you think I'm stupid? You won't shoot me while I'm holding your precious son," he retorted, as he moved the baby further up his body to create a protective shield.

"You're right. I won't, but you're not going anywhere until you hand him over. I'm positive I'm much better at the waiting game than you are."

"You think so, eh? Chris, you're such a fool. I know how to fly that helicopter. Now I'm going to get in it and fly out of here, and there's nothing you or anyone else can do to stop me."

Chris heard the sound of a chopper above him.

"What the hell," he said, as he watched a UH-60M Black Hawk lower itself toward the second helipad. After it landed, a soldier exited the helicopter. Chris could tell by his uniform that he was an officer. The officer lifted a wheelchair from the helicopter and then put a woman into the wheelchair. The soldier pushed the wheelchair over to Chris.

"I'm not going to ask how you got Colonel Samuels to fly you here in a Black Hawk," Chris said, with a knowing look. "What I want to know is what the hell you're doing here? First of all, it's damn dangerous, and secondly, you should be in the hospital recovering," he said.

"I couldn't stay in that hospital knowing that my son wasn't safe. I knew that I wouldn't be able to live with myself if I didn't do something to help."

Tara closed her eyes.

"Don't bother trying to get into my head, you little bitch. I can block you out. He's my grandson, and I'm leaving with him right now," Wolf yelled as he started to walk backward toward the helicopter.

Chris watched Tara's head slumped back and began to shake. He'd never seen her in such a state before. *There must be one hell of a battle going on*, he thought. Wolf's body vibrated as he fell to his knees. He held Connor tightly while his body jerked. Chris looked back to Tara; blood dripped from the side of her mouth.

"What the fuck's happening? We have to stop this," he said.

No sooner had the words left his mouth than Chris heard the gunshot and saw the exit wound on the left side of Wolf's head. In slow motion, a collage of flesh, bone, and blood vomited through the air. Wolf's shocked face turned white. His black eyes greyed like the coals of an extinguished fire. He collapsed, still clutching the baby with his last morsel of strength.

Weeping, Una fell to her knees, involuntarily letting go of the gun. It somersaulted across the roof before landing.

Chris ran to his screaming son and tugged him from Wolf's death grip. Pulling Connor to his chest, Chris held him close, attempting to comfort him.

"You could have killed my son!" Chris raged.

She lifted her head and choked out a muffled response: "It's finally over."

Chris followed Una's pain-stricken eyes as they locked onto Tara's slumped body.

"Will you ever be able to forgive me, Tara?" Una asked.

Tara's eyelids flitted as she slurred the words, "I already have. Chris, bring me our son."

Chris knelt in front of the wheelchair and placed Connor on her lap, holding him there while Tara regained her strength. Gradually, her eyes opened more, and she lifted her hand and stroked baby Connor's face.

"Thank God!"

Nick and Blake arrived simultaneously, yelling, "Is everyone okay?"

After a short pause, Blake said, "Chris, we have to go. Carl's down front with the van and he's injured. He was grazed by one of the guards' bullets when he broke through the gate."

Chris glanced over at Una, and his anger changed to pity.

"Una," he said, "Come with us."

The five of them emerged through the front door of the mansion. Chris stopped to look around, remembering the first day he had arrived at the Ostermann Estate. He had been excited about his cushy, new job as a babysitter for a naive twenty-year-old, making three times more money than at the CIA. Now all he saw was a killing field; dead bodies were strewn across the grounds.

The stench of blood assaulted his nose. Chris fell to his knees; his stomach heaved, and he threw up. He had not done that for years. He wondered if being sickened by evil meant that his humanity was returning.

CHAPTER FORTY

TARA KNEW THAT SHE had done the right thing as she read the headlines of the *New York Times*—TERRORIST ASSASSINATIONS A HOAX, SUPER SHIRT STOCK PLUMMETS. She also knew that she would have to set many more things right if she wanted to redeem the Ostermann name. It didn't matter to her that no one else knew the atrocities that her father and ancestors had committed. It only mattered that she knew, and she would never be able to live with herself if she didn't use her gift to undo it.

LaVergne, TN USA
08 October 2009
160197LV00003B/16/P